Dandelion

S. Belle

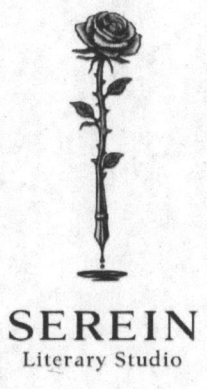

SEREIN
Literary Studio

ISBN: 979-8-9944538-0-3

Published by Serein Literary Studio

First Edition, 2026

Cover art by S. Belle
Edited by Nicole Taylor

Content Warning

My books are dark romance and are not for the faint of heart. Reader discretion is advised, and for those who do choose to read my books, I highly encourage self-care and self-awareness practices while reading.

That being said, if you wish to proceed, I welcome you to the most dangerous safe space you've ever entered. Come ready to explore yourself and your boundaries. All are welcome.

There a content and trigger list begins on the back of this page. For those who prefer to go in blind or do not have triggers, this list contains inherent spoilers and may be skipped for the best experience. For those who need it, we have done our absolute best to include as many relevant triggers as possible. While thorough, the list is not exhaustive, and everyone has their own unique triggers. Individual experiences may vary.

Please proceed with caution. If you need a break while reading, take one. If you need help, ask for it.

<u>Trigger Warnings</u>

In no specific order, this book contains:

- Descriptive violent sex scenes (consensual/dub-con)
- Sexual exploitation
- On-page sexual assault
- Kidnapping/abduction
- Presence of a stalker including stalking behavior (on-page surveillance)
- Torture
- Murder
- Criminal activity including but not limited to gang-related activity and gun violence
- Mention of drug cartels
- Mention of child neglect
- Mention of gambling addiction
- Mention of sex trafficking
- Mental illness including on-page panic attack

<u>Kinks</u> (in no particular order)

- Impact play
- Light humiliation and degradation
- Orgasm control
- Predicament bondage
- BDSM (D/s dynamics)
- Cockwarming
- Praise kink
- Anal play
- Breath play

This one is for the girls whose love is so pure, it saves us all from our monsters.

Now go be a good girl and let your broken boy use you to feel whole again.

Dandelion (the playlist)

Track	Title	Artist	Duration
1.	Electric Love	BØRNS	3:38
2.	all-american bitch	Olivia Rodrigo	2:46
3.	Control	Zoe Wees	3:51
4.	Hey Brother	Avicii	4:14
5.	Captain America	Cal Scruby	2:56
6.	Power Over Me	Dermot Kennedy	3:27
7.	10,000 Hours	Bugus	4:04
8.	Tonight	FM Static	3:39
9.	Bronco	Canaan Smith	3:54
10.	Way Back	Brantley Gilbert	3:39
11.	Gravity	Sara Bareilles	3:55
12.	DNA	Lia Marie Johnson	3:37
13.	Dandelions	Ruth B.	3:54
14.	Dress	Taylor Swift	3:50
15.	NASTY	Russ	1:56
16.	Earned It (Fifty Shades of Grey)	The Weeknd	4:38
17.	Levitating (feat. DaBaby)	Dua Lipa	3:23
18.	Lost in the Moment (feat. Andreas Moss)	NF	4:03
19.	Daddy Issues	The Neighbourhood	4:20
20.	War Of Hearts	Ruelle	3:46
21.	DiE4u	Bring Me The Horizon	3:27
22.	Terrible Lie	Nine Inch Nails	4:39
23.	Anybody Out There	Tyler Shaw & Amaal Nuux	3:20
24.	Hurricane	Thirty Seconds to Mars	6:12

25.	Rescue	Lauren Daigle	3:36
26.	I Will Follow You Into The Dark	Death Cab For Cutie	3:09
27.	Falling like the Stars	James Arthur	3:33
28.	Marys Song (Oh My My My)	Taylor Swift	3:35

https://bit.ly/Dandelion_ShadowsofAbilotte

Dandelion (Spotify Playlist)

CHAPTER 1

Logan

Catching a glimpse of myself as I pass by, I take a step back and face the mirror. My hair is in total disarray from running around the townhouse, so I flip my wallet into my left hand with my coffee cup while holding my keyring between my teeth. Using my now-free hand, I finger comb my dark brown curls back into place. Giving myself one more look, I drop my keys back in my hand and head out the door to work.

I smile as I see my custom Bronco Outer Banks Edition that my brother helped me buy. The muted lavender-soft gray pearlized vehicle appears off-white with a glimmer of purple in the soft morning sunlight. It's a one-of-a-kind ride that reminds me every morning how much he loves me. I really wanted a vintage Bronco to match my best friend, Dallas', but Royce insisted I needed a newer model for safety. I climb in, throwing my coffee in the cupholder and my wallet haphazardly on the dash, starting the ignition and heading off to another day at The Camellia Club.

S. Belle

Once on the main road, I head to my recent calls on the infotainment center and call Dallas, knowing her shift should've wrapped up recently.

"Hey! You heading into work?" she answers before I even have the chance to greet her.

"Yes! How was your day at the hospital?"

"Nothing too crazy, Just the usual; a broken arm, a heart attack, and a few cases of flu. Oh! and a pregnant lady whose husband was insistent her Braxton-Hicks contractions were her delivering their 22-week old fetus and threatening to sue us for malpractice for not giving her medicine to stop the premature labor. Which, shocker, wasn't actually happening."

Laughing, I ask, "First time parents?"

"Of course! I put on my best friendly face and ensured them that their baby would happily stay right where they're at as long as she got some more water in her system." I can practically hear her shaking her head. "What's your day like today?"

"Nothing too crazy. I have our monthly staff meeting, and I have a new event coordinator I've got to continue to train-up, but she's doing really well so that's been fairly easy."

"I still don't understand how you *enjoy* managing an entire social and athletic club. I would be pulling my hair out dealing with all of those people constantly."

"Dallas, you talk to patients all day long. How is that different?"

"Because treating patients is way different than management. Once they're out of my ER, I hopefully will never see them again. Nowhere near the amount of social politics you play all day every day, by choice."

10

I catch myself chuckling as I respond, "Fair. Outside of work, I also have my weekly sibling dinner with Royce tonight."

"Speaking of Royce, have you seen Blake since he moved back to town?"

"No!" I say, probably a little too enthusiastically. "Why would I?"

She teases playfully, "I don't know, he is your brother's best friend, and you two were close once. Plus, he's not exactly hard to look at. I thought maybe since he's back in town you two might've seen each other."

"Well, no. We haven't. He hasn't gone out of his way to see me, nor has he put much effort into talking to me much since he left for college and law school, so I don't see any reason to be the one to reach out."

"Okay, whatever you say. You think he'll come to dinner tonight?"

"Girl, I hope not." Dallas laughs way too hard at my response. "What are you laughing for?"

"You have had a crush on him since we were like ten years old! 'I hope he doesn't come to dinner,' yeah, okay. Let's see what you end up wearing to dinner tonight now, 'just in case' he does come."

She keeps laughing, "I'll be wearing a t-shirt and leggings, thank you very much."

"Yeah, with that t-shirt tied up to show off how good your ass looks, maybe."

"Dallas!"

"What? You know the first time he showed us that hidden bike trail behind the park and the tree house he and Royce built you were head over heels for him."

"That tree house was just three pieces of plywood nailed to some branches to make platforms."

"Yeah, but it was all we needed. And you can bet I'll be awake when dinner's over so I can hear how it went," audibly smirking at herself.

"I hate you so much sometimes," I snicker.

"No you don't. I—"

"Before you start whatever story you're about to start, I'm pulling into the club right now."

"Okay then I'm going to get my butt to bed as soon as possible. Text me after dinner!"

"If you insist," knowing that if I don't text her, she'll be texting me anyways. We hang up while I'm parking and I head into the club.

When I stroll in, I'm greeted by our receptionist. "Hey Logan, that dress is adorable!"

"Thanks!" I do a quick twirl as the chiffon cap sleeves and wrap hemline flutter with the motion. "It's one of my favorites. Hope your morning is going well!" I call out to her as I walk past her desk towards my office. I drop my keys and wallet off at my desk, then head towards the back of the club where the tennis courts are.

I see Ana out on the second court, which happens to be her favorite to train clients at. She's setting up some of her equipment for a client and gives me a smile when she sees me approaching. She's been one of my favorite employees since I started working here and has been my biggest supporter as I moved into the lead manager position at the club. At twenty-eight, not everyone on staff was happy with my promotion, but I've been working here doing different jobs since I was in high school, so with my college degree and inside knowledge of so many different facets of this social and racquet club, I was more than prepared to take it on.

"Hey Ana, how's your morning going?"

"First client should be showing up any minute! Did you bring me any coffee?"

"No, but I can grab you one from the break room if you need it."

"No, no, it's okay. I've already had plenty this morning, but if you wanted to have a cup ready for me at the staff meeting this afternoon I wouldn't be complaining."

"That can be arranged! How's Nina's soccer camp going?"

"She is absolutely loving it. I'm glad I caved and signed her up. I was going to make her wait one more year since she barely made the cut-off by turning eight during camp, but she was so determined to play that I let her. It was definitely the right decision."

"Do you have any special plans for her birthday tonight?"

"Just going to get some pizza and ice cream after camp, but honestly camp will probably be the highlight of the day for her."

I notice a woman in her late fifties that is heading towards us, and nod to her while making eye contact with Ana. Ana greets her, and I slip off to do a lap around the facility, my morning ritual to ensure everyone has what they need for the day and help everyone see me as an extra set of hands as much as they do their manager.

After a busy day at work, I head home before dinner. Dropping my keys and wallet on the entry table on the way in, I can't get my mind off tonight. Would Blake come to dinner? Surely Royce would tell me if he invited Blake. Royce knows I hate surprises; he wouldn't blindside me like that. Plus, Blake just moved back to town last week. He has to still be unpacking and settling in at his new firm and apartment; there's no way he'd be ready to be casually going out to dinner with friends yet. Still, I wonder if I should freshen up a bit for dinner and change, just in case he comes. Dang, Dallas really did predict that one, huh? I could just text Royce and ask, but then that would look like I care, which obviously I don't.

I glance at my watch, well aware I didn't really have time to come home in the first place. I must've already subconsciously decided I was going put in a little extra effort tonight given that I decided to come home at all instead of going straight to the pub. I speed walk upstairs to the bathroom, and quickly run through a mirage of options of what to do with my hair, ultimately just leaving it alone and running a brush through it. Touching up my foundation and mascara, then changing into some jeans and a navy blue floral blouse that has a low v-neckline, I balance putting in more effort without being overdressed if it is just me and Royce.

Heading back downstairs, I throw on a pair of black sandals to finish off the look and am out the door in under fifteen minutes. I shouldn't be noticeably later than normal, especially with how inconsistent Royce's schedule is. I jump back into the Bronco, and wonder why there's a twinge of excitement in my gut as I pull back out onto the road.

CHAPTER 2

Logan

O'Brion's Pub is one of those places that looks like it's been around both twenty years and two hundred years simultaneously. I dodge the specials sign on the sidewalk and make a friendly smile at the girl sitting at the outdoor table when I make eye contact after my near-miss with the sign. Pulling open the dark green painted door, the warm ambiance of the pub is accompanied by the chatter of a full house and some guys at the bar yelling at the soccer game on TV.

I spot Royce in our usual booth about halfway down the long narrow pub, and plop into the booth seat across from him. "I didn't realize Abilotte United was playing tonight?" I question, pointing my thumb back at the rowdy bar crowd.

"They're not, they're rewatching Sunday's game."

"Then why are they getting so worked up?"

"Doesn't everything seem more exciting after a whole pitcher of beer?" he laughs. "It's good to see you. How was your day at work?"

"It was good! Our new event coordinator is doing really well. And she enjoys her work, so she's going to make my life ten times easier once she knows her way around all the systems and protocols and can start to willingly take things off my hands."

"Good. Was Ana working today?"

"Yes, which I can't believe she was. It's Nina's birthday today and she didn't take the day off."

"Well, why not?"

"I guess Nina was excited for the pool day at summer camp today. And I suspect she wanted Nina to get to have time with her friends without having to coordinate an actual birthday party. So she decided if Nina was going to daycare, she might as well work."

"That makes sense. I would've loved to have a summer birthday as a kid. Pool parties would've been a blast."

I laugh at the ridiculous notion, "Because Dad would've thrown us so many parties. Guess what else Nina is doing this week."

"What?"

"Soccer camp! With the Abilotte United guys running it. Apparently, she really likes 'Coach Boston,' and I think Ana might, too, from the way she tells the stories." I can hear the grin in my statement.

He pauses to look at the TV screen playing last week's match, "As in midfielder Boston McLeod? And our Ana?"

"I don't think anything has actually happened, but she definitely wouldn't be opposed if it did."

"He's like the most notorious playboy in the city, and that's coming from me. There's no way he'd consider a girl with a kid."

"Maybe she just wants a fling." Royce bursts out laughing at that.

"Isn't that how she got Nina in the first place?" he quips with more laughter following suit.

"Royce!" I scold as I chuckle along with him. "We're done talking about Ana. How was your day? Do you have any new properties in the works?"

"Just the same old stuff. Meeting with clients, showing off the potential of buildings, lots of paperwork looking at new options. Nothing nearly as exciting as one of my friends trying to hook up with a professional athlete." He smirks and diverts the conversation back to taunting me, "Is that why you're so dressed up? Are you and Ana going out tonight? Those aren't your normal work clothes."

I don't want to admit the real reason why I went home to change, and I don't want Royce remembering this too well to ask Ana about it later. "No, I've got plans with Dallas afterward. I figured I'd change on my way here. Ana has birthday plans with Nina, remember?"

He laughs playfully at me as we continue to catch up about our days. I do most of the talking; Royce has a way of being the center of the conversation without sharing much about himself in the process. I know he does it to avoid telling me things he doesn't want me to know. He makes most of his money now in commercial real estate, but I know that's not his only source of income.

Growing up, our father wasn't around much, and Royce put in a lot of effort to make sure I felt like the center of his world and never noticed that I went without the parental affection every kid deserves. Somewhere along the way, I think it just became part of our relationship that he was my biggest supporter, and still is. But part of that support growing up was him doing whatever it took to make ends meet when our dad didn't come home for months and bills were due. I guess some habits just don't die like we wish they would. Regardless of what he may or may not do behind closed doors, I can't imagine my life without him. His presence is warm, and he has a way of reminding me that nothing is as bad as it seems. He doesn't make life feel perfect, but he makes the bumps seem smaller, which they usually are compared to what my mind is making them out to be. Our weekly sibling dinners are one of the most grounding parts of my week.

I look him over while we sit at the pub, sitting in comfortable silence while we eat. His tattoo sleeve on his right arm shows beneath his short sleeve t-shirt, and his golden-brown hair falls into his face as he bends over to eat. He looks up at me and smiles a lopsided grin, and I can't help but think back to the number of friends over the years who have tripped all over that grin. He's got faint lines at both the corner of his eyes and between his eyebrows. Proof he smiles as much as he stresses, and I wish there was a way I could ease the burden he carries around with him to care for us both, even though I'm far old enough and capable of caring for myself.

We finish eating dinner, and hang out long enough for both of us to finish our drinks. Royce walks me out to my car, and gives me a hug before confirming we're on for dinner, same time same place, next week. I start the Bronco and watch as he walks over to his black Levante and climbs into the driver's seat. I pull out, and head back to my townhouse.

Dropping my keys on the entry table when I get home, I catch a glimpse of myself in the mirror. It's ridiculous that I bothered to get ready for Blake without even knowing whether or not he was coming. He and I may have been close as kids, but by the time he left for college we were hardly speaking. We've never so much as kissed, and while he's never been in a serious relationship that I know of (much like my brother), I heard from Royce that he's had his fair share of women over the years. Me throwing on a little extra mascara and running a brush through my hair surely wouldn't impress him. I'm still kicking myself for acting on my school-girl crush when I get a text from Dallas:

Dallas: *How'd it go? Was you-know-who there?*

Me: *No*

Dallas: *You don't sound happy about that*

Me: *Because I changed clothes assuming he would be, but Royce didn't invite him. So I'm going to have to admit I may have put in some effort for him*

Dallas: *HA. I knew it! Maybe he'll come next week?*

Me: *Maybe*

Dallas: *What'd you end up wearing?...*

Me: *Shut up.*

Dallas: *Maybe you should invite him to next week's dinner*

Me: *Absolutely not. That would be so out of pocket. If he comes, it's on Royce.*

Dallas: *You could see if Royce wants to help him settle in. You could even see if he's got new sheets he needs help trying out*

Me: *OMG Dallas!*

S. Belle

Dallas: *What? When was the last time you got laid?*

Me: *You're incorrigible. I'm not hooking up with my brother's best friend to break a dry spell*

Dallas: *If you don't, maybe I will*

Me: *lol you would never do that to me*

The conversation goes on with twenty different ways Dallas schemes for me to coincidentally spend time with Blake. She's been my best friend since we were little, and she's seen every phase of me and Blake's relationship. From being my older brother's best friend, to someone I hung out with one-on-one at the lake and felt like I could confide in unlike anyone else, to him completely betraying who I thought he was as a person and us barely speaking. I'd do anything to go back to how we were before that happened, but it happened and we've never really been the same since. He did his best to fix things afterwards, but I don't know if I could ever trust him again. Which is why when he stopped trying to reach out, I never reached out either. I suspect he was hoping time would help me forgive him, but it's been so long I don't know if I've moved past it or just buried it.

I move through my evening routine, and continue to wonder if there was even any potential there. My rational brain concludes that there shouldn't be. He betrayed my trust and if it happened once, it'll happen again. But I can't help but wonder if he put himself out there if I'd fall for it again like I did when I was a teenager.

CHAPTER 3

Logan

I'm sitting at my desk, working on this quarter's budget breakdown when I get a text from Royce telling me that he's currently hanging out with Blake and wondering if it's okay for him to invite him to sibling dinner this week. I read the message on my lock screen, but don't open it while I debate a reply. I keep trying to work on the spreadsheet, but my mind is teetering about how to respond to Royce.

Part of me wants to say "absolutely not;" that's our time together and I'm not sure I want to see Blake at all. The other part senses the nervousness in my stomach, making me wonder if I am actually excited by the possibility of seeing Blake. I know Royce probably really wants to spend time with Blake, and asking is his way of trying to respect our time together. What kind of sister would I be if I tell him he couldn't hang out with his best friend who just moved back to town after being gone for over a decade? I sigh to myself and pick up my phone, typing out a message

S. Belle

with a level of excitement that takes way more energy than it should. I give him the green light to invite Blake, and he quickly replies telling me that I'm the best.

A soft smile forms on my face knowing that he's happy with me—before it registers what I did. I groan and swipe out of my messages with Royce and straight into Dallas', giving her an update and wondering what the hell I was thinking.

While waiting for a message back from Dallas about my little spiral, I slouch back in my chair and stare past my computer to the wall. My brain drifts to one of the first times I looked at Blake as more than just my brother's best friend...

19 years prior...

I'm sitting on the swings between Dallas and Olivia when Olivia notices her brother and Royce down by the water.

"What are they doing?" Olivia squints to try to see better in the bright summer sunlight.

A few ripples begin on the surface of the lake, and Dallas responds, "It looks like they're skipping rocks."

"Oh! I've always wanted to learn how. Let's go see if they'll teach us." Olivia jumps off her swing and runs down the hill without even waiting for us to respond. I laugh with Dallas as we rush after her. By the time we get to the bottom of the hill, Olivia is squatting between Blake and Royce, and Blake is telling her what to look for in a rock. Royce fills Dallas and me in, and we both start looking as well.

Dallas quickly finds a rock, and Royce grabs one of his own, demonstrating how to throw it properly. I pause to watch as Dallas makes her first attempt, and Royce coaches her through it, with Blake doing the same thing for Olivia behind them. I go back to looking for a rock, and find a couple possible options. But Olivia and Dallas are already getting the hang of it, what if I can't do it and embarrass myself? I casually pass on a good rock and keep looking, pausing to watch my friends and brother all skip the rocks three to four times before it sinks below the surface. I look back down and notice a shadow approaching the rocks in front of me.

Blake squats down, getting eye level with me and handing me a rock. He tells me it's a good one, then talks me through what to do. He demonstrates again himself, then sensing my hesitation, offers to guide me through the motion before I try on my own. I nod, and he stands behind me, grabbing my arm and showing me what to do. My first attempt only skips once before sinking, but it wasn't a total fail and Blake quickly hands me another rock. He's extra reassuring and telling me I got the throw right, I just need to hold the rock in my hand a little differently. He positions it in my hand, then encourages me to try again and I get a good three skips in. He's focusing on me and lights up when I get excited with my success. It's the first time anyone besides Royce has ever been outwardly proud of me, and I can't help but get excited for a completely different reason.

My mind drifts back to reality, and I shift my focus back to the spreadsheet in front of me. I send a message to our new event coordinator asking her to come by my office when she gets a minute. We have some extra funds in the budget for the quarter and I want to see if she has any ideas for how we could use it. I'm also hoping her presence will keep me focused on my job and stop me from thinking about Blake for the next two days straight until dinner.

There is a part of me that can't wait to catch up with Blake. I want to hear about what his life was like before he moved back home, how law school was, college, see who he's become as a man. He was truly one of my best friends for years. But I know I'm risking forgiving what he did to Royce, and setting myself up to get burned by him again. I know myself well enough to know I'll give anyone far more chances than they deserve, so seeing him with Royce at our sibling dinner, in an atmosphere that feels safe and light, will take away the feelings I should be holding onto. I don't know if I'm ready for it. My anxiety about the whole situation starts settling in. I need that coordinator to get to my office, like, thirty seconds ago.

The next two days pass in the slowest time warp I could've ever imagined. I've been both dreading tonight and feeling an unwelcomed excitement about it. I took a little extra time this morning getting ready; curling my hair and putting on a full face of makeup, which makes it easier to simply touch up and change clothes after work before heading to O'Brion's. I grab a pair of dark-wash jeans, brown booties with a matching belt, and a pretty dusty blue blouse with a faux wrap that shows off more than its fair share of my chest before heading back out.

I realize I'm going to have to start changing every time for Royce to not be suspicious at this point, but it's worth it to see if Blake will see me and give me the same look he did when we were teenagers; the look that made me wonder exactly what he thought of me and who I really was to him. What will I do if I do get that look? Probably nothing. He was always my brother's best friend—I think that's why neither of us ever did anything about the feelings I know I had, and assume he had, back in high school. But beyond that, we're strangers to each other at this point; strangers who ended on a sour note. I can't imagine anything unfolding, but it would be nice to see if I still warrant a reaction out of him and pretend maybe he's been wondering about me all these years like I have been.

CHAPTER 4

Blake

Royce is sitting across from me at a booth asking me about the move and settling into the new apartment. I tell him about the moody black limewashed walls and warm hardwood that give it a great masculine energy with an incredible view over the city. The brick walls in the bedroom leak heat, but having a place with character is worth it. We drift to talking about the new job, and he asks if I'm starting to take on new clients of my own yet.

"Yeah. The partners knew the work I was doing in New York. I'll still have periodic supervision to make sure I've got the firm's practices down, but otherwise they're letting me take over a few clients of theirs and have a nice lineup of potentials for me as well. Why, do you need representation already?"

"It never hurts to have a lawyer you trust."

I take a quick look around before asking my next question: "So what exactly are you selling these days?"

"I think that'll require a signed retainer before I spell it out in black and white for you."

"Are you still working with the cartel?"

"I work with, almost, everyone these days."

"Well, that rules out—" I shut my mouth as I see Logan approaching us down the long aisle between booths. Her multicolored eyes find mine. In the warm, low lighting of the pub, it's hard to see the chunk of dark brown at the bottom third of her otherwise hazel left eye, but as she gets closer it's easier to see that tell-tale coloring that makes her even more beautiful than any other girl I've laid eyes on. Her espresso brown hair is curled down her back and I catch a whiff of her sweet and creamy vanilla perfume drift across the table as she slides into the booth beside her brother.

Earlier this week, I brought up Royce and Logan's sibling dinner in conversation, knowing my best friend well enough that he wouldn't be able to resist inviting me. But if I was actually allowed to come, that means she gave her approval. It's not much, but it's a crack in the door to try to insert myself back into her life. Years ago, she was the only person I let see inside my head after Olivia, even Royce didn't have that privilege. Letting her go when I could tell she wanted nothing to do to with me was one of the hardest things I've ever done. But I'm home now, and she's going to have a hell of a time pushing me away again this time.

As she greets Royce with a hug, I admire her thicker frame and toned legs through her skin-tight jeans. I wonder if she dresses like that every time she comes out to the pub with Royce, or if the revealing blouse in my favorite shade of blue was done just for me. She turns to face me, and I greet her. "Hi Logan, it's been a long time."

"Hi Blake. How's the move been?"

"It's been good. I was actually just telling Royce about how nice the new apartment is. Maybe you two should swing by and check it out some time."

There's a flash of a panic in her eye as Royce eagerly replies how that sounds like a great idea. I pick the conversation back up, "He was also telling me you're still working at the Camellia Club as the manager now?"

Her eyes soften into a smile. "Yeah, I really do love it there. The grounds are beautiful and there's just so many different moving pieces, it keeps it exciting and entertaining. And honestly the people there are great."

"Oh? Meet anybody interesting working there?" When she makes eye contact with me, I'm sure she can tell exactly what I mean by that question.

She answers, "Just a really good friend, Anastasia. She's one of the tennis pros there. There're a couple other girls there we've hung out with a few times. But she's the only one I'd consider a good friend. She hangs out with me and Dallas a lot, and her daughter is the cutest kid I've ever met and so funny, I swear."

"Yeah, Nina is pretty adorable; almost makes me want to have a kid of my own, she's so cute," Royce chimes into the conversation.

"Yeah? And which fling would you pick to have a kid with, exactly?" I laugh as I throw Royce's comment back at him.

"Not a single one of them, which is why I don't have one yet. But maybe one day."

"Well, you'd have to show interest in a girl for more than one night for that to happen," Logan teases her brother, and he laughs while shaking her off.

"On that note, you seeing anyone, Logan?"

Before she can answer, Royce chimes in, "Nope, and I'd know. After the last guy not going so well, she knows to give me all the details even if it's too early to really be doing that."

My expression must clearly be asking what he means because Logan adds to his statement: "When I broke up with the last guy I was seeing, he didn't take it well."

"What exactly does that mean?"

Royce cuts Logan off, "He blasted pictures of her and her cell number all over the internet. Encouraging people to hit her up if they wanted, *attention*."

"You're kidding..." My tone is anything but amused.

"Nope, after the third guy tried texting me, I explained the situation that it was an angry ex, but I wasn't 'open for business,' and he posted on the thread he saw my information on that it wasn't legit."

"Yeah, but that didn't deter everyone."

Logan rolls her eyes at Royce's comment. I ask her directly, "What does he mean by that?"

"He means some people have been more persistent. Even knowing it wasn't a real ad."

Royce glares at her, still looking in her direction when he says, "She had stalkers."

"Multiple?"

"Yeah, I've dealt with all but one. He's been more difficult to find."

"And I'm not worried. You'll find him!" she huffs, clearly annoyed by the topic of conversation. Royce gives me a nervous look, and I have full intentions of getting more details out of him later. Having no desire to ruin Logan's night, I let it drop for now and wave down the waitress for Logan to put in her drink order.

After Logan orders her drink, Royce steers the conversation back to me. His energy is contagious and both Logan and I can't help but get a little buzz from him. He's obviously happy to have me back in town, and leaving him behind is one of the biggest regrets I have. He was my best friend, but to get myself through all my schooling and knowing I wanted to go to law school, I had to put a little distance in our relationship. We still spoke regularly throughout the years, but we haven't seen much of each other in person. He's one of the main reasons I moved back home. I was able to establish a strong reputation for myself in New York, knowing that I always planned to lean on that reputation in a big city to become a Junior Partner early in my career back home in Abilotte.

The night continues with another round of drinks, and as everyone is finishing their last few bites of food, Royce comments on how enjoyable it was to have everyone together. I tell him, "I agree, it's been great catching up with you both. Thanks for letting me crash your sibling dinner."

"You know you're welcome any time. You're basically family anyways." My eyes flicker over to Logan at his comment. Her lips part slightly, caught off guard by the comment. My mind briefly wanders to what it would feel like to have her lips against mine before it registers her pressing those lips into a hard line. I smirk at her and tell him, "Well then, you can count on seeing a whole lot more of me." I pull my wallet out of my pocket and drop some cash on the table, rising to stand as I slip out of the booth. Royce follows suit and nudges Logan out of the booth.

We do a quick hand grab and shoulder pat as our goodbye. As I'm turning away from Royce, I pull Logan into a hug before she can register what's happening. She's stiff in my arms as I whisper, "See you next week," through

her hair, my hand subtly tracing down her back. At 6'4",
her 5'3" frame lines her face up with the center of my chest,
and I feel her soften into me slightly with the familiarity of
our hug. Not wanting to push her too far in one night, I
release her. The slight flush on her chest and the dilation in
her pupils are all the reassurance I need—she isn't as
disinterested as she's pretended to be for the past decade. I
walk out with quiet confidence, knowing I'll have her in my
arms again soon.

The next day sitting at the office and paging through
case files on a new client, my assistant knocks before
opening my door. She walks in, case file in hand. "Hi Mr.
Weber. I have a new file for you to review of a potential
client."

I close the file I was looking at before taking the one in
her outstretched hand. I open it and begin reviewing the
details. My mood quickly sours, and a frustrated
expression flashes across my face as I slam it shut. "Damn
it, Rachel. I told you I have no interest in representing
clients charged with kidnapping or abduction. I know I
spoke about this with the partners and you previously.
Why did you bring me this case?"

I see the fear flicker across her face. She hesitates before
speaking, "He's believable. I know you're not interested in
representing child abductors or kidnappers in general, but
I thought you might want to hear him out so you can judge
if you think he's innocent—"

Cutting her off, I sigh. "Rachel, it's not about their
guilt. I am not interested in trying those cases. If you think
he's innocent, take his case to someone else. TJ maybe. But
don't bring me another."

"Yes, sir." She scurries out of the room, probably grateful my rage dissipated quickly and not wanting to test her luck. My head drops into my hands, elbows propped up on my desk as I close my eyes trying to shake away the memory flashing into view. As it fades, I sit up and reach into the bottom drawer of my desk for the bottle of Jefferson's and a glass. Eleven in the morning is far too early to be drinking, but this is why I don't try kidnapping cases. I bring the glass to my mouth and let the warm bourbon coat my lips as I sip on it. Leaning back and resting the glass on my desk, my mind wanders to the one person who could distract me from the weight that comes with those memories.

17 years prior...

Walking along the sidewalk that wraps around the park and heads down to the water, I notice a small frame kicking rocks with her hood up. Feeling even heavier at the sight of her, I slow my strides deciding if I want to deal with another person right now. I came out here to be alone with my miserable self, but before I can turn around the responsibility sets in, and I drag myself over to her.

Approaching her slowly, I put myself in front of her path. She notices me when one of the rocks she kicks skips past my right foot. She looks up at me with an exhausted, splotchy face. I know why she's crying and it's my fault.

"You know you shouldn't be out here alone," I scold her gently.

Her eyes drop as she responds softly, "I'm not, you're here."

"I wasn't a minute ago." She just keeps looking at her feet as she walks past me, moving like a zombie. She must feel as numb as I do. I sigh and spin around, walking a few feet in front of her then sitting down on the rocks. I'm in her line of sight and in her

walking path. As if it takes too much energy for her to walk around me, she stops and reluctantly sits down next to me. She wraps her arms around her bent knees and places her chin on them as she stares out at the water. I wonder what she's thinking and find myself drifting between watching her and looking out at the water lost in my own misery.

She breaks the silence, nearly a whisper, "It's so hard to come here now."

"I know," my voice cracking in response. "I used to come out here and skip rocks all the time. I can't anymore."

"We used to pick dandelions."

I hesitate before asking, "Do you want to do that now?"

As hard as it would be to do it with her, seeing the tears silently rolling down her cheek, it breaks me to see she's not even phased by the feeling.

"No, I can't. I—" the words cut off as she chokes on a sob. I wrap my arm around her and pull her into me, her head pressed into my chest, she starts blubbering about all the things they should've been doing this summer now that they were sixth graders. When she's out of words, she continues crying into me as I stroke the back of her head.

An incoming text breaks the memory. I look down and see Royce's name on my lock screen asking if I can meet him for lunch. When I tell him I can if I'm back in an hour, an address to a Mexican restaurant comes across with the promise that it'll be quick. As I'm heading out the door, I get an email notification that he's signed my retainer for both him and his company and has sent the necessary retainer fee for both accounts. This should be interesting.

The Mexican restaurant looks like your standard hole-in-the-wall spot. Faded orange walls and tile flooring with a row of tables on one side and a friendly host who is already grabbing menus when he sees me through the glass door. Before I can step through the doorway, a hand wraps around my forearm, pulling me to keep walking past the building. I see Royce leading the way around the corner and release the door behind me, knowing better than to ask questions yet.

When we get a few yards down the alley, I question him, "Am I actually going to get to eat lunch today? Or are you planning on showing me why you didn't hesitate to pay such a large retainer?"

Royce gives me a look over his shoulder before facing the keycard scanner in the alleyway. I hear the buzz and unlocking of the steel door as he answers, "Business first."

We walk up a flight of metal stairs and head into the building. Royce leads me to a giant loft overlooking what appears to be a four to five story old warehouse workspace. A metal catwalk leads to the far wall where a set of stairs wraps around the building back down to the first floor. The interior brick and exposed metal beams show off the industrial history of the building.

"What do you think of the space?"

"Depends what you're planning on using it for."

"I want a new headquarters to run business from."

"For the company? I think your employees might miss their modern office space a bit, even if you are primarily a renovation-based commercial real estate development business."

"It wouldn't be for them." His tone is detached but firm, the way he always gets when he talks about his illegal endeavors.

Shifting gears, I comment, "It's big enough to give you privacy in the city, but this is a pretty nice part of town."

"I know. It's going to be more heavily patrolled, and things will get noticed more quickly, but if we patrol it properly and cover our tracks well it should work fine."

"Do you have a plan?"

"I was thinking a food hall and residential apartments in the floors above. There's already garage entrances for food trucks to drive straight onto the main floor. Rotating various food trucks through along with a few staple restaurants we can build in, it'd be easy to justify various trucks coming and going at all hours. Plus, residential space justifies random people coming and going when needed."

I ponder the idea. I don't love being involved, but I don't want him getting caught—and if he does it's now my mess to clean up. "Are you planning on having any vacancies in the units?"

"No, all real tenants, but some may be working the night shift at the food hall. If there's any money that needs cleared, it'll go through the food hall since a lot of cash flows through those businesses anyways."

"Well, it sounds well thought out."

"Do you see any problems?" He looks at me for the first time in the conversation, and I see the doubt behind the mask.

"No, just the surveillance issue but realistically I think your plan will work. Will residents be able to access this space after the food hall closes?"

"No, and I'm planning on splitting the space anyways. The food hall will run on the back half of the week with access from the front of the building. We came in from the back, which I'm planning on sectioning off and only having access through the back door or through secured office space. The back portion of the first floor and this loft space will be secured and soundproofed."

"I'd like to see the design plan to make sure you've got all your bases covered the way it sounds like you do."

"I'll need some paperwork drawn up for the acquisition," Royce says coyly.

"Don't you have a real estate lawyer on staff for that?"

"Doesn't your firm have a real estate lawyer on staff that I now pay for?"

"You want me reviewing it and securing it, don't you?"

He smirks and nods towards a long card table propped up in the space downstairs with two bags of food on it. I walk down and catch the scent of Mexican wafting towards me. I yell up at him, "This has been here the whole time?"

"Is that a yes, you'll take care of it?" he calls back as he starts following me down.

I'm quickly unwrapping the burrito he got me and taking a bite as I answer through a full mouth, "Yeah, asshole. I'll take care of it. Just don't hold out on the food next time." He laughs as he plops into the seat next to me, pulling his gun out of his waistband and dropping it on the table beside him. After I've got about half my burrito down, I pause and look at him eating. His features have hardened as he's aged, and the sight of him comfortable with a gun is so far from the kid I knew.

"Why do you still do it?"

His eyes cut up mid-bite. He lowers his food and shrugs his shoulders, averting eye contact as he says, "What else would I do with my free time?"

"Fuck?"

We both laugh as he lightens up, "Probably. But that's just a different kind of trouble. If I'm going to be making a mess in my free time, might as well make money while I do it. At least I'm not moving drugs anymore, that shit was the worst."

I nod and let the conversation drop as I go back to eating my food. There's not much else to say about the topic really. Pushing him to get out of that world has never worked, no matter how hard I've tried over the years. I'll always encourage him to let it go, but I know at this point it's part of who he is, and I understand it.

After we're done eating, we pack up the trash from the Mexican and head out, walking back past the Mexican restaurant as if we'd just eaten there and were heading back to work with our leftovers.

CHAPTER 5

Logan

Ana turns the knob of Dallas' apartment door and shoves it open for me as we drag in bags of hibachi, sushi, and several bottles of wine. Dallas is sitting on her rich orange loveseat when we come through the door. The modern boho space fits her perfectly. Warm creams and terracotta are the primary colors in the palette with pops of teal, mustard, and deep red. Frida Kahlo-inspired prints decorate the walls, and the plants in front of every window on tables, stools, and stacks of books make her home feel fun and bubbly, but comfortably relaxed at the same time.

She springs off the couch and meets us in the kitchen. I drop my bags and start pulling out the various entrees and Dallas grabs large plates for all three of us to pile an assortment of food onto. Ana finds a corkscrew, three glasses, and quickly hands out full cups, finishing the first bottle between the three of us.

As we're dispersing everything, Dallas speaks to Ana, "Is Arielle coming?"

Ana rolls her eyes in response, "No. Graham is throwing a fit about us doing girls night too often. He wanted her to spend time with him tonight."

"Well, that's stupid," she replies as she stabs a fork into the pile of hibachi chicken on her plate.

"It is. But I think you're really annoyed because you were hoping for some eye candy tonight."

Dallas dramatically places her hand on her chest, "Me? I would never objectify our friend like that."

Ana chimes in, "I mean, her ass is amazing," and everyone breaks out into laughter.

"Anyway! How was everyone's day at work?" Dallas redirects the energy as Ana starts talking about the different clients she had today, and I babble about operations at the Camellia Club. "Who would've guessed that you'd be the manager there after starting in the dining room rolling silverware at fourteen?"

I answer Dallas, "Honestly? Me. I loved that place the minute I walked through it. The elegance, the variety, I can't imagine doing anything else."

"Well, I'm glad you're there. I can't imagine anyone else being my boss."

"Thanks, Ana. I'm thankful somebody feels that way."

Ana hears the frustrated tone in my voice, "You can't make everyone happy, Logan. That's part of being the boss. If some people," she fakes a cough, "Lindsay" and then fakes another, "want to be a pain in the ass, they're going to be no matter what you do."

"I know; I just hate it when I can't give people what they want."

"Which is why you're a great boss." Ana leans into my shoulder playfully.

"Where's Nina tonight?" Dallas asks with a half-full mouth.

"She's with the grandparents for a few hours so I could come hang out." I ask how soccer camp is going, to which she responds, "It's over now. Today was the last day, but that girl loved every second of it. I'm glad I caved and spent the money for her to go. She had so much fun."

"Is she any good?"

"Actually, yeah! She was doing really well, even one of the players on the team commented about how much potential she has."

"That's awesome! Wait, players?" Dallas questions.

I add, "Some of the Abilotte United guys were the coaches at the camp."

"Yeah, it was definitely a nice perk of the camp." Ana giggles at her own implication.

"Speaking of... Logan, do you have anything you'd like to share with the group?" Dallas smirks at me, knowing I haven't told Ana anything about my encounter with Blake. I've avoided giving Dallas any details, too.

"Nope, absolutely nothing."

Ana cocks an eyebrow at me, "Oh?"

When I don't respond, she glances over at Dallas to elaborate. "Someone had an extra guest as sibling dinner this week."

"Wait, who?" Ana's excitement radiates through her tone.

"Royce invited Blake to come," I say quickly before looking down and busying myself with a spicy tuna roll.

"That's all you're gonna tell us?"

"There's nothing really to tell. He moved back to town, and Royce gave him an open invitation to come, so I'm sure he'll be around."

"Logan, if you don't give us the details right now, we may just come watch from the bar next week."

"What do you want to know exactly, Dallas?"

Dallas speaks first, but they take turns peppering me with questions: "How good did he look?" "Did he try to flirt with you at all?" "Is he seeing anyone?" "Did he ask if you were seeing anyone?" "Did he hint that he missed you at all?" "Are you hoping he'll come next week?" "How did seeing him make you feel?"

I laugh at their ridiculousness before answering, "It was... interesting seeing him again. Obviously, we've known each other forever and there's a lot of history, so there were a lot of different feelings flying around all night."

Dallas huffs, "Wow, way to answer without actually answering." I burst out into laughter before she comes back with one more question. "Fine, one last question. Are you planning on shaving next week, just in case?" She joins in my laughter at the end of her question.

Time passes quicker than expected, and before I know it, I'm strolling into O'Brion's for yet another sibling dinner. I can't wait to catch up with Royce. He genuinely loves hearing about the antics of girls' night and I've got some great stories for him. I mentally prepared for Blake to be here, since he said he would be last week, so when I find them both in our usual booth, I'm not caught off guard by the sight.

Royce's back is to me, with Blake sitting across from him. I make eye contact with Blake from a distance, his jade-green eyes holding my gaze. He shifts back in the booth, still watching me as he runs a hand through his sandy-blonde waves, tousling the subtle curls that find their way back to his forehead. His hair is cut shorter on the sides, leaving just enough length on top to feel professional but stylish. He rubs the back of his neck as he looks away from me, his broad shoulders and biceps straining against his white button-up. His sleeves are rolled up to the elbows, and you can see the veins in his forearms trying to escape from under his skin. He's bulky but proportionate for his height, and my heart skips a beat thinking about the things he could do with that strength.

I redirect my mind as I come up beside Royce. He picks his motorcycle helmet out of the booth and hands it over to Blake so I can slide in beside him. I greet them both, and can feel the heat from Blake's gaze on my skin and I look at Royce to talk. Am I imagining that? I look back over at Blake and see those striking green eyes fixed on me.

Under the weight of Blake's gaze, I turn back to Royce to speak, "Can you order me my usual when the waitress comes back? I'm going to run to the bathroom to wash my hands before we eat."

"Sure," he smiles coolly at me, seemingly unaware of the tension between Blake and me.

As I slide out of the booth, I hear Blake comment, "I think I'm going to do the same, actually," and I can feel him walking close behind me as we head toward the bathrooms. When we get to the hallway where the bathrooms are, Blake lengthens his strides. He gets even with me on my right, brushing up against me in the narrow hallway. He leans over to whisper near my ear, "You look absolutely stunning tonight."

My step stutters at the comment, and he spins around to place himself directly in front of me, our bodies nearly touching with how close he stopped. I see a smirk pull at his lips, which annoys me that he's finding my reaction so amusing. Irritated, I snap back, "Well, you look like a backstabber to me. I don't know how Royce trusts you honestly."

His smirk falls and his eyebrows furrow into a frown. "What exactly do you mean by that?"

"You were more worried about protecting yourself than protecting him. The things he does? The risks he takes? It's all because you left him behind and left him with no other options."

I try to step past him, but he blocks my path, getting even closer into my space until my neck strains to glare up at him. When I don't speak, he does: "You're still mad at me after all this time? I had his record expunged as soon as I could, the second I got out of law school. Did he ever tell you that? I know I shouldn't have let him take the fall himself, but he insisted. We were teenagers, for Christ's sake. He's forgiven me—he was never even mad at me since it was his idea. What exactly would you have me do to warrant your forgiveness?"

Truthfully, I didn't know that he had gotten Royce's record cleared. My anger falters for a minute as I debate whether he's remorseful about the situation. He just justified his actions and excused them with his age and Royce's complicity in the situation. He's acting like his ability to make it go away resolved the issue, but that would've been nearly eight years later before his record was expunged. Royce had to live with a record for eight years before he "fixed it." His life path was set by then; it was too late. No, he doesn't get my forgiveness. He deserves my resentment.

My anger rises back up, and as I open my mouth to speak, Blake's deep, paternalistic tone cuts me off, "Whatever you're about to say, don't. You're just picking a fight because you want to be mad at me. You don't want to feel this thing between us because you want to loathe me." He pauses, and in the silence I feel my body recognizing exactly how close we are. My breath picks up as I look down at the measly space between us. Looking back up at him, I feel him shift his weight forward, causing his firm abs to graze against my breasts.

"It's fine if you don't want to admit you've always been just as attracted to me as I am to you." His left hand finds the underside of my jaw, lightly tipping my head back farther. His touch is like electricity and causes my eyes to flutter shut. He speaks softly. "It's fine if you don't want to admit it, Dandy. You couldn't handle me anyways."

Before I can process his words, his hand is off my face, the weight of his body in front of mine a phantom as he breezes past me back to the table, not bothering to wash his hands like he pretended he was going to. I watch over my shoulder as he walks away from me, not bothering to look back.

I head into the bathroom, washing my hands and trying to process the conversation that just happened. What does he mean I couldn't handle him? I know more about him than anyone else on Earth, or at least I used to. Also, why do I care? It's not like I trust him. Him fixing Royce's record and staying close with him over the years doesn't change what he did.

I walk back out to the table and grab my seat. I have a difficult time staying engaged in the conversation because my mind is busy contemplating if I could ever forgive Blake. I shouldn't; he doesn't deserve it. Besides, what would it really change? I'll be friendly towards him for Royce's sake no matter what, and if he thinks I "can't handle him" then whatever attraction he feels the need to expose doesn't matter. I try to suppress the bitterness and practice being polite to him, since he's clearly going to be around now more than I would prefer. As I shove the resentment away, I can feel a different level of annoyance come back. I desperately want to know why he thinks I can't handle him, but I can't exactly ask that in front of my brother.

My racing thoughts come to a halt when I see a text from a blocked number come through my phone. It's a picture of Royce, Blake, and me sitting at the booth talking accompanied by the message:

Blocked: *Inviting new people to dinner?*
I expect a warm welcome next week.

I drop my phone on the table and look over to the left near the bar where the picture would've been taken. There's nobody there that looks suspicious. When I look back, I see Royce glaring at my phone. He fires off an angry text, presumably to someone on his team to try to track the message, then slides the phone over to Blake.

"This is what I was talking about. This guy has the balls to show up in person and take pictures of her. I think he waits to send them until he's long gone though, because I've never seen him, and I've been in several."

Blake scowls at the phone. "You've never been able to track the messages?"

"Never. His encryption is better than anything I've ever seen. But he's going to fuck up at some point."

"Have you thought about hiring security?"

I speak before Royce can. "He has never threatened me, I think it's stupid to have another person following me.

If I can't tell when I'm being watched, why would they be able to find him any easier?"

The two men share a look that tells me they don't approve of my decision, but Royce knows better than to force my hand. Blake looks at Royce when he speaks. "You'll tell me if anything escalates?"

"Of course."

I hate being treated like a child. I know Royce's protectiveness is just part of how he shows he cares, but it's still frustrating feeling like I'm not capable of taking care of myself. I try to push past the feeling and shake off the incident so I can enjoy the rest of dinner, but I can't help but feeling like the night has been soured thanks to my annoying stalker.

CHAPTER 6

Logan

The alarm on my phone pings, and I squint as I turn it off. The clock reads 4:15 a.m. and I groan, forcing myself to pull the blankets off. I flip on the lamp as I shuffle over to my closet to pluck out a pair of lavender leggings and a matching sports bra. I grab a white tank top with a reflective silver stripe down the back and work on changing into my running outfit. Even half-awake, my mind starts racing about last night. I slept horribly, probably because my subconscious couldn't stop thinking about Blake's behavior last night. Was he just messing with me? Was it a taunt trying to push me to try my luck? Was that his subtle way of rejecting me by telling me not to bother? I pull my ponytail tight and shake my head, partly testing out the pony's strength and partly trying to shake the thoughts out of my head.

I brush my teeth and scold myself for letting Blake be the first thing I think about in the morning. Then I go back to wondering if I have any anger left in my heart for him, or if he's right and I was just trying to distract myself from wanting him. Maybe holding on to being angry with him isn't worth the energy; maybe I'd be better off just letting it go. It'd be easier to be around him if I could move past it. I lace up my running shoes and head out the front door into the dark morning. I head down the front steps of the townhouse, onto the sidewalk, and take off.

12 ½ years prior…

I wake up to knocking at the door and glance over at the ancient brown alarm clock on my nightstand, 3:12 a.m. Who the hell is knocking right now? The knocking gets more aggressive, and I sit up to peek out the bedroom window. The second I glance at the window, I recognize the tell-tale blue lights and jump out of bed to race down the hall to the front door. As I'm coming around the corner, I hear a strong voice project, "Mr. Cooper? This is the police. Please come to the door."

I'm not shocked at all that they're looking for my father. I am surprised when I timidly pull open the door and see Royce standing between two police officers, handcuffed. "Royce?"

His apologetic eyes find mine, the sorrow not leaving as he says, "Hey, Logie."

The cop glances at Royce before speaking to me. "What's your name, miss?"

"It's Logan."

"Are you Royce's sister?"

"Yes."

"How old are you, honey?"

"Fifteen."

"Unfortunately, we can only drop off your brother into the custody of an adult family member. Would you mind going to get your father for me?"

"He's... at work." Royce gives me a subtle nod of approval at the lie. I have absolutely no clue where our father is right now, but sharing that is surely not going to help the situation.

The other officer speaks, "What about your mother?"

My eyes drop and I don't have the heart to answer, so Royce speaks up. "She skipped town and ditched us when I was six. Your guess is as good as mine on where she is."

The second policeman gives me a look of sympathy before saying, "If we can't drop him off with a parent tonight, we're going to have to take him to the police station and book him."

I fight back tears, "Please, don't. What happened? What did he do?"

The officers both look at Royce to let him answer, and he simply shakes his head no. The officer on the right asks, "Do you want us to go ahead and call your father?"

"No! Please, don't. Logan," Royce begs me, "please don't call Dad."

"Royce, if I don't, you're going to go to jail."

He just looks down, repeating himself, "Please don't call him."

The cops both give me a long look before I reluctantly shake my head. I sense the pity coming off them both. They have no idea what would happen if we bothered our father with this. Realistically, he probably wouldn't even answer or show up to help. But if he did, he'd probably just make the whole situation worse. Then he would lay into Royce, and it wouldn't even be worth it.

It took a full three days before Royce walked through the front door of our house. It was the most miserable three days of my life, even worse than when Mom left us. He ended up getting kicked off the baseball team over the arrest and had to do a million hours of community service to avoid jail time. He was charged with possession with intent to sell, along with criminal trespassing. The charges were right; he and Blake were dealing marijuana at school, but they broke into the school that night just to have somewhere to hang out. Blake was already eighteen at the time, so Royce took the fall for everything, hoping he could get it sealed as a juvenile record. His public defender was able to get the intent-to-sell dropped based on the quantity but was too lousy to get everything processed before his eighteenth birthday. He ended up with a record, and everyone at school looked at him differently after that. He tried to hide it from me, but I know he looked at himself differently too, like he was somehow lesser because he got busted. He lost most of his scholarships to college, and some even withdrew their admission offers.

Nothing was the same after that. Without baseball to distract him, he got into more and more trouble. He got deeper into dealing, saying he was doing it to help pay for college, ended up in fights, and started hiding things from me. That's how I knew it was bad. He started surrounding himself with new people and keeping me and Blake away from his "new friends." I tried to convince him to move past it early on, but over the years, I gave up, knowing the argument was falling on deaf ears. I never knew Blake was trying to help, too. Maybe if I had, we could've worked together to pressure Royce to be done. That's probably why he never told me his record was expunged. He didn't want me to know.

As I'm debating with myself about how to act, I can feel the bitterness towards Blake leaving my body. Apparently, I'm going to forgive him after over a decade of resentment. I can't believe myself. I make it to a stoplight and bend over, hands on my knees as I try to catch my breath from the run. When the light changes, I cross the street and make a left, running past Royce's real estate office. It's amazing what he's made himself into in the last decade. He has an entire building on 2nd Street full of employees who help him run his international company. It makes it easier to hide his supplemental income. I just wish he could see himself the way we do; maybe it would be enough to make him walk away.

I focus on my run, the route getting harder and long enough that my brain doesn't have enough energy to wander. That's the best part of my morning runs, even more than the physical benefits and runner's high, it's the quietness in my mind that accompanies the finish line. I push myself on the last leg before getting back home, and when I walk through the door, I kick off my shoes by the entrance so they're ready and waiting to be slipped back on tomorrow morning.

CHAPTER 7

Blake

I walk back into my office from meeting with a new client and drop the file next to a pair of size 10 Johnston & Murphy shoes that are currently propped up on my desk.

"TJ, what the hell do you think you're doing?"

He gives me an ornery smile before answering. "Convincing you to go out with me tonight."

"Why on earth would I want to do that?"

"Because it's Friday night, we're single, handsome criminal defense attorneys. I've been waiting for someone fun to join the firm since LaFleur got married and left me as the last man standing."

"I have closing arguments on my manslaughter case today."

"Exactly! Celebratory drinks and war stories for the ladies at the bar!"

"I would rather shove my dick into a meat grinder than go out tonight."

"This invitation isn't up for negotiation, Weber."

I glare at him. "Fine, if you insist on drinking tonight, then you can come over and have some beers with me while I finish unpacking."

"That is not what I had in mind."

"Well, that's the offer on the table."

He ponders it, then drops his feet off my desk and pushes out of the chair. "Boring, but deal. Only because I'm convinced I'll get you out of the house before the night is over." He claps me on the shoulder as he passes by, and a chuckle escapes me at his persistence. I wouldn't have expected to make friends with someone at the office so quickly; I'm normally fairly reserved. But Tyler Jethro, "TJ", Buckley wasn't taking no for an answer, and he's quickly weaseling his way into my circle. Quite frankly, everyone at the office loves him and I understand why. He's got one of those personalities that entertains everyone, even when he's being abrasive. Royce would like his energy. That thought prompts me to invite Royce over for drinks with TJ tonight.

A few hours later, TJ is tipping his Uber as he walks in the front door.

"You Ubered?"

"I'm not planning on being sober enough to drive home."

"Beer's in the fridge." He walks to the kitchen, grabs one, and cracks it open. He turns to look out the floor-to-ceiling window in the living room. "Your view of the city is amazing, man."

"Thanks, it was a pretty lucky find. It's not a bad commute to the firm, either."

"I don't see any boxes to unpack. I thought you said you needed help."

"Were you actually planning on helping?"

"Absolutely not."

"That's what I figured. I finished the last few while I was waiting on your slow ass to get over here." We continue bantering and Royce shows up shortly afterward. Him and TJ introduce themselves, and Royce quickly warms up to TJ's constant instigations. We order burgers for dinner, and down a few more rounds. Empty bottles and wadded-up wrappers litter the coffee table as the casual conversation continues. I actually enjoy myself more than I thought I would've, and TJ has only tried to change my mind about going out about once an hour. The last time, though, Royce sided with TJ saying it'd be fun for us all to have a night out together. I had to promise another time to get out of it.

It's nice to see Royce relaxed, though his phone hasn't stopped going off and I think he's just bringing the third beer to his mouth without actually drinking it. TJ, on the other hand, has already put down a six-pack himself and I'm not sure he has any clue where his phone is. His place could be on fire, and he wouldn't even be bothered.

A groan escapes Royce's lips. "Logan and her friends are drunk."

My pulse picks up instantly. TJ asks, "Who's Logan?"

"My sister. She wants me to come get them and take them home."

"Oh! Let's all go!" TJ is way too enthusiastic. I point out to him we'd be going to take them home, not to stay out. "Sure, but maybe one will want some company."

"As long as it's not my sister, I don't care." Royce chirps back as he stands up, checking his pockets for his keys and wallet.

S. Belle

"Bet." TJ is up and moving before Royce can finish replying to Logan that he's on his way. "You coming with, Weber?"

I shake my head. While I'd love to see how Logan acts around me drunk, crammed into Royce's SUV with Royce, TJ, and whoever else is present is not how I want that going down. "I'm good here. Royce, do you mind dropping TJ off, too?"

"Sure, you ready to go?" Royce asks TJ, and TJ is out the door in response. Royce laughs. "Well, this should be entertaining. You sure you don't want to come and watch the show?"

"Nah, I'm good. But I can't wait to hear about it later."

"Alright, have a good night, man." He pulls the door shut, and I slump back into the couch, finish off my beer and pray TJ doesn't think going after my girl is a good idea. I don't want our friendship to end with me rearranging his face.

CHAPTER 8

Logan

Dallas and I are standing at the bar when I feel my phone vibrate. I assume it's Ari or Ana asking for another drink when I see an unknown number. I subtly turn my phone away from Dallas as I open it. I haven't told any of the girls about my stalker; I didn't want them worrying, but when a picture of us standing at the bar comes through, I have a hard time hiding my nerves.

"Something wrong?" Dallas questions me.

"Just getting tired. I think I'm going to text Royce to pick us up."

"Boo, one more round of shots then."

"Okay, fine, but let me get him to agree first." She chugs the glass of wine I just ordered for myself, knowing I won't drink it, and waves down the bartender again for a round of shots. Once I get confirmation that Royce is coming and will take everyone home, I reach for the shot and throw it back. The liquid courage has my thumbs moving as I trail behind Dallas back to where we left Ana and Ari. I respond to the unknown number:

Me: *Too scared to come say hi?*

I know provoking him is a terrible idea, but I do it anyway. I'm so tired of this bullshit. A minute or so later, my phone pings with a "message undeliverable" notification. Well, I guess Royce can't be too mad at me then.

I'm trying to continue dancing, funneling some energy off Ari who's currently grinding against a random guy that is getting exceptionally handsy with her, but she doesn't seem to mind. She looks completely in her element, keeping rhythm with the bass of the song blaring through the club. Dallas has slipped in next to her, and the two of them are scream-singing to each other while they dance. Before I know it, I feel a hand on my shoulder and nearly jump out of my skin before realizing it's just Royce.

He clocks my reaction. "Everything alright?"

"Yeah, all good!" I spin to pull him into a hug with a major wobble.

"Woah, how much have you had to drink, Logie?" I giggle at my nickname.

Maybe I am more drunk than I realized. "Enough, clearly." I spin back to face the group, one arm still draped around Royce. I feel TJ's arm drape over mine, and hear him addressing everyone:

"Hey ladies, I'm TJ. Royce did not do you justice with just how beautiful you all are."

Ari doesn't even acknowledge his comment, Dallas laughs and rolls her eyes at him, but Ana seems to enjoy the simple line. Royce shrugs TJ's arm off him. "Why did TJ come with you? Also, who is TJ?"

"He works with Blake, and he wanted to tag along, hoping a drunk girl would invite him in."

"Hey! Don't tell them my master plan, dude. Not cool."

Ana laughs before adding in, "Well, I'm not opposed to the suggestion. Dallas, what do you think?"

"I think you're all nuts."

Royce redirects the conversation. "Is everyone ready to get going?"

Ari complains, "Come on guys, can't we stay for one more song?" She wraps her hand around the head of the guy dancing against her, and her engagement ring flashes in the strobe lights.

The guy behind her seconds her request. "Yeah, come on guys, just another song or two," his hand squeezing the hem and waistline of her shorts together so tightly her red thong's waistband is slightly visible.

I hear my brother's voice growl beside me. "Absolutely not." He's glaring at Ari. She ignores his comment and continues dancing. He slips out from beneath my arm and approaches her. "I'm not going to stand here and watch you be disrespectful. Your ride is leaving, let's go."

The guy behind her speaks. "It's fine man, I can take her home."

"I'm sure her fiancé would have feelings about that." Ari's eyes cut over to Royce at that comment and she freezes.

Whatever passes between them, Royce turns to leave, and she grabs Dallas' hand to follow her. Dallas grabs me, and I reach back and grab Ana. TJ has his arm snaked around her waist, so I'm not worried about him being left behind. We all make it out of the club and are leaning on each other for support as we approach Royce's Levante.

"Ooh, a Levante. Good choice, big bro." Ari inspects the car as we approach it.

"Just get in already," Royce grumbles as he climbs into the driver's seat. I hop in the passenger seat next to him, hoping I get him past disliking Ari. He's never actually met her before, though he has heard a lot about her, and that wasn't exactly a good introduction. I watch as the four left in our group figure out how they're going to fit in three seats. Ari climbs in the seat behind me, and TJ climbs in behind Royce, leaving the middle seat open.

"Who wants the middle and who wants to sit on my lap?" TJ asks Ana and Dallas.

Ana climbs over him slowly, acting like she's going to sit on his lap, then moves past him and sits in the middle. TJ gives Dallas a questioning face before she slams the door shut and walks around the car to hop in Ari's lap.

"Oh, come on. Really?" The whole backseat breaks into laughter, and I even see Royce crack a smile out of the corner of my eye.

Ari wraps her arms around Dallas and whispers something to her that warrants a giggle, and I notice Royce scowling at her again through the rearview mirror. I nudge him enough to make him look at me. "Can we go?" gently encouraging him to drive. He shifts into drive and pulls out as the banter from the back seat drifts forward.

"So, what does TJ stand for?" Dallas asks him.

"Tyler Jethro. Tyler Jethro Buckley," he grabs her hand and kisses the back of it. "It's a pleasure," he says in his smoothest voice he could muster.

Dallas almost falls out of Ari's lap laughing, and Ana throws her arms around his neck. "Hey, I thought I was your favorite!"

"Don't worry, there's plenty of me to go around."

"Even some for me?" Ari chimes in from behind Dallas. Royce comes to a hard stop, sending everyone forward in their seat. I ask him, "What was that for?"

"Dallas, it's your stop," he says, ignoring my question.

Dallas drunkenly hugs everyone in the car, and Royce is softening watching her in the mirror. She's getting ready to get out of the car, then turns back dramatically. "Wait! TJ! We need to add you to the GroupChat."

"Oh?"

"Yeah, that way you can come out with us next time. We can be your wing-women!"

"Or you can just be my women."

Her eyes roll while laughing. "See? That humor is worthy of the GroupChat. Ana, can you add him?"

"Already on it!" and she's got her phone out shoving it towards TJ. He finishes putting his number in her phone, and Dallas takes that as a good enough time to shut the door. Royce pulls off and heads to the next stop, dropping Ana off next. She climbs out on TJ's side of the car, facing him when she passes over him to get out. He slides his hands on her hips, pausing her so she's straddling him. "Don't miss me too much tonight," she teases.

"It'd be a lot harder to miss you if I was in your bed."

She laughs and gives him a peck on the cheek before continuing to get out.

"You could probably follow her in if you want," Ari suggests to TJ. Before he can think twice, Royce pulls away.

"Sorry, man. Maybe next time." Royce laughs at the frustration he just caused TJ.

My townhouse is close to Ana's place, so it doesn't take long before Royce makes it there. I thank him for picking everyone up and taking them home.

"No problem, I just have to get these two home, and I'll be in bed at basically the same time as usual. It's no big deal." I know he's downplaying it so I don't hesitate to need him again in the future.

"I know, but really, thank you." I give him a quick hug, then look back at the backseat. "Leave Ari alone, TJ. She's engaged."

"We'll see about that," TJ jokes. I raise my eyebrows at the two of them and climb out of the car, not wanting to know what happens next.

The next morning, my alarm for my run goes off, and I completely ignore it. However, I jolt awake a few hours later when I realize I promised Ana I'd go to an Abilotte United game with her, Nina, and Ari. I curl up in a blanket and make my way out to the kitchen, the cream walls reflecting far too much morning sun for my pre-coffee hangover headache. I quickly finish my first cup, then refill it and start getting ready for the game.

Before I know it, I'm in the stands near midfield, sandwiched between Ana and a drunk guy who's heckling the referee way too loudly. I look down the line and notice Ari at the far end staring at me.

Still looking at me, she asks, "Want to switch?" Clearly my suffering is exceptionally visible.

"No, it's okay."

"Alright, then." She climbs over the back of her seat, using the three empty seats between her, Nina, and Ana to get closer to where I'm standing. She pulls the hat off her head, then leans down to Ana. "Cover Nina's ears."

Ana doesn't even hesitate. The second Ana's hands are on Nina's head, Ari smacks the dude next to me in the shoulder with her hat before yelling, "Hey asshole, it's a damn soccer game. The more you yell at him, the more he's going to call shit against us. So politely, shut the hell up."

He scoffs at her, then turns back to the game. She's halfway back to her seat when he yells something again. She mutters under her breath, "For the love of God…" Turning back around, she grabs him by the shoulder and squats slightly to get near his face. "I swear on everything you find Holy, if you don't stop yelling, you'll see just how dark the bottom of Maiden Lake is."

He looks back at her, and whatever he sees in her eyes makes him give a soft nod. She releases his shoulder, walks back to her seat and plops down in it, resting her elbows on her knees and holding her head up like that interaction took every ounce of energy she had left in her. Ana and I both make eye contact, Ana fighting back a laugh over the situation, which causes me to shake my head and smile.

The halftime whistle blows, and the players make their way over to the bench before heading into the locker room. With our seats in the fourth row behind the bench, we have a great view of some of the players.

"Man, these seats were worth every penny. Do you see how good Lucas Clark looks?" Ari drools over the players down below.

"Don't you have a fiancé?" I joke.

She waves a hand in the air. "Eh, what he doesn't know won't kill him."

"Speaking of, how's the wedding planning going?" Ana asks her.

"My mother is going to be the death of me, I swear. And I think Graham intentionally encourages her just to see how much I can take. It's been bru-tal."

I've been mostly staying out of the way with the planning, but I try to be reassuring. "It can't be that bad right? I'm sure she's just excited for you."

"She's not even letting me design my own dress."

My mouth falls open. "I mean, I knew she had feelings about our dresses, but you can't design yours?"

"I didn't really even get to pick it. I was basically just a catalog model for her while I tried on nine million dresses before she found one she thought was both 'flattering' and 'worthy of a Rhodes woman,' whatever the hell that means."

Ana retorts, "I really hate that she didn't let you design your dress. I mean, it's not like you have your own wedding line or anything."

"Trust me, I know. At this point, though, it's not even worth the hassle. As long as there's wine and I'm married at the end of the trainwreck, if it floats her boat, then so be it."

Not sure what else to say, I shift the subject slightly. "Do you know when our bridesmaids' dresses will be in?"

"Oh! They're here actually, so you can stop by whenever to get fitted for alterations."

"You're going to do them?"

"Why not? Saves y'all some money, right? I can't imagine either of you plan on re-wearing those dresses."

"Yeah, a black satin mermaid-style gown with a Swarovski crystal belt is actually my usual Sunday luncheon attire. How'd you know?" Ana retorts with her best posh accent.

"They're definitely styled for someone a few decades older than us, but they're not completely unflattering at least."

Ari rolls her eyes at my comment. "It's okay, Logan. You can admit you hate them along with the rest of us." She shifts her gaze down to Nina, "The best part of the whole day, though, will be getting to spend so much time with my flower girl!" She pulls Nina into a side hug and gives her a soft shake, which elicits a laugh out of her.

"Mom, when do I get to try on my flower girl dress?"

Ana responds, "I'm not sure yet, sweetie, but we'll go soon, okay?"

"Okay! Aunt Ari, will you let me help you with the alterations for my dress?"

"Anything for my favorite human ever."

"Is it okay if I stop by next week?"

Ari looks at me when answering my question. "Sure, just text me a heads-up day of so I can make sure I don't have another client when you're coming. No point in sitting around waiting for me if you can avoid it, right?"

"Of course."

Our conversation trails off as the players take the field for the kickoff. About ten minutes into the second half, I notice Ari's eyes fixed on Ana.

"Ari, what are you looking at?"

"Well, Ana's head doesn't always look downfield when the ball's downfield, so I'm trying to figure out which player she's watching."

"I don't know what you're talking about," Ana quickly responds with a giggle.

"Is it Clark? I wouldn't blame you. I can share. Or maybe it's King? Or both? I hear they like to share." Ari grins at herself.

"Hey! Little ears over here!"

Nina laughs. "Mom, Aunt Ari says adult things around me all the time. It's okay."

My eyes bug out of my head at Nina's statement, and Ari is laughing way too hard. Ana, however, is too focused on the game to even react appropriately. The player in possession of the ball at the time is none other than the team's biggest playboy, Boston McLeod.

"Wait, is it Boston?"

"He was one of my coaches!" Nina adds. "He was so nice. And he kept telling Mommy how good I was."

"Interesting." Ari's sly grin grows wider as she inspects Ana's reaction. She's playing it too cool, which gives herself away.

I ask her, "Anything you have to say for yourself, Ana?"

"No comment," she says, fighting a laugh.

Mid-morning the following Thursday, I meet Royce at Atelier Rhodes, Arielle's flagship store for her bridal and couture collections. Royce is hovering outside of the building, coffees in each hand. He smiles warmly at me and passes a cup over as I get close to him.

"Thank you so much for coming with me."

"What are big brothers for?"

"I feel bad dragging you here just for me to try on one dress for five minutes."

"Logan, stop feeling bad. I offered to tag along."

We head in, and are greeted by Ari's assistant, "Hello, my name is Alyssa. Are you here to browse Serein by Arielle Rhodes, or Fleur de Lune this morning?"

"Hi, Alyssa! I'm actually here to meet with Arielle. She's doing a fitting for my bridesmaid dress for me."

"Oh, did you have an appointment with her? I don't see anything on her calendar…" She quickly clicks through a few screens on her computer behind the desk in the entryway of the store.

"No, she told me I could just drop by whenever today because she wasn't very busy."

"Okay, well, let me go up and let her know you're here, Miss…?"

"Logan. Logan Cooper." I answer her with a smile.

"Okay, Miss Cooper. I'll be back shortly. Please feel free to look around while you wait."

As she disappears to the back of the store, I see Royce already looking around Ari's couture collection, grazing his hands over the fabric of a few pieces. As he peruses, he stops, grabbing a silky red dress, rubbing the fabric between his fingers. "Did Arielle really design all of these?"

"Are you impressed?" Ari's voice comes from behind me, strolling towards us with a gentle smile on her face.

Royce's gaze at the dress is broken as he looks over at her. "Not really."

Her face drops, and she squints at him before flicking the gaze over to me. "Why did you bring him exactly?" Dragging an unexpected laugh out of me and a soft chuckle out of my brother.

"Follow me," Ari spins towards the back of the store with a head nod and leads the way behind a drawn curtain to reveal the fitting room. There's a trifold mirror with a pedestal to stand on, a few hanging racks on the wall next to the mirror, and a sewing machine with some thread reels and fabric on the walls, along with various scraps of lace, beadwork, and other materials she may need to reference for clients to visualize an alteration. Past the mirror are six large changing rooms, black tile flooring, white walls, and deep red curtains throughout the space.

"Ari this space is so cool. I don't think I've ever been back here before."

"Why would you need to be? That's your dress on the first rack there. You can use any of the rooms you'd like to get changed. Did you bring your shoes?"

"Yes, ma'am!" I hold up the strappy black heels after pulling them from my bag.

"Perfect, go get changed. Royce, you can hang out on the couch there if you want."

I make my way back and pick the second fitting room on the left. I can hear conversation between Royce and Ari while I change, but the sound doesn't carry well in the space, so I can't really hear what they're talking about. I quickly change into the subpar dress Ari's mother bullied her into making us wear, then plop onto the gold stool while I strap up the heels.

The dress is a little loose, but not a terrible fit. I find myself shifting around in it, trying to make it a little more comfortable as I make my way back out to the main space. When I get out there, Ari is sitting on the couch next to Royce, and they look like they're actually getting along. Ari notices me out of her peripheral vision and jumps up, flying into motion.

She grabs a pin cushion off the sewing machine, and quickly starts pinning around my hips and ribcage to tighten the dress appropriately. "I think we need to pull in the hips and your ribcage area a bit. Does that feel okay?"

"Can you loosen the top a little bit?" She nods in response, pulling the pins out and giving me a few millimeters more room that will make all the difference. She squats down, pinning around my hemline to account for my short stature, then bounces back up.

"What do you think? Does it feel okay?"

I do a quick twirl and step off the pedestal, taking a short lap to test the length, before hopping back up. "Yeah, it feels good."

I run my hands over the shoulders then down the sides of the dress to the belt. "Royce, what do you think?"

"Dude, why are you asking him? It's not like men really notice that level of detail. He doesn't even know what to look for."

Royce clocks her in the mirror before speaking. "The belt looks like it's sitting a little low if it's supposed to hit her natural waistline. Can you bring the torso piece up a bit?"

I just raise my eyebrows at Ari, and she glares at me, the look really meant for Royce. I try to contain my laughter as she pulls up slightly at the top of the shoulders, bringing the boat neckline up a bit further and dragging the belt to the right height on my hips. "I'll adjust the neckline through here," she runs her hands along the top hem that's currently pressing into my neck a bit too tight, "that way it's not choking you. But do you like that better with how the belt hits your waist?"

"Yeah, I do." I catch the satisfied smirk Royce is sporting in the mirror.

"Alright," Ari replaces several of the pushpins with safety pins, "That should hold in case you knock any out changing. Go get dressed, and you can leave the dress in the changing room."

I strip out of the dress, throw it on the hanger, then change back into my regular clothes. When I come back out, Royce is standing near Ari with his arms crossed casually over his chest. They both stop talking when they notice me coming.

"You ready to go?"

"Yep. Thank you, Ari, for doing the alterations."

"Absolutely, it's the least I can do for making you wear that dress."

Ari leads us out as Royce asks, "You picked bridesmaids dresses you don't like?"

"My mother did, trust me, it's a long story."

"And I have no desire to hear it." I smack him on the shoulder over that comment.

We quickly say our goodbyes to Ari and her sweet assistant, Alyssa. Standing on the sidewalk, I notice Royce's Ducati Diavel V4 parked on the street a few spots past the storefront, the opposite direction of my Bronco.

"Alright, I'm this way," I say, throwing my thumb over my shoulder. "But I'll see you tonight for dinner?"

"Absolutely. I'm probably going to be a little later than usual, so feel free to grab drinks and food without me, and I'll order when I make it there."

"Everything okay?"

"Yeah, I just have a lot of loose ends for an upcoming deal that I want to make sure are moving in the right direction before I head out tonight. Nothing to worry about, just a couple end-of-day meetings to make sure it's all good."

"Alright, well then I'll see you tonight!" He starts walking toward his bike but keeps watching me over his shoulder until I make it into the car and drive past him safely, waving goodbye as I pass.

CHAPTER 9

Blake

I get to O'Brion's just before our standing meet-up time. I'd pretend I was just early, but, truthfully, I was itching to see Logan again. Sibling dinner has quickly become the highlight of my week, knowing I'll get to see her. I grab our usual booth, positioning my back to the door so she'll have to walk past me to get to the other side. The waitress is friendlier than usual when she notices I'm alone, and I order a beer while I wait.

I feel her presence before I see her, catching a whiff of her perfume as she passes me. She smells like my perfect kind of heaven. She drops into the seat across from me and gives me a strained smile before she tells me, "Royce let me know he's probably going to be later than normal."

"Oh, he didn't mention that to me."

"Yeah, he said we can go ahead and order food and everything. Sounds like he's expecting to be seriously late."

"Alright then, do you want to get any appetizers?"

"Appetizers?"

"Yeah, food before the main meal. Surely, you've heard of them before."

She rolls her eyes at my joke, then looks down at the menu. "The pretzel bites are really good, but I don't usually get any."

"Why not?"

"Oh, I don't need them. My meal is more than enough."

Before she can tell me not to, I make eye contact with our waitress. She heads over, asking if Logan needs anything to drink. "Just a water is fine, thank you."

The waitress starts to walk away. "We'll also have an order of pretzel bites and a bottle of rosé." I glance over at Logan, "You still like rosé, right?"

"Of course, but—"

"That should be good for now, thank you." The waitress smiles at me before walking off. There's a stretch of silence as I inspect her appearance. Her hair is in soft curls as usual, and her makeup is natural, but pretty. She's wearing a navy-blue wrap dress that I assume she wore to work, but there's enough cleavage to catch my eye. I can see her heating up under my curious gaze until she finally pipes up. "What are you looking at?"

"You. You look stunning, as usual of course. I'm just appreciating it."

She's clearly caught off guard by my statement. She opens her mouth to speak, then stops several times before pinning me with her eyes and asking, "what did you mean when you said I couldn't handle you."

"Oh, sweet Dandy..." A smile tugs at my lips as I answer. "Why do you care, exactly?"

She thinks for a second before responding, "I just wanted to know if that was more of an insult toward me, or an insult to yourself."

I shake my head, "I'd never insult you. But, if you're really interested in finding out what I meant," I switch seats and slide into her booth, forcing her to move closer to the wall, "I'm more than happy to show you."

Our waitress comes back with the bottle of wine, noting the change in our seating arrangements and appearing a little disappointed. I couldn't care less about her interest though; my eyes are focused on the girl I currently have trapped to my left. After she pours us both a glass and leaves, I turn to face her in the booth.

"What did Royce tell you about me over the past few years?"

"Not much," She averts her eyes, clearly lying.

"Did he tell you about the women I was seeing?"

"Were you seeing someone? Because the only stories I heard were the few times he came to visit you."

The few times I saw Royce in person, we almost always went out, and it usually ended up in one or both of us taking someone new home. Not that those hookups ever amounted to anything, but she doesn't know that.

"Did those stories bother you?"

"Why would they?"

"Because thinking of anyone else kissing those perfect lips of yours drove me mad. Just curious if you had the same thoughts."

I can tell she wasn't expecting my admission. Before she has a chance to speak, I continue, "When Royce told you had a boyfriend during law school, I imagined those pretty lips of yours wrapped around his dick and wondered whether I knew enough to get myself out of a manslaughter conviction."

She glances around us, "Jesus, Blake, we're in public. You can't just say that stuff."

Expecting her dismay, I calmly note: "And that right there, that reaction, is why you can't handle me, Dandy."

There's a softness that flashes across her eyes when I call her by her nickname. I don't want to push her away, just challenge her enough to push her out of her shell. I shift tactics, "I'm sorry, that was a bit bold of me. I just get carried away when it comes to you. Always have."

There's no lie in that statement, but it tells me this gentler approach will help bring her guard down faster. I let my hand drift to her inner thigh as I ask my next question, "But you never answered my question."

"What question?" She asks, genuinely confused.

"If it bothered you, thinking of me with other women." I push the fabric of her dress out of the way, allowing my hand to rest on her bare thigh.

"It wasn't my place to be jealous."

"But were you?" I squeeze a little on her thigh, and she instinctively shifts so her legs spread slightly. I glance from her legs up to her eyes and catch them dilate briefly. "It's okay if you were."

She shrugs her shoulders and watches as the waitress brings the pretzel bites and drops them off at the table, not pulling away from me in the slightest. She plucks a pretzel from the basket before dipping it and plopping it in her mouth. A slight moan escapes her as she closes her eyes, enjoying the taste. When her eyes open, she sees me smiling at her.

"What? They're really good!"

My grin gets bigger at her clearly not realizing what she just did to me. I feel a pulse in my dick thinking about all the different ways I could get another of those moans out of her. She must sense my thoughts, "Stop looking at me like that."

"I can't help it. You just look so delicious."

"If you're hungry, have a pretzel bite." She grabs one, dipping it for me, then bringing it to my mouth. I open and wrap my tongue around the bite between her fingers, then close my mouth so my lips trail across them holding eye contact through the motion. She blushes, not prepared for me to be so bold.

I finish chewing before I ask, "Does my directness make you nervous?"

"No, I just…" she glances down, trying to decide what she wants to say, "I'm just trying to figure out what to do with you."

"What do you mean by that?"

"You're my brother's best friend; I don't want to sleep with you casually and then things be weird for the foreseeable future."

"If there's anything you think is casual between us, you're delusional." I can see her trying to decide if she believes me or not. I ease off for now and ask about her week.

We chat comfortably, though she's still wary of what's going to come out of my mouth. My hand hasn't released her thigh as we talk, order our food, and when it finally comes, I drag her leg across my lap before letting it go, making it clear my intention is to be touching her the remainder of the night. She tries to act like she's unaware of the contact, but I can smell her desire through her vanilla perfume. We finish our food and the bottle of wine, and she's more receptive to my flirting.

The waitress comes to check on us. "Do y'all want another bottle of wine, or maybe some dessert?"

"I think we're good with the checks."

"I was kind of looking forward to dessert. Can we get a brownie à la mode?"

"Of course," The waitress trots off to grab our food.

"Blake, I'm full. I really don't need dessert."

"Trust me, you'll thank me tomorrow. Besides, I'm really looking forward to hearing you moan in pleasure again."

The waitress quickly brings out the dessert, ice cream melting quickly on the warm brownie. Logan dives in, the brownie eliciting a similar reaction as the pretzel bites earlier in the night. I love that she enjoys her food, enjoys the treats in life. I'd buy her cake every day if it meant I got to see the pure bliss on her face. She's nearly a third of the way through the dessert before she realizes I'm massaging her thigh lightly with both hands, not touching the treat.

"Are you going to have any?"

"No, I got it for you."

"There's no way I can finish all of this."

"You can, and you will. For me." I hold her gaze as she takes another bite, the warm ice cream slipping down her lip and chin slightly. She reaches to wipe it away, and I grab her hand, bringing my own thumb to clean it before slipping my ice-cream- coated thumb in her mouth. She swallows her bite and sucks my thumb into her mouth, holding eye contact with me as she runs her tongue over it, licking it clean. She continues to suck a second longer than necessary, then releases.

"Good girl," I coo at her. "Now finish what you started." I nod subtly toward the remainder of the dessert.

She works her way through it, and I watch intently as she eats. My dick throbs in my pants as I imagine her mouth around it. We don't speak as she eats, but her pace picks up the further my hand drifts up her thigh. When she finishes, she's nearly panting and looks at her water glass, realizing it's empty. She glances over at mine before looking up at me. "Do you mind?"

"Say please for me."

She starts to roll her eyes, and I quickly stop her, "I wouldn't do that. You're handling yourself well tonight, but I'm not sure you could handle what happens if you roll those pretty eyes at me."

Her eyes focus on mine. "May I please have a sip of your water?"

"Of course," I grin as she takes several large gulps from my cup.

She looks for our waitress, who reappears. "Everything good?"

"It was wonderful, thank you."

"You sure I can't get y'all one more round?"

I glance at Dandy, debating it before I answer. "No, we're good. Just the check, thanks." When the waitress comes back, Logan tries to ask for a separate check. "I've got it." I tell her.

"I can pay for myself."

"I know you can, but I've got it." I hand the waitress my card and shoo her away before Logan can put up too much of a fight.

"Why did you pay for me?"

"Are you going to question every time I want to do something nice for you?"

"Potentially, if I don't know why you did it."

"Because feeding you tonight was enjoyable for me, and I wanted to pay for my treat. And maybe me doing this for you will motivate you to do something for me later. You know, if you think you can handle it." My innuendo is obvious. I don't truly expect anything out of her tonight, but I do want to be abundantly clear the door is open if she's daring. The waitress returns with my card, and I slide it into my wallet.

"Do you feel okay to drive home?"

"Yeah, it was just two glasses over a few hours, I'm good."

"You sure? I can take you."

"No, I'm good. I promise."

"Okay then, I'm going to head out." I lean over toward her like I'm going for a kiss. She doesn't move towards me but doesn't pull away either. I continue to lean forward, past her face towards her ear, and slip a business card in the pocket at the seam of her dress as I whisper, "Goodnight, Dandy." My hand trails across her waistline as I climb out of the booth, not looking back to judge her reaction.

CHAPTER 10

Logan

I'm still sitting at the booth, astonished by everything that happened tonight. Blake was forward, and it was so damn hot how unapologetically he pursued me. It's hard to associate the man he is now with the boy I knew in my head. When we were younger, he never flirted with me like that. Sure, I always wondered if he looked at everyone the way he looked at me, but he never said anything. He never let his hands roam when he held me, and even his top-of-the-head kisses always felt platonic enough. But after tonight, there's no question about whether or not he's interested, which I guess was his point. I can't exactly deny how much I enjoyed it either, but what would Royce think? What happens when it inevitably falls apart? Royce would always take my side, but he'd lose a friend over it, or at least it would be a lot more strained between them. I don't want to do that to him.

Heading out to my car, still thinking about Royce, I take my phone out to text him to see if he's okay. I was so caught up with Blake tonight that I didn't even register how late it had gotten. When I pull out my phone, there's a text waiting:

> **Royce:** *Hey, I'm so sorry for missing dinner. Things took a lot longer than expected. I'll make it up to you next week?*
>
> **Me:** *It's okay! Did everything get taken care of?*
>
> **Royce:** *I think so.*
>
> **Me:** *Good, well I'm glad you're okay! I was getting worried.*
>
> **Royce:** *I'm sorry, again. Get home safe.*

The next morning, my 4:15 a.m. alarm goes off, and I silence it, flopping over on my back to stare at the crease where the wall meets the ceiling. My brain refuses to stop thinking about Blake. I had exceptionally vivid dreams last night, all about Blake. Some were essentially flashbacks from when we were kids, images of moments together as teenagers before everything fell apart, all with shifts in the memory where he kissed me, or I kissed him. I wonder if he thought about trying something back then, or if this infatuation is new.

I know I thought about it all the time back then. I wasn't even subtle about it. Dallas was well aware of my crush on him over the years. And fifteen-year-old me would've given anything to have the attention Blake is giving me now. But I can't help wonder if it's real, or how long it's been going on in his head. Has he wanted me the way I want him all these years? If so, where did all this confidence come from? I can't imagine the heartbreak if I let him back in the way we were before, let him in even further, and then this obsession fades away. I thought the betrayal hurt before... If he did something like that to me or Royce again when we are together, I don't know if I'd survive that devestation.

I roll over and look at his card on the nightstand. Pulling myself up on my elbows at the edge of the bed, I grab my phone and the card, plugging his number under the contact name "B." I don't know exactly what I plan to do, but I do know if anything happens, Royce cannot find out about it. I guess it wouldn't be weird for me to have Blake's number, but Royce notices a lot, and I don't want to give him any reason to ask any questions.

Do I text him? He clearly wants me to. But if I open that door, can I really go where it's leading? I twirl the card around in my fingers a few times before dropping it back on the nightstand and lugging myself out of bed. I start getting ready for my run: dressing, pulling my hair into a ponytail, and brushing my teeth. Stopping with the toothbrush still in my mouth, I pick up the phone and type out a text, hitting send before I can think better of it.

> **Me:** *When my run sucks this morning, it's your fault for feeding me so much wine last night.*

I finish getting ready, then head out for my run. I'm already regretting sending the message, but I focus on my run to avoid allowing myself to unsend it. I'm about a half of a mile away from getting back home when I feel my phone vibrate. I pull it out, continuing to run as I see a text back.

> **B:** *What the hell are you doing up so early?*

Me: *My workouts are best in the*
morning

I type my response back quickly and check my surroundings as I take the last turn to head home. Unlocking the door to go in, I hear another ping. I pull out my phone, thinking it's going to be Blake, when I see a picture of myself, holding my phone in front of my waist while running:

Unknown: *Who are you texting, Logan?*

God, I want to tell this guy to fuck off. I quickly look around me, then unlock the door while still watching over my shoulder. I get into the house, lock the door, and slump against it as I forward the messages to Royce. I don't have to give him any context, he'll know.

I'm getting ready to take a shower when I hear another ping. A little nervous to check it this time, I peek at my phone and relax when I realize I'm finally getting a message back from Blake.

B: *I'll remember that. How long do you*
run?

Me: *It depends on the day, usually a*
couple of miles. Sometimes, longer.

B: *Don't you think that's a little*
dangerous, especially with your stalker?

Me: *I stay on the main, well-lit roads.*
And I keep my phone on me. I'm as safe
as I can be.

B: *I think you should run with someone.*
Or at least use one of those running apps
that track you.

Me: *I'll take it into consideration.*

The conversation dies as I go through my morning routine. I'm a little disappointed I don't get a response, but I decide it's not worth sending another text. Either he's getting ready for his day, or he doesn't want to talk to me. Neither situation makes me want to bother him.

I finish drying my hair, styling it, and getting dressed for work. My phone pings, and I see a picture of two different dress shirts hanging side by side on the handles of a wardrobe. To the left is a full-length mirror that caught a glimpse of a shirtless Blake and the waistband of his sweatpants in the picture. I study the half-sleeve of tattoos on his upper arm and catch a couple I can't quite make out running down his side as well. I didn't realize he had any tattoos, but I guess by the placement that's the point. I can feel my mouth watering at how massive his arms are, and his chiseled chest makes it hard to answer the question attached to the picture:

B: *Which one?*
>>> **Me:** *The white and blue pinstripe.*

I pick quickly without much thought because I spent way too long looking at the picture. I'm still staring at it when another one comes through. It's a selfie of him in the full-length mirror in the dress shirt I picked, a pair of fitted navy slacks, brown shoes with a matching belt, and freshly styled hair.

B: *What do we think?*
>>> **Me:** *I think I made a great decision.*

Am I really doing this? And what exactly am I doing?

S. Belle

We continue texting and flirting as I drive into work. I hear from him a lot less as the day goes on, but I try to remember he's a lawyer and can't just pick up his phone whenever I want him to, and he never makes me double-text, so I take that as a win. I can't help but get excited every time my phone goes off, and I get a little annoyed when the girls' GroupChat starts popping off around lunch because I can't tell the difference between those texts and Blake's.

At one point, Ana comes to hang out in my office. Blake texted within the first two minutes of her being there, and I had to pretend I wasn't more interested in my phone for the whole half hour she hung out with me between clients.

As I'm heading out to my car at the end of the day, I debate what I'm going to say next to Blake. We were talking about my favorite food near his building. He told me where he's staying, and it's just over three miles away from my townhouse. Chewing on my inner cheek, I quickly type out my message.

> **Me:** *Would you want to grab drinks tonight at one of these great suggestions of mine?*

I immediately regret sending the message. Well, not really. But I'm concerned I'll wreck my car while driving since I'm about to be so in my head waiting for a response. I climb in and check my phone for a message. I see the three little dots pop up, signaling that he's typing, and then they disappear. It happens again, then the third time the dots pop up, it's quick before a single word comes across.

B: *Yes.*

The nervousness in waiting for a response is replaced with anxiety about having just invited him out on a date. He's typing again almost immediately, and I sit staring at my phone with the car in park, waiting for the next message to come through.

B: *Pick somewhere close enough for you to walk.*

Me: *How about Rosemont's?*

I share the Maps link with all their information, including the website, when I send the suggestion.

B: *Looks good to me. I'll see you there at 8.*

The nervous energy feels like excitement about the situation as I drive home and blast some Taylor Swift on the ride. Once I walk in my front door, though, the panic sets in. What the hell am I going to wear? I look down at my dress I wore to work today. It's a cute floral, babydoll style dress but it's definitely not what I'm wearing tonight.

I head to my room and toss the dress in the hamper, standing and staring at my closet. I try on a cute green dress first with brown sandals, then peek at myself in the mirror. Is this too innocent? It's pretty, but maybe it's too sweet. I don't want him looking at me like a little kid if this is a new feeling for him.

I take off the dress and throw it on the bed to hang up later, and undo the sandals, walking out of them as I walk back over to the closet. I throw on a skirt and a cute black bodysuit. I like the look, and try on a pair of black boots. They feel too heavy for a night out in July, so I try on a pair of strappy black heels next. That looks good, but does it look like I'm trying too hard?

Fuck.

I think it does.

Well, off those heels go. Flat sandals look frumpy with this skirt, so I think I'm going to have to try something else. The outfit comes off, launched onto the bed with the dress I tried on. I grab a pair of dark wash jeans, my go-to, and focus on my different shirts. I pull out a pretty, light pink blouse with flouncy sleeves, throwing it on. It's okay. I rock my head side to side, twisting in the mirror and inspecting myself from different angles.

I look cute.

Flirty but not overdone.

God, why am I trying so hard? This man has seen me in every state of disastrous appearance over the years. Do I really think he's going to care what I'm wearing?

Still determined to impress him, I head into the bathroom. Freshening up my makeup and fixing my curls now means it should have time to settle and not look too fresh before I leave in a couple hours. I debate if I should text Dallas and tell her what's going on. I decide against it, at least for now. I'll probably fill her in after the night's over.

Actually, maybe I won't. She doesn't talk to Royce, but I don't want her to be put in a situation where she needs to hide it. I guess I'm keeping it to myself. I don't know what I'd tell her anyway. Admitting I invited Blake out on a date, knowing he wants something serious with me, but I have no clue what I want with him isn't a conversation I want to have. She'd just ask me why I'm resisting it when I always wanted him. Truthfully, there's so much of me that wants to fall back into him and see where it goes, but there's still something holding me back from being excited about the idea of a relationship with him. Maybe it's just my fear of things going south and putting Royce in the middle. Maybe I haven't forgiven him as much as I want to, and I need to keep working on trusting him again. But until I feel comfortable truly committing to a relationship the way he clearly wants, this has to stay between us. Assuming he even meant what he said last night. But honestly, the way he said it, I know in my bones he was serious. That may be the first thing I've never doubted.

When I'm done primping, I go make myself some salmon, rice, and broccoli, flipping on the TV to distract myself for the next hour before it's time to head out. I grab a glass of wine with dinner and am sipping on it after I finish eating. The episode of my latest Netflix binge ends, and I look at the clock, realizing it's already 7:54 p.m. The bar isn't far, but it'll take me ten minutes to walk there. I loathe being late.

I quickly stand up, scrambling to clean up my dinner. I rinse out the bowl, and in my haste, I turn on the water and splash myself in the process. It'll dry by the time I get there in the summer heat, but I can't tell if I got anything on myself or if the spot will leave a mark. Shit, I should just change.

I finish getting everything rinsed and throw it in the dishwasher, no longer worried about splashing the shirt I intend to take off in thirty more seconds. I rush back to the bedroom and pull off the pink top. I walk over to the closet and grab the first thing my eyes settle on. It's a sheer olive-green bodysuit with long sleeves and a deep crossover V shape that mimics a wrap top. I swap my bra to a lacy black bralette since you'll be able to see it through the shirt, and pull down my pants just enough to clasp the buttons of the bodysuit under me before pulling them back up and checking the final look.

I decide it's good enough, not wanting to make myself any later than I already am. I throw on a pair of chunky heeled sandals and move as fast as I can towards the bar while trying to avoid breaking a sweat.

When I finally make it there, I catch the back of Blake's head sitting at the bar, nursing a beer already. I take a deep breath, the speed of the walk and rushing out of the house helping distract me from my nerves that are trying to edge their way back in. I slide into the barstool next to him, resting my feet on the rail that runs underneath the bar. Turning my head to the right and glancing past Blake, the bartender notices my presence and walks over to me.

"What can I get you?"

"I'll have a Frosé, please."

"Do you want to open a tab?"

As I reach for my purse to grab a card, Blake chimes in, "You can just put her drinks on mine, thanks."

The bartender looks at me, silently questioning if I'm okay with that. I turn to Blake with a soft smile, "Thank you."

The bartender disappears down the bar to make my drink, and Blake's eyes roam over me unapologetically. They drift down my body, lingering somewhere between my breasts and ass, though I can't tell the exact hold up, before he finishes moving his gaze down my legs to my shoes, then quickly flashes his eyes up to meet mine. There is no doubt what's going through his mind, though his face looks a little frustrated.

When he doesn't speak, I fill the silence, "You have to stop looking at me like that." The bartender slides me my drink, and I look around to see if anyone is watching how intently Blake is staring at me right now.

Warmth fills his tone, "Looking at you like what?"

"You look like you want to eat me."

"Maybe I do. Did you wear that outfit for me, or are you trying to get the attention of every man in this bar? Because either way, it's working."

I can feel the heat rising to my cheeks, which softens the apparent jealousy that had a hold on Blake's face. I slide my drink over, and take a sip out of the straw, leaving the large cup on the bar top and looking up at Blake as I drink.

"Damn, Dandy, you keep looking up at me with those eyes I'm going to have to take a picture to use later." I nearly choke on my drink, coughing a bit as the unexpected comment makes my drink go down the wrong pipe. "Or maybe I'll just use your mouth later so I can hear the sound of you choking again." His smile has turned into a full-on ear-to-ear grin, and a hearty laugh escapes him as he looks at me, jaw on the floor. He takes a sip of his beer before speaking, lips brushing across the rim as he talks, "What? Cat got your tongue?"

"I just don't know what to say to that, you caught me a little off guard." I laugh through my statement.

"How about, 'Please Blake, make me come with your dick down my throat and then finish across my pretty little face'?"

"I think I'm going to need more alcohol for tonight." I say, shaking my head and smiling to myself as I take a long sip of my drink. Any doubt I had about his intentions is officially miles away.

"Why's that?" He has his body turned so his knees are facing me, elbow propped up on the bar as he continues to sip his beer in a causal posture.

"I was expecting a lot more conversation like, 'Hey Logan, how was your day?', 'What's new with your life since we've hardly talked the last decade?' and was completely unprepared to be bombarded with your very direct ideas of what you'd like to do to me." It probably sounded a little judgmental, but maybe it was. I can't deny the effect of hearing those filthy words come out of his mouth with such ease, but he could at least treat me like a human, not just something he's trying to stick his dick in.

"I'd apologize, but I'm not sorry for what I said. I absolutely intend to catch up, but I guess with how much Royce has talked about you over the years, I don't really feel like I've lost a lot of time knowing about your life."

My annoyance softens at his admission. "Sorry, I didn't mean to make you feel bad about it."

"Don't apologize for being honest with me."

I give him a gentle smile, "So what have I missed over the years?"

"Not much. I've mostly just been focusing on school and work, and you know the highlights of that."

"Did you like New York?"

"The work was interesting. Bigger city means bigger cases and more volume than I'll probably ever have here."

"Was it everything it's hyped up to be?"

"Yes and no. It was fun the first few years because there's so much to see and do, but it's not home."

"Is that why you came back?"

"What do you mean?"

"Did you miss home?"

His eyes close as he takes a long swig, polishing off his beer. When they open, there is an air of sadness in them. "Yeah, I missed the people here."

"Royce?"

"And you. And…" he trains off, dropping his gaze to the empty bottle he's twirling around in his hand. He looks up, peering at the bartender until he turns around. He tips the bottle at the bartender who nods at him, quickly pulling out another and opening it on his way to drop it off with Blake. "I missed being somewhere I could feel her. I thought leaving may help the memory fade."

"Did it?"

"Only in the worst ways." I nod in understanding. Leaving Abilotte made him feel like he was leaving Olivia behind. I've never really contemplated leaving, Royce has always been here, but I couldn't imagine even trying.

"Sorry, I didn't mean to bring down the mood."

"It's okay, I miss having someone to talk to about this stuff who gets it." His eyes look at me with so much meaning behind them. My body reacts, feeling tugged toward him in the way it used to when we were in high school. My hands are itching to reach out and touch him, which I'm sure would be well received, but I'm just not sure it's the right move in the moment.

"Well, I'm glad you're back."

"Are you?" he asks playfully, the smile not quite reaching his eyes yet.

"I think so," My joke lands, and the corner of his eyes crinkle a bit, meaning I'm being successful at pulling him away from the memories that haunt him.

I'm looking up at him expectantly, my body now facing his in my chair. His hand finds my knee as he leans forward, "In that case, is that an admission that you wore this outfit just for me?" His thumb rubs back and forth on my inner knee.

I nod at him, a little nervous to admit it. "I may have gone through a few outfits trying to decide what to wear."

"You did well." He pulls his chair closer to mine, bringing his legs around me and placing both hands on my knees, continuing to rub them. "So, have you had enough to drink that I can go back to telling you how undeniably sexy you look tonight?"

Laughing, "I don't know. Law school really enhanced your way with words."

"I love seeing you get flustered by them."

"You do?"

"Yes. I imagine the way your lips part slightly in surprise is the same way they will when I slide into you. It's a perfect visual." He pauses, inspecting me, "And the way you're trying to fight the pant coming over you right now, I bet it's' the same way you look when you're fighting an orgasm, and I'd say anything to get to see that over and over again."

I can't deny he's right as I take a mental inventory of myself. I can feel my skin prickling with sweat, my uneven breathing, and I can feel my wetness soaking through my panties and dripping onto my bodysuit. I look up at him, feeling exposed at how easily he can read me. Nobody has ever spoken to me like this before, and to hear the words from his lips... Any hesitation about how much I wanted him is gone. But it makes me nervous how easily they affect me. Am I really this easy? Or am I just this easy for him?

My eyes must give away my internal panic, "Relax, Dandy. You look perfect so turned on. But if you keep looking at me with those eyes, you're going to have a long night ahead of you."

My face scrunches a bit, "What do you mean—" the last word of my question getting warped into a soft squeal as his hands reach up to my hips and pull me out of my seat towards him. He guides me to spin around, and dumbfounded, I do without resistance. When he pulls me back into his lap, I can feel his erection through his jeans. Fuck, is that real? There's no way...

I'm snapped out of my head when he reaches around me to slide my Frosé to me. "Drink," he commands.

I stop, already starting to get a brain freeze from the wine-based slushie. "People are looking at us."

"Let them look. I need you to finish that drink."

"I'm getting a brain freeze."

One of his hands releases my hip and reaches up to rub circles into the back of my neck. My eyes flutter closed, and my head falls back in a groan. "Tell me about your friends I don't know, Ana and Ari."

Keeping my eyes closed as I talk, I tell him about the girls. "Well, you already know the basics about Ana. Tennis pro at the Camellia Club. Daughter Nina. She was one of the few people who was supportive of me becoming the manager so young, and we're the same age, so we ended up getting close. And she's how I met Ari."

"Is Nina's dad around?"

"I've never met him. She normally redirects the conversation whenever he comes up, so I don't push it."

"What about Ari? What's she like?"

"She was Ana's college roommate. She's a lot different than I expected her to be when I first met her."

"How so?"

"Well, Ana is so friendly and warm, so I expected Ari to be the same way. She just wasn't what I expected for Ana's best friend. At least until I got to know her better and realized that sassing each other is their primary form of affection and how Ari shows love."

After another minute or two, I realize the distraction helped the brain freeze pass faster. His fingers on my neck stop moving, and the ones on my hip press into me just inside the bone, nerves firing down my pelvis straight to my clit. He continues to rub little circles there as he directs me again. "Keep drinking."

I chug it, and when I get to the bottom, a slurping sound confirms I've finished. "There. Done. Now what's so bad I needed to chug my drink for you to say?"

He subtly thrusts his hips—not so much anyone at the bar would notice, but enough to press his hard cock deeper into my flesh. "Feel that?"

"It's kind of hard not to." I try to sound playful, but it comes out breathy and needy.

"Good. You're going to help me take care of it."

"Am I?"

"Yes. Would you like to hear how?" He takes my silence as permission to continue. "We're going to go back to your apartment, you're going to let me come in, and we're going to go to your bedroom. You're going to take off this pathetic excuse for a shirt and let me see that lace up close," his hands drift up to the edge of my bralette and trail across the edge on my sides, indicating what he's referring to. "Once I'm satisfied I've etched into my brain how perfect you look waiting for me, you're going to show me that pretty pussy of yours I've been fantasizing about for years, and I'm going to taste it until you're begging me to let you come."

Oh, my god. He pauses, watching my reaction over my shoulder from behind. I'm openly panting at this point. Trying to smooth my ragged breathing, I wonder, "I don't see how that helps you take care of this," I say, lightly grinding myself against him.

"Trust me. That's just the warm-up. After you see just how well I can take care of you, we're going to test how much you trust me. I'll show you exactly what I need from my sweet little toy." He leans forward, his voice lowering, "Tell me, do you have enough rope for me to tie you up the way I like, or do we need to stop at my car on the way out?"

He *brought* rope with him? Jesus. I was not ready for that. I want him so badly right now, I feel like I'm already shaking. He's watching me intently, and my mind is so foggy from desire, I'm not even sure if he's spoken since the rope comment or not. Worried my voice will fail me, I turn towards him, reach to grab his beer, and chug it.

"Close our tab."

"We just got here," he says casually.

"Please," I plead desperately, "close oour tab." I look him dead in the eye, and he doesn't look away as he puts his hand up, waving the bartender over. The bartender brings the check, which he hastily signs. He stands us both up, him holding me tightly in front of him as he guides us both out of the bar, murmuring in my ear, "Whatever my girl wants."

We make our way to my townhouse, and he stands close behind me, watching our surroundings as I unlock the door. When I open it, I look back at him, silently asking him to follow as I step inside. He steps through behind me and shuts the door as I drop my things in the entryway. I turn to face him and before I can reach for him, he directs me, "Go to the bedroom."

I lead us upstairs and into my room. In the heart of the room, I turn to face him. He steps toward me and delicately slides the top of my shirt off my shoulders. It falls down into a pool around my waist, exposing my bra. I remove my hands from my sleeves and wrap my bare arms around him, reaching up toward his neck. A hand finds its way into my hair, gripping firmly at the base of my head. He pulls it sideways as he begins trailing kisses down my neck to my collarbone, walking me backward toward the bed as he does. I feel the back of my legs hit the mattress, and I sit backward onto it. I try to turn my head slightly and his grip tightens, holding me in place. A slight gasp escapes me, and he releases, dropping to his knees in front of me.

I watch as he works to remove my shoes. They thud to the floor, and the second the sound reaches my ears I'm pulled to a stand by the nape of my neck. He brings me up toward him so high that I have to rise onto my tiptoes to ease the pain. I tilt my head up toward him, desperately trying to reach his lips. He bends toward me, his breath ghosting over my mouth as he whispers the words, "Stop trying," both punctuated firmly. He continues dipping his head, kissing from just below my ear down my jawline to my chin. Then he pulls back and releases my head to focus on unbuttoning my pants and peeling them down my legs, squatting as he does.

I step out of the jeans, him holding the bottom of the ankle to make it easier. He looks up at me.

"Do you want me to stay with you tonight?"

I nod.

"Use your words," he says, frustrated with me.

"Yes." A pathetically breathy pant escapes me with the word.

He pauses for a moment before asking in a husky voice, "How much have you had to drink?"

"Just the one Frosé at the bar."

"That was quite a big drink." His arms rest on his knees as he continues to squat, looking up at me.

"Yeah, but it was probably just, like, two at most."

"And how many did you have before you met me at the bar?"

His hands reach up to press my hips backward against the mattress again, "I may have had two or three more before I got there."

"Two or three?" His voice is firm, demanding an actual answer.

"Okay, I had three."

"So, almost a whole bottle of wine."

I giggle at his statement as he starts kissing my inner ankle. He mutters against my skin, "So, you're drunk, huh?"

I giggle again in reply. Apparently, I am. He groans harshly and starts kissing up the inside of my calf, tilting my outstretched leg to access the back of my knee, then continuing up my inner thigh. I moan and fall back against the bed, and the kissing turns into a firm bite on my inner thigh. I gasp, my chest lifting off the mattress as I try to pull my leg away from him. His strong hands hold my thighs in place as he continues to bite, pulling the skin and muscle into his mouth before kneading it slightly. The shock and pain eases to a wave of pleasure, and his teeth release as he continues to suck hard on the area before releasing it, clearing intending to leave a mark. He moves a couple of inches farther up and toward the back, his nose grazing the crease of my bikini line as he bites again. I groan his name, "Blake," which causes him to bite harder. I gasp at the pain. "That hurts," I plead, begging him to release me.

He eases off enough to talk, teeth still pressed into my skin. "Too bad." He resumes his plan of destroying my inner thigh. I squirm and squeal beneath him as he continues to play with how hard he's biting and sucking on me, never moving too far so that the entire area stays sensitive. When he finally lets go and starts to pull his head away, I urgently grab the back of his head, trying to press him down toward me.

He chuckles. "Sorry, that's not happening tonight." I groan, continuing to try. When he easily stands upright, my size and strength no match for his, a wave of disappointment washes over me. I prop myself up on my elbows, looking up at him. I wonder if I did something wrong until he cups my face with one hand, looking into my eyes as he speaks. "The first time you come on my face and I tie you to this bed railing, you're going to be sober. I'm going to fuck you so hard your pussy will be swollen, and you'll be begging me to quit, and I want you to remember every last second of it. If you think you can handle that, text me your safe word, and I'll decide when you're ready."

He kisses the top of my head, then turns to walk out of the room. The gentle affection after leaving me so harshly has my emotions all twisted up. My eyes drop in disappointment until I hear his low voice call out to me, "And, Dandy," I look up to see he has paused in the doorway, looking back at me. His large body fills the frame as he hovers there, his eyes raking over my body. "If you want me to kiss you, you're going to have to crawl on your hands and knees and beg me to fuck your face. And if you do a really good job and take my cum down the back of your throat like a good girl, I'll lick the tears off your face and let you taste them on my tongue. That's how you get a kiss out of me."

Then he leaves.

CHAPTER 11

Blake

Peaches.

I wake up early. My sleep schedule for work has trained my body that 7:30 a.m. is basically the latest I can possibly sleep in. I check my phone and see the text from Logan. *Peaches.* I guess she remembered our conversation last night well enough to recall me asking for her safe word. Well, I'm not sure "asking" is the right word to describe what I did. I groan and roll over in bed with my phone. My dick is furious with me for leaving last night, and I woke up hard as hell after dreaming about all the things I could've done to her. She was so pliable drunk last night. Hopefully, I'll get the chance to have her like that again, after we've established through lots of trial and error, exactly what she's comfortable letting me do with her body.

I respond back, wondering what she's doing this morning.

Me: *Your safe word, I assume?*

Dandy: *Yes.*

Her message pops up quickly. It took me over two hours to wake up and see the original text since she sent it. I can only imagine how bad her anxiety spiral was waiting for me to reply.

Me: *You sure this is what you want?*

Dandy: *I was until just now, haha.*

I smile at my phone. God, I haven't smiled at my phone since... high school? She used to make me smile a lot. I'm not sure anyone else has really been successful since.

Me: *Okay, do you have any hard limits that you know of?*

Her typing bubble pops up then disappears again, clearly thinking of a response. A few minutes later, her reply startles me from nearly dozing off again.

Dandy: *Uhm...fisting.*

Dandy: *And don't stab me!*

I chuckle to myself. I need to readjust my dick in my boxers before responding; flashing through my mind is the image of her tied up, trying to squirm away from me as my four fingers stretch her wide enough to start trying to work my thumb in.

Me: *Alright, no fisting. And lucky for you, trips to the hospital are not my thing.*

Dandy: *Does that mean punching me from the inside is?*

God, I missed this girl and her sense of humor. It's crazy to think how long I've gone without her. I hadn't realized how comfortably numb I'd gotten, but she's reminding me what it feels like to feel have sunlight in my soul again. I start to type a reply, but a message from her comes through before I can hit send.

Dandy: *I have one other rule, if that's okay.*

Me: *What do you need from me?*

I'm not sure I like her trying to establish rules like she's in charge, but if she needs something to feel comfortable with me, I'll do whatever it takes. She types for a minute, then the dots disappear. I stare at my phone, waiting for the message to come through. Is she going to send anything? I'm getting ready to give up and lock my phone when the message that makes my heart sink comes through.

Dandy: *Under no circumstances can Royce find out we're sleeping together.*

Sleeping together. Is that all she thinks this is to me? She knows me better than anyone else on this planet. I've let her see inside my brain in ways nobody else ever has, yet she thinks all I want from her is to sleep with her? I guess we'll have to keep working on that. I focus on the main point of her message, Royce. She doesn't want him knowing about us. I'll admit, he knows enough about my sex life that I wasn't looking forward to telling him I was fucking his sister, but he also knows how much I care about her. If there's anyone who would understand how protective of her I'd be, of how hard I'd work to avoid her ever feeling an ounce of true pain, it's Royce. I feel a burn in my chest, the anger settling in as I realize that she wants to keep us a secret. I've been in love with this girl for as long as I can remember, and she wants me to keep that from the person we care about most. I hate it. Hopefully, I'll be able to change her mind about this, but if it's what she needs for now, I'll agree. Reluctantly, I type back a message I don't feel at all.

> **Me:** *I agree, probably best he doesn't know. In exchange for my silence though, I need you to know something.*

Dandy: *What's that?*

> **Me:** *I don't share.*

Dandy: *You don't want me sleeping with anyone else.*

> **Me:** *What you've heard about your brother doing... it's nothing compared to what I'll do if another man lays a finger on you. You're mine.*

Dandy: *What about you?*

I know what she means, but it's the silliest question she'll probably ever ask. I know she needs the validation, though, so instead of teasing her about it, I answer honestly.

> **Me:** *There will never be anyone I want more than you.*

Dandy: *Okay.*

> **Me:** *So, we're in agreement?*

Dandy: *Yeah, we agree.*

I don't respond as I crawl out of bed to make myself some breakfast. I crack a few eggs into the pan and throw two pieces of bread in the toaster to start the day. I make my way to the gym, hoping a good hard workout will get some of this tension out of my body. By the time I leave, my muscles are shaking without any resistance, and I'm exhausted, but unfortunately still desperate for my girl. Showering when I get home, I find myself daydreaming of her again when I close my eyes to rinse my face. I think about her rubbing her ass on me at the bar; how all I wanted to do was bend her over right there for everyone to see, to mark her as mine in front of everyone.

My hand finds my erection in the water. I'm not sure my dick has been soft since she slid in the barstool next to me last night. Frustrated, I start stroking myself, aching to feel some sort of relief. I think about her laid back on the bed, legs wide and eager for me to touch her. I think about her smell, warm, creamy vanilla mixed with the sweetness of her soaking her panties as I marked her thigh. My hand picks up speed as I visualize her uneven breaths, the flush across her cheeks and chest when I get her worked up; how needy she sounded when she told me the bite hurt. I could tell she liked the pain. I try to imagine what her face would look like when she comes, moaning my name. All too soon, I'm coming all over my hand and down the shower drain. At least that will provide a little relief before I'm stone-hard over her perfect body again. Drying off, I rake through my hair with some gel to help it dry properly, then fire off a text.

Me: *Have you eaten lunch yet?*

It doesn't take long for her to respond.

Dandy: *Nope, you?*

> **Me:** *No, but I'll be at your place in 20 to fix that.*

Not waiting for a response, I get dressed and grab the keys to my Audi SR7 Sportback. Its metallic dark gray exterior shimmers in the sunlight as I climb in. I flip on the vented seats, even in the parking garage, the black leather seats still catch some sunlight and get hot quickly in this July heat.

I pull up to her front doorstep, debating if I should park and get out or just text her that I'm here. Before I can make a decision, I see her front door opening, and a pretty round face checking her surroundings before turning her back to lock her door. As she gets closer, I see her look around one more time before approaching the car and climbing in.

"Scared someone will see me with you?" I half-joke as she climbs in the car.

"Honestly, a little. Yeah." She admits while strapping in her seatbelt.

"Royce doesn't have anyone watching you. He respects your autonomy, which I think is stupid given the whole situation."

"I wasn't talking about Royce. I was worried about *him* seeing me with you."

I snicker, "I'm not worried about it. If anything, I hope he sees me with you so he realizes just absolutely how little chance he has with you."

"I'm scared it'll just make him mad."

I look over at her, trying to read her body language quickly as I drive. "Has he said anything that makes you think he'd escalate?"

"Not exactly, but I don't know, his persistence just feels like maybe he would. Plus, Royce can't catch him, which means if he were to try something, I don't know what would happen."

I can feel the reality of the situation radiating off her, "Do you want me to take you to file a police report about it so they can investigate?"

"What's the point? If Royce can't figure out who he is, the police definitely can't. He has access to creative solutions they're not allowed to use, and he's still stumped."

"Okay, well if that ever changes, you call me. Got it?"

She nods at me, and I change the subject. "Hello, by the way. Your dress is cute." She's wearing a blue and white floral sundress that hits just shy of mid-thigh. I reach over to touch the hem of the dress, then let my hand trail down to settle on her leg.

She smiles. "Hi to you too, and thank you. So where are we going to lunch?"

"Royce took me to this Mexican restaurant close to my office the other day and it was pretty good. I was thinking that if you're up for it?"

"Absolutely." She smiles at me, and I can't help but feel like driving through town with her in my passenger seat on a Saturday afternoon is exactly what I'm supposed to be doing with my life. We get there quickly, neither her or I live too far from this place, and we stroll in. I try not to look at construction crew at Royce's newest acquisition. If he's got them working on a Saturday, then he must intend to have the space ready for use soon. I hold open the door for her and she walks under my arm to the hostess stand, getting a booth. Instead of sitting across from her at the table, after she slides in, I sit right next to her. The waiter comes and asks what we'd like to drink. We both just get waters, and he brings them back with a bowl of chips and salsa.

As we're waiting for our food, I tell her what I can about some of the cases I'm working on to keep her entertained. She fills me in on her staff, and tells me more about her friends and the details of her life I couldn't know about from stalking her social media. Once the food comes out, we eat in a comfortable silence, my leg pressed firmly against hers the entire time. I finish first, and watch her while she eats. Nearing her last bite, I go ahead and break the news to her.

"Just so you know, we have plans after this."

"We do?" covering her mouth to continue chewing when she asks the question.

"I'm taking you shopping." I say with a cheesy grin across my face. "We also have a dinner date at Ikeda on Monday. You can't say no because I already made the reservation, and they have a cancellation fee."

I actually couldn't care less about the cancellation fee, but I know she's too kind to blow me off if she thinks it'll cost me money. Ikeda is one of the nicest Japanese steakhouses and sushi bars in the city, which I know is her favorite food.

"You don't have to do all of that, you know."

"I'm aware." I smile at her as she finishes eating.

"Also, it's a little bold of you to assume I don't already have plans on Monday."

"Do you?" I ask, indifferent to the answer.

"Maybe."

"Well, too bad. I've been waiting to have you since I was thirteen. I have no intentions of slowing down with you." That makes her blush in the way I love.

17 years ago...

I'm walking through the park, looking at the empty swing set. It's near dinnertime, so nobody is out here. I make my way across the playground, picturing her on the swings with Logan and Dallas. I see her laughing, throwing her head back, golden-blonde waves matching mine falling down her back. I close my eyes, which are watering with the memory. When I open them, I turn toward the hill that leads down to the water. I can see Logan off in the distance. She's out here almost every time I am, clearly as haunted as me. Her head hangs between her knees, and walking down the hill, I can see the heaving and shaking of her upper body. Trying to stop my own tears, I bat them away and pluck a dandelion from the hill, approaching her. I use my other hand to protect the seeds as I get closer. She hears me coming and continues to try to control her breathing. No more tears stream down her face, but I can see the streaks on her cheeks from where they ran before. She looks up at me, her face so swollen and splotchy you can barely see her freckles through all the discoloration.

I tuck the dandelion behind me and sit down next to her. She continues watching me as I settle. Once I stop moving, she starts and shifts so she can lay her head on my shoulder. We've been doing this a lot the last few months, coming out here and being broken together. I rub her back and try to soothe her through the hyperventilation, just hoping my presence can help settle her a bit. I watch her silently as her breathing finally starts to level out. She must feel calm enough to speak, because she fills the air with a gentle voice.

"I miss her so much." Her breath appears in the cool early spring air. She shivers against me, and I wrap an arm around her. She snuggles in deeper, her hat being pushed out of the way as she presses harder against me. "I can't believe it's been a year. It's

been so hard doing everything without her. *Things happen and I still get excited to tell her, and when I remember she's gone it's like I lose her all over again."* She looks up at me, shifting slightly in my arm. *"I don't know what I'd do without you, Blake. I don't have anyone else to talk to."*

"You have Royce." I try to remind her.

"Yeah, but he doesn't feel it the way we do. He's sad about it too, but us," she looks out toward the water again, *"we hurt the same."*

I look at her, wondering how she thinks I'm the one getting her through this. I'm a disaster. She's the one who sits here and argues with me for as long as it takes to convince me it's not my fault. She's the only reason I can sometimes look at myself in the mirror without the guilt causing me to bash my own face in. She's my rock, not the other way around.

Her eyes look so distant. I lost a sister, but she lost a best friend. A confidant. In her life, she doesn't have many people she trusts, and it's my fault her circle got smaller. If I can't bring Olivia back, then I need to take care of her people. My heart aches for Logan almost as much as it misses Olivia. As she zones out, I rub the stem of the dandelion in my hand. Shifting, I move so Logan is sitting upright. It shakes her out of her trance, and she looks at me curiously. I pull the dandelion from behind me and show it to her, causing her to vigorously shake her head, no.

"I... I can't." She starts sobbing and quickly heads toward hyperventilating again.

"Hey, hey, hey..." I slouch so my head is slightly below hers, directly in her face which forces her to look at me. *"Yes, you can."* I sit back up slowly, making sure her eyes follow my face. Holding the dandelion in front of her, I continue to speak. *"Just breathe. Think about how much fun you three had picking dandelions on the hill. Think of her laugh, how happy it made you all trying to find the best one without a single seed missing."*

Her crying stops, and she looks at the weed in my hand before dropping her gaze and shaking her head again. "I can't, Blake." Her words barely more than a gasp for air.

"Yes, you can. Think of her standing next to you, blowing the seeds into the wind. Hold on to that image. Remember her, and make her happy by doing what she can't. Keep wishing on dandelions for her."

She looks up at me, my words registering. She looks back down at the dandelion, grazing my fingers with her own as she takes it from me. She turns toward the water, takes a shaky breath in, and closes her eyes as she blows. Her upper lip trembles as she runs out of air, the dandelion now only stem as the seeds flutter away. Feeling her hand touch mine, her body radiating warmth beside me, and seeing her lips pucker, I feel a stir in my stomach I've never felt before. My eyes search her face as she fights the urge to cry again, and I admire her. Her strength to keep us both going each day, her vulnerability to be honest with me, her tenderness that I feel I've lost, she still shows even with a rougher life than mine. She is so beautiful. That's when I place the stir in my stomach—the butterflies. My eyes find her lips again, and I realize, I want to kiss her. Royce's little sister; Liv's best friend. I want to feel her against me, show her just how much she means. But I can't risk losing her; she is my safe place, and I'm hers.

She looks over to see me watching her, so I smile softly at her, and I do the only thing I can. I pull her into my chest for a hug, whispering into the side of her head, "Feel better, Dandy?"

My mind comes back into focus, and Logan is watching me, swallowing her last bite of rice. Before she can ask, I offer up, "I was thinking about the day I gave you your nickname," kissing her on the temple. She clearly remembers the day, and I watch her start to drift into the past. I feel guilty, knowing she's thinking about Olivia, but there's good in those memories too. I watch her dazed look as I call over to the waiter, hoping the sound of my voice will break the spell. He brings me the bill, which I pay. She's still lost in her head, so I have to nudge her gently to get her attention. "Come on, let's go." She forces a smile as she follows me out, and we start walking straight past the car.

"Where are we going?"

"I told you, I'm taking you shopping," her short legs struggling to keep up with my pace. We walk a block, then turn around the corner. As we approach the store front, I distract her, "I want to pick out something for you to wear on Monday."

"I have plenty of clothes, you don't need—" her eyes widen when she sees me moving to open the door, her assumption that I was buying her clothes was obviously incorrect. "No, no, no. This is very not necessary."

"I want to, appease me?"

Knowing she has a hard time saying no and disappointing people, she loses the internal battle and walks in the store with me. One of the workers greets us.

"Hello, how may I help you both today?"

"Oh, just looking around," Logan answers, trying to divert the employee's attention.

I put my arm around her waist, my hand resting comfortably on her hip. "Would you mind taking her back and getting her measurements on file for future use?"

"Oh, do you have an account already, Mr. ..."

"Weber, and no, not yet, but please open one under her name." I take out a card for the file.

The employee smiles politely and nods, then glances over at Logan. "Okay, Mrs. Weber, please follow me."

"Oh, it's not—"

"You can just call her Logan. 'Mrs. Weber' makes her uncomfortable. But please do make sure the account is set up for Logan Weber." I smirk at her, watching her freak out about how to kindly inform this woman we're not married. Somehow, I need to force her to pick something up for herself so she has to call herself "Logan Weber." I can imagine the discomfort already.

Satisfied with aggravating my favorite person, I begin looking around, grabbing a few pieces before Logan gets back. When I see her approaching, I grab another employee and ask her to get the correct sizes for each piece, and bag them for me to pick up later, informing her it's a surprise for my girl. She glows at being able to help in the fun, and nods before discreetly doing as I asked.

"Hey, everything go okay?"

"Yeah, all good. Find anything good while I was gone?"

"Nope, I was waiting for you to come back for all the fun."

I watch her as she looks around, taking mental note of the different pieces she touches—the fabrics, colors, and styles. By the end of it, she's down to three different pieces, and I try to convince her to buy all three. She says no, which is good because one is already in a bag for her behind the register. I point to a different one and tell her it's my favorite, so she puts the other two back. I make a mental note to grab the second one when I come back to pick up her other bags. We check out with the girl who helped Logan with her measurements, and we thank her before leaving.

As we're walking back, I hand the bag over to her.

"They're yours, take them." She does and smiles as I use my now free hand to caress her shoulders. "You're welcome to use that account anytime, with my card. But if I see the charge and I don't get to see my purchase within 48 hours, I'm going to assume you bought it for someone else and that's not going to end well, got it?"

"You don't have to worry, I'm not going to do that."

"You understand I want you to, correct? I wouldn't have set it up if I didn't."

She doesn't respond, so I stop us on the sidewalk.

"Alright then," I say, taking the bag back from her. "These will be at my apartment. You can get them at the end of your running route, which will now conclude at my apartment. I'll be back to the store later to pick up a few more things, and for the foreseeable future, you will stop by my place every morning to see what you'll be wearing that day." I pause, waiting for a reaction, but all I get is shocked silence. "If you don't show up one morning, I will assume that means you are going commando for the day, and I'll require proof in the form of a picture. Said picture will be taken in a public place, not a bathroom, your office, or any room with a door that can be shut easily without question so I can ensure you haven't just removed them for the picture then put them back on. I will need to see that you are wearing neither a bra nor panties, preferably in one picture but given the public space requirement if it takes two, I will be understanding there." She continues looking at me, dumbfounded. "I also want daily confirmation that you did indeed wear whatever was received from me in the morning. If I don't have that confirmation by lunchtime, I will come get it myself."

She tries to speak, then stops twice before coming up with the worst excuse I've heard. "But, I've never been to your place before."

"True, but you know where it is, we've talked about it. And we can take care of that next if you'd like to come over." The wheels are spinning in her head so fast, I feel like I'm getting dizzy watching. "Or, you can admit I'm too much for you to handle and this can end here. But I need this from you, Logan. I need you to let me have the control; to dress you up and know you'll be ready for me when it's time for me to remind you exactly who you belong to."

"No." She shakes her head looking up at me earnestly. "Take me home."

We finish the walk to the car, and I start driving her home, riding the short distance in silence. We pull up to the front of her townhouse, and she looks over at me confused. "Why are we here?"

My brows furrow. "What do you mean? You asked me to take you home." I have to admit I was a little disappointed at the request, but I did my best to hide it.

"I meant your home. You know, when you offered to take me to your apartment?"

"Oh, for fuck's sake," I burst out into laughter with her. "I thought I'd traumatized you already. Hold on tight. We're going to see how fast this thing goes." I peel off, racing to get us to my place before she changes her mind.

CHAPTER 12

Logan

I follow behind Blake as we walk through the front door of his apartment. It opens into his living room, the kitchen is tucked halfway behind the wall with the TV on it. There are floor-to-ceiling windows showing off the city's skyline, and the warm, masculine energy with exposed brick and dark tones fits Blake perfectly. I've never seen a space so masculine and warm at the same time.

"This place is incredible, Blake."

"Thank you," He responds, walking over to the fridge and pulls out a beer. "Do you want one?"

"Sure," though it's not my drink of choice, I could use a little liquid courage to be here alone with him. He walks over to me, handing me the opened beer bottle, then makes his way over to the couch. The buzz I was feeling across my body a few seconds ago shifts to confusion. I thought we were coming up here to have sex, but the way he sprawls out on the couch, flipping the TV on, implies otherwise.

I make my way over to the couch and sit down beside him as he sips on his beer. He eyes me out of the corner of his eye, then sits up and places his beer on the coffee table. "What do you think you're doing?"

Nervous, I answer, "Uhm, sitting on the couch watching TV with you?" I feel very off-balance right now with whatever the hell is going on.

"Is that what you want to be doing right now?" His face is serious, tone dripping with implications I can't quite read.

"Honestly, I just like being around you." The admission spikes my heart rate, waiting for a response.

"Why do you say that like it's a bad thing?" the absence of any sexual tension in his voice is notable. He sounds almost, disappointed?

I take a swig of the beer, trying not to make a face at the taste, "I guess I just feel guilty toward Royce about it, and honestly, maybe Olivia a little too." I feel my eyes starting to water, and I try to hide it, but the way his posture slumps tells me he saw it.

"Olivia wouldn't be mad at you. You know that right?"

Turning my head away, I swipe at a rogue tear trying to escape.

"Logan, when we were kids she used to make jokes all the time about wanting me to marry you or Dallas so you could be 'sisters for real.'" He finishes the statement with air quotes to indicate those were her exact words. Olivia wanted me as a sister, and now that can never happen because she's gone. Fuck. The information just floods my system with more emotions than I know what to do with, and more tears start falling. I hate that I'm crying right now; I'm sure this is really what he was hoping for when he invited me over. The frustration with myself leads to even more tears, and now I'm practically hyperventilating.

His arms wrap around me and pull me into his chest. I try to resist at first, feeling absolutely ridiculous, but when he won't let me go, I stop fighting, allowing him to lean back and pull me with him so I'm essentially lying on his chest crying. He rubs gentle circles into my shoulder and upper arm, the stimulation soothing and distracting from the disaster in my head. Eventually, the tears start easing up, and my breath levels out.

"I'm sorry, I know this probably isn't what you wanted."

He looks at me with such sincerity. "Logan, I want you. All of you. I know exactly who you are. This," I feel his thumb brush away the wet streaks on my face before he tilts my chin up toward him, "doesn't bother me one bit."

My heart pounds in my chest. His eyes hold mine and I feel like I'm a teenager all over again, and he's got that same look in his eye. "Blake, I—"

"Wait, let me talk for a second, okay?"

I nod at him anxiously.

"When I said I didn't think you could handle me, I didn't just mean sexually." He pauses, trying to find his words. "Losing Olivia, losing you, losing bits of Royce over the years… It changed me. All that weight I carried, it's just gotten heavier. And that doesn't even take into account the clients I've failed over the years." He shakes his head to himself before focusing on me once again. "But what never changed is how much I wanted you as mine, and I don't want to risk losing you again because I was too afraid to do something about it."

"You don't seem afraid now."

"I am. I'm terrified you'll see what I've become and that image you had of me will burst. You'll decide I'm not what you want. Not someone you can trust anymore. And I don't know what I'd do with myself, because you're all I've wanted for years. I'm not sure if you'll walk back through that door when I let you go tonight."

I hesitate, trying to say the right thing. Trying to say what I mean. "I don't want to be anywhere else."

As he looks over my face, I'm not sure how much time passes. I'm stuck in a trance where it's just me and him. It's as if he's trying to memorize the moment, and I am too. He's letting me back in, and even if I don't have all the details yet, he's trying to show me the parts of him that were always only mine. I want to give him the reassurance that I'm his too, any way I can.

He senses my breathing pick up and presses his forehead to mine. "Do you trust me?"

Do I?

I nod. He gives me a forehead kiss in response, then sits me upright. "Stay here," he instructs. I watch him disappear to what I assume is his bedroom. I wait patiently, and eventually he returns with a blindfold dangling from his arm, a hair tie on his wrist, and a hairbrush in hand, ripping off the packaging and tossing it on the coffee table. He looks up at me. "Tell me your safe word," his voice authoritative.

"Peaches."

He sits on the couch beside me. "Kneel in front of me, facing the TV."

I do as I'm told, and I feel the hairbrush lightly pulling through my hair. He makes three passes through all of it, then begins to braid it. My eyes close through the process, the brushing and light pulling of his fingers running through my hair while he braids soothes me into a level of calm I've never felt before. He ties the braid off with the hair tie and gives it a soft tug, tilting my head back toward him. When I don't straighten my head myself, he cups the back of my head, tilting it forward and putting the blindfold over me. I open my eyes under the blindfold and feel him adjust it, making my world go completely black.

I feel his hands land softly on my shoulders, sliding down my arms, and then pulling me up. I stand at his guidance and feel the cool air of the apartment as he pulls my dress down. He kisses my waist and trails a few down my side and over my hip before removing my bra. I let it fall to the floor and wonder where his hands have gone as I stand there, waiting to feel him again. The next touch I feel is on my outer hips, his thumbs and index fingers making their way into my panty line on either side of my body. He pulls them down slowly, and I shiver with anticipation as I step out of them. Again, his hands are gone and I wait to feel his next touch. Instead, I hear his voice, "sit down." I sit slowly, feeling the fabric of the couch on my bare ass.

I hear his footsteps walking away, and I call out to him, "Blake?" My voice doesn't sound like my own. It's breathier and weaker, and it warrants no response from the man currently tormenting me. I hear footsteps returning and the sound of several items dropping beside me on the couch. I'm tempted to reach over and touch them, but before I can, I'm lifted to my feet again, feeling Blake push past me to sit directly behind me.

"Kneel."

And I do, returning to the same position we were in when he braided my hair, except for the fact that I'm now completely exposed. I wonder if he's still dressed, and if he's hard for me yet. Two hands pull my arms backward at the elbows, bringing them close to touching behind my back. A rope is quickly wrapped around both of my upper arms individually, slightly tighter than comfortable. He continues by tying the two sections of rope together, giving them a strong pull and forcing me to push my chest out to get any sense of relief from the strain in my shoulders caused by the position. I feel the rope being wrapped around my ribcage, and on the second wrap, he gives it another tug, making my arms extend straight against my body and evidently tying them flat against my back.

The position has me pressing my breasts out, and the rope wraps underneath them and pushes them up slightly. There's strain in my entire upper arm from the position, and my hands are forced to rest together at the small of my back. The rope is knotted at my upper arms, securing the band across my ribs, and then runs delicately down to my wrists. He ties each wrist individually, and instead of joining them together, he binds them to my ankles. He gives me little slack from wrist to ankle, forcing me to slightly push my hips forward to avoid the strain in either spot. Other than being able to spread my knees, I have been effectively locked in place. Any movement of one joint pulls so hard on another it quickly leaves me breathless, and I try to find comfort in the position. I can't seem to find relief but am distracted in my search as Blake turns me to face him.

I feel his breath on my cheek as he holds my head in place. His voice is low when he speaks. "Do you like how it feels to be tied up, completely at my mercy?"

There's a danger to his voice I wouldn't have expected. I feel myself dripping down my thigh thinking about what he may do next. There's peace in knowing I have no power in this situation, that he's unrestricted to use me as he likes; it's freeing. I respond to his question, nodding silently.

"Words, Dandy. Use your damn words." The whisper comes out harsh, like he's furious he can't hear my voice.

"Yes."

"I'm going to go easy on you today, but don't get used to it. I will only give you grace once. If I have to correct you after that, you'll be punished. Is that clear?"

I nod in response.

"I'm sorry, what was that?"

Quickly realizing I again failed to speak, I say, "Yes, I'm sorry." I hesitate before asking, "When you say 'punished', what do you mean?" I ask, looking toward where I imagine his face is.

"If you're really interested in finding out, don't answer me when I ask you a question again." I try to judge if he's annoyed, but there's no harshness in his statement. Just a clear understanding that if I don't speak when he wants me to, he will not give me forgiveness again. "Now, be a good girl and open your mouth and stick your tongue out for me."

I do as directed and wait to feel his dick on the tip of my tongue. A minute passes, then another, and… nothing happens. Feeling stupid, I start to close my mouth, my tongue beginning to retreat—until a firm grip on my jaw yanks me forward on my knees, lifting my feet off the ground and nearly tipping me sideways. Blake stabilizes me by holding my head in place, forcing me to use my abs against the ropes to keep from falling over.

"What the hell do you think you're doing?"

All I can do is gulp, the grip on my jaw not malicious but overly firm nonetheless.

"You're going to sit there with your mouth open and ready, waiting for me to use you like the good little fuckhole you are. Now, open."

I do as directed, sticking my tongue out like last time. This must satisfy him because he releases my face, and I feel him shift back. I sit there waiting. How long is he going to make me stay like this? After what feels like ten minutes, my jaw starts to cramp. I've never done anything this intense before, and my body fights against it. My jaw starts getting so sore, I don't even notice the pain in my upper body anymore. I feel my jaw twitching to shut, but fight it as best I can.

"Is your jaw cramping?"

"Yes," I answer quickly before resuming Blake's required position of my mouth. The movement of talking gives me quick relief, followed by even more strain in my jaw when it has to hold itself open again.

"When I ask you a question and you can't use your words, it's okay to nod or just do your best. But do not close your mouth again unless I give you permission. Clear?"

I nod in response.

"Good, would you like me to help give your jaw some relief?"

Again, I nod, more frantically this time. Desperate to please him but also desperate to ease this ache.

I hear his zipper and feel him shifting below me, presumably to push his pants down slightly. He pulls me forward by my head, causing me to fall forward on my knees into the couch. I quickly adjust my legs wider for balance, but all my weight rests on them, as my ankles are pulled into the air by the position. He adjusts my head slightly, and I feel his dick resting on my tongue, in the center of my mouth.

"You can use my dick as weight to help keep your mouth open. I'm going to finish this movie before you're allowed to move your mouth any further. If I feel you licking me, or your mouth closing around me, you will be punished the first time."

I nod, causing my tongue to rub the underside of his dick. I feel it twitch slightly, before falling back on my tongue. I can feel a smile tug at the corners of my mouth, as he breathes out, "Fuck Logan, stay still, or I'm not going to be able to hold back."

I do my best to hold out, but my knees ache from supporting my bodyweight in the awkward position. Even my neck starts to cramp from trying to hold my head the right way. The only positive of all the other pain in my body is it distracts me from how my jaw feels. I can feel myself dripping down my thigh, making a pool on the carpet below me. I'm drooling down my chin and tongue and surely making a mess of his couch. I try to listen to the movie, which I don't recognize, to distract myself, but all I find myself doing is guessing how much is left. After what I guess is another twenty or so minutes, I can't take it any longer. My head falls forward and my jaw relaxes, closing my lips around the head of Blake's dick. I taste precum when I do and find myself flicking my tongue to lap it up.

Lost in the relief and pleasure that comes with finally getting to curl my lips around Blake's dick, I start to register how large he feels in my mouth. Trying to slide a bit more in, I realize his dick was probably close to hitting the roof of my mouth the whole time I sat there with it open. As I continue exploring, I feel it being tugged away from me. My groan turns into a gasp as I'm easily lifted up onto the couch and thrown on my side. He laces his fingers through my braid and tugs me toward him by my hair, pulling me so my head lays on his abs between him and his dick that's pressed up against my face.

"You really wanted to see what punishment looks like, huh?"

He grabs for something beside him, and I feel two fabric cuffs being placed around my legs just above my knees. He spreads my knees wide with his hands, and I hear two metal clicks. When he lets go of my knee, I try to let it fall, only to feel a metal bar forcing them apart.

"That's called a spacer bar, if you've never used one before." I feel him shift again, and hear another click as my legs are pressed even further apart. I start to feel the tension immediately in my hips as I feel even more resistance. Another click, indicating it's locked in place. My hips burn up my thighs and into my glutes, my inner thighs straining to make space for the bar.

"Blake, I don't think I can do this." I can feel the tears start to swell behind the blindfold, and my voice wavers.

"You will. Or you'll use your safe word. You either trust me to give us both what we need, or you quit." His silence fills the air, and the tears start to fall from the pain. It burns, yet my clit is throbbing. I don't understand what's going on with me. I feel a tear roll off my cheek and land on his abdomen. He runs a thumb over it then speaks again. "Do you want to use your safe word?"

"No," my voice cracks as I say it.

"Good girl."

The praise immediately floods me with endorphins, and the wave of pain coursing through my body wafts to extreme pleasure. I moan audibly, shifting, and all the pleasure quickly turns back to pain at the movement. He pulls my head up by pulling on the end of the braid, and when he releases, I feel his cock trying to press into my mouth. I open and begin to slide down. I keep going, and going, until he hits the back of my throat. I swallow what I can but still haven't reached the base of his shaft yet. I start to pull up, but his hand quickly finds the back of my head and holds me there. He rocks his hips slowly, giving me time to adjust as I cough and gag around his dick.

"That's a beautiful sound, Dandy. You choking on my dick is all I've been thinking about since last night. Keep going." He coos encouragement at me. It starts getting easier and he picks up the pace slightly.

Just when I feel like he's satisfied with my rhythm, a sharp slap finds the top of my breast. *Was that a—* My thought is interrupted by another slap, this one harder straight across my nipple. The initial sting fades to a burn, then wafts to pleasure. That was definitely a paddle. I feel like I'm in a lucid dream as he speaks, "Are you ready for your punishment?"

"Yes," I try to say around his dick, but it's mostly a jumbled gargled mess.

"You're going to take ten slaps to each tit, and twenty to your pussy. You will count for me, and if I can't understand you, that hit doesn't count. If you get the number wrong, we start everything over. You ready?"

"Yes," I work hard to enunciate, struggling to breathe as I continue getting a dick slammed down my throat.

At first, he goes easy, one slap to each breast, and one to my pussy between each breast. He gives me time between the hits to speak, and easily counts my words. As he continues, I get closer and closer to an orgasm, and forming words becomes harder. He reduces the time between hits, and I miss getting one out on my left breast before he hits the other. When he circles back, I forget that he didn't count the last one, and I have to start over.

This time, he doesn't start easy, and I struggle to keep up. He changes where he hits across my breast, but always hits my clit with significant force. I have drool all over my face, and my own fluids across my breasts from the paddle spreading them everywhere. During the second round, he shoves his dick down my throat as far as he can go and repeatedly slaps my nipple so quickly and so hard I swear he's going to break the skin. He pulls out of my mouth completely and asks me what number we were on, and I fuck it up, again. I start sobbing, knowing we're starting all over. The third time through, he does the same thing to my clit, and I get so close to the edge I scream when he refuses to hit it again until finishing all twenty on my breasts. The last four on my pussy he drags out so slowly, I wonder if he'll ever really let me finish. But when I get to twenty, he quickly throws the paddle on the floor and turns his hips to face me, sliding his legs on either side of my body. He starts thrusting quickly and harshly into my mouth over and over again until I taste his cum down the back of my swollen throat.

He pulls me off him and up onto my knees. I feel my wrists release from my ankles as he cuts the rope, cutting my arms free from my body next. They're still tied behind me, legs spread wide, as he pushes the blindfold up my face and licks away all my tears.

As he's tasting the salt across my face, I try to turn toward him for a kiss. He pulls back immediately, and I fall forward with the loss of support from his body.

"Did you think you earned a kiss?"

I look at him, hopeful and fearful at the same time. "Didn't I?"

"I told you, until you crawl to me and beg to choke on my cock, that's not happening." He holds my face still as he places a delicate kiss on my cheek. "You did great, beautiful." His tone is soft as he tries to ease the heartbreak he must see flicker across my face. He continues untying me until I'm completely unrestrained, then pulls his pants back up. He squats in front of me, getting in my face, "If you want to try for a kiss again later, I might let you." His tone feels cold, genuinely implying that he also may not allow it. I watch as he stands up and walks away toward his bedroom without another word.

I cannot believe he just left me here on the couch alone. Why would he do that? My whole body aches from being restrained for so long, my throat is swollen and coated in cum that I can feel when I swallow. My clit throbs, dying for a release that it didn't get, and I'm covered in sex. I look around the room and see pools of fluid on the floor, spots on the couch, and chunks of rope scattered across the space. I should just go home, this is infuriating. So why do I feel like I want to stay and try to earn his praise? Frustrated tears well their way up when Blake strolls back out to me.

"Follow me."

The anger at his nonchalant command as if he did absolutely nothing wrong has me fuming. "Seriously?" there's no doubt in my voice that I'm pissed.

"Yes, get your ass in here." He says it firmly, but there's no bite behind it.

I glare at him and nearly stomp my way in, but my anger at him is sidetracked by my curiosity of observing his room as I enter it. I notice the dark décor, the brick windowsill below the large glass pane, and a few pictures scattered across the nightstand and walls. He guides me to the bathroom, and I'm still trying to steal more glances at his room when my nose catches a waft of... lavender?

I turn to see the room lit solely by candles around the tub and vanity, a fresh bath still sloshing from where he turned the water off a mere minute ago. There are bubbles filling the tub, and when I step a foot in, I realize the water is pink and glittery from a bath bomb.

"I put some Epsom salts in there too to help with the aches."

The gesture diffuses a lot of my anger, and leaves me with disappointment that he still hasn't kissed me. He ventures out of the room briefly, coming back with both our beers in hand. He passes me mine before sitting on the bathmat next to the tub.

He watches me as I settle into the water, then breaks the silence with the most unexpected question. "Do you ever have to work weekends or are you always just a normal business week?"

"I'm sorry, what?" I would've never guessed he would ask about work after everything that just went down.

"Do you ever have to work weekends? I don't think that's a complicated question."

"Uhm, not really. I may work different events if I think they could use the extra hands, but that's part of the benefits of the promotion, I'm never forced into weekend shifts if I don't want to."

He continues peppering me with questions about my life, none of which are remotely close to addressing what just happened in the living room. At a brief lull in the conversation, I've regained enough strength to be bold.

"Can I ask you a question?"

"Of course," He's leaning casually on the edge of the tub, watching me intently.

"Why won't you kiss me?" It comes out more desperate than I meant for it to, but that is how I feel so I guess it's only fair.

"I don't kiss any of my hookups."

Hurt wafts over me. Did he really just call me a hookup? I risked my relationship with Royce, my relationship with him, for a hookup? I look away, and he quickly speaks again realizing my dejected behavior, "Sorry, let me clarify that please. I never kissed, past tense, any of my hookups because the only person I ever really wanted to kiss was you."

I glance back over at him; he's so close to my face from edging closer, trying to get me to listen to him just now. "That doesn't make any sense." It's not harsh when I say it, just confused.

"I always had it in my head that you'd be my first kiss. I guess after learning how to avoid kissing a girl, it just became a habit, since I never really wanted to kiss anyone else."

"That's not what I meant. If you never kissed anyone because you only wanted to kiss me, why won't you kiss me?" I can hear the pain in my voice when I repeat the original question.

He sits back a little, looking down in thought before speaking, "I keep telling you how much I want you, and you keep pushing me away. Hiding me." He looks back up at me. "I just need to believe you want me as desperately as I need you."

He intentionally pushes up to a stand quickly after that comment, signaling the end of the conversation. "Take your time in here. I put you through a lot. When you're ready, there's fresh towels on the rack and a robe for you in the linen closet if you want it." Like he does best, he walks out of the room, leaving me alone with my thoughts.

CHAPTER 13

Blake

The TV flashes in front of me, but I'm not really watching it. Logan is in my bathtub, naked, and I'm out here by myself. She looked so damn perfect bound and desperate for me. I never thought I'd get to have her like that, so eager. It still wasn't enough though. She let me manipulate her body however I wanted, but only after I coaxed her into it. She never puts herself out there for me, always trying to dance around the edges to avoid embarrassment. As if she needs to keep her distance and hide herself, like it's just a game we're playing here.

If she's going to deny me in front of everyone that matters, the least she could do is tell me behind closed doors that she wants me. I feel guilty for not kissing her when I know she wants me to, but I deserve to feel wanted when I have my first kiss. I never thought that would be an issue with her, but I've seen her look at me like I was everything important in the universe; I know how it feels to matter to this girl. I need to feel that when I kiss her for the first time. I didn't hold out this long for it to be meaningless between us. Until she begs me to let her in the way I've been forcing my way back into her life, I'm not going to let her take that from me. If she can't understand that, then she's changed beyond anything I can fix.

I bring the beer bottle up to my lips again and realize it's empty. Heading to the kitchen to grab another one. I feel dazed, moving feels like a drag as my body slugs with my mind. How can I be so thrilled to have her here, and still feel like I'm only getting scraps of the dream I've been wishing for? Sinking back into the couch with a fresh beer in hand, I try to focus on the documentary on the screen.

Something catches movement out of the corner of my eye, and I look to see Logan standing in the bedroom doorway, hair falling out of her braid and curled up in the robe I left for her. She looks nervous, and I pretend I don't notice.

"Feel better?"

She nods. I swear she does that just to piss me off. I need to hear the sound of her voice, let it linger in my ears for after she's gone, but she just fucking nods. I can't punish her for it right now; we're not in a scene and she has to be wrecked from how intense the last one was. I look back toward the TV and sip on my beer to hide the twitch of my lip as I fight my own dominance.

She takes a few steps into the room then cuts to stand in front of the TV. Turning to face me, she slowly unties the robe and pulls it off her shoulders allowing it to fall to the floor, exposing herself to me. My dick stirs in my pants, eager to see what she does next. She holds eye contact with me as she gets down on her knees, and to my surprise, crawls toward the coffee table, around it, and kneels just beside my right knee. I can't take my eyes off the way her body moves on all fours as she approaches. She looks up at me, those beautifully distinct eyes looking up at me as she asks, "May I suck your dick?"

My body tries to answer for me. I see what she's trying to do, and while I appreciate it, I need to know that she means it. Against what my body's craving to do, I glance back toward the TV and tell her, "No."

I don't look down to see how she reacts, though I desperately want to.

"Why not?"

When she speaks, I look down to see her face scrunched in confusion.

Leaning forward, I lightly run a hand down the back of her head, then reach my thumb around, brushing down her cheek in an affectionate yet domineering gesture. "Not right now. Maybe later."

With that I release her and slouch back into the couch, my legs spread far enough that my knee is pressing into her shoulder and my leg blocks her from being able to move forward.

"Please," her soft voice breaks my focus on the TV as she asks again. It was still eager, waiting for me to say yes to her.

"No, Logan. Not right now." I swing my leg over her and push her forward with my foot on her backside. "I do appreciate you kneeling for me though. You can do that right in front of me."

She crawls a few feet forward at my nudging and kneels looking up at me. Placing my legs on either side of her, I'm sure she can see clearly how hard I am through my pants. I continue to ignore both the boner and her as I watch TV. She speaks again, and I'm losing both my patience and my will to fight her. "Please, Blake, I want to taste you again."

I sigh and look down at her, knowing I need to really test her, "I fuck desperate sluts like you when I'm ready. If you want me so badly, you can wait until I'm bored enough to use your easy mouth again."

I look at the bottom of the TV, mostly watching her reaction out of my periphery but not allowing her to know that. Her confidence falters; her eyes fall and her shoulders slouch, when she looks back up to speak to me, there's a tremble in her voice. "Please, Blake. Please let me suck your dick. I... I need this." she swallows the lump in her throat that's been making her voice unstable. "I need you."

Those words break my restraint. "You need me?" My tone is harsh, trying to hide the truth of how much she's affecting me just now.

"Yes," the desperation in her voice palpable. I look down at her, and I see her vulnerability spread across her. This plea is real, and if I tell her no again, it'll be over.

"Alright then, take it out."

She springs forward on her knees, her hands shaking as she quickly tries to undo my button and pull down my zipper. She pulls my dick through the hole in my boxer briefs, and immediately puts her warm lips around the head. She's frantically sucking my dick, as if she's desperate for another taste of my cum. I let her work at a rapid pace until I'm close to finishing, watching her worship my cock. When I feel like I'm about to burst, I pull her head off me by the very bottom of her braid. She tries to fight it at first until I pull so hard I know it hurts. She releases me with her mouth and watches as I pant trying to catch my breath. I hold her there for a minute, two, thinking of anything and everything to get myself soft. I'm not fully there, but I see her watching as my dick grows limp.

I release her braid. "You can continue."

As she tries to get me hard again, I fight against it, wanting to see her break a little more thinking she's not doing it for me. It's cruel, but knowing she'll do anything to try to please me makes me want to test her. I reach behind her, pressing her head into my crotch as I grab my beer. I hold onto it and continue to drink as I grow hard in her mouth. She's slowing down, getting tired and having to switch strategies. She swallows as much of me down as she can with each thrust, and I try not to look down at her. I drag it out as long as I can, but I feel the buildup approaching and I again have to stop her so I don't finish yet.

I let the wave pass, and when I'm confident I'm not going to come the second her lips touch me again, I shove her back onto me. This time, I thrust into her face repeatedly, but still refusing to look down at her as I use her. Edging myself has caused it to be harder and harder to get close to coming, and it takes me pounding her face for a long time, working gags from her over and over again, before I get close to the edge. She must feel the pulse in my dick as I get dangerously close, because she starts trying everything to get me there, I even feel the flick of her tongue on the underside of my balls. I nearly come and shove her off me by her forehead. I breathe deeply through my nose, willing the urge to go away. When I pull her back toward me this time, placing my head on her lips, she simply sits back on her heels.

"What do you think you're doing?"

"I've been sucking your dick for almost an hour."

"Your point? If you want to suck my dick, you'll do it for as long as I allow you." I pull her head back toward me and continue to try to press into her mouth without looking. When she continues to resist me, I let go and stare down at her, demanding her to say something.

She sighs, "I just want to make you come."

I push her. "Then beg for it."

Frantically, she looks up at me and pleads, "Please, Blake. Please come in my mouth." She tries to start sucking it again and I stop her.

"Not what I meant. Beg with my dick down your throat through your pathetic little gags when you can feel me pulsing in your mouth, and maybe if I feel sorry enough for you, I'll let you taste me again."

A wave of understanding crosses her eyes, and I use both hands to shove her head down my full length. The desperation she had at the beginning returns, and though it takes a long time, she manages to bring me to the brink again. I can feel her swollen throat trying to swallow me deeper, tears streak down her face, and I barely even notice the choking and gasping for air between thrusts until she starts trying to form words.

"Pl—," *choke*, "pleas—," *gasp*. The tear stream gets stronger as she pushes all the way down my dick, her lips brushing against my pelvis as she speaks around my cock, "please come," she uses her tongue to massage my balls as she holds her position, and I finally lose it. I pull her back halfway then thrust into her twice before I'm filling her mouth. She wasn't prepared for me to take control so she's snorting through it trying to breathe as I keep coming. She gags, and I feel the tightness of her throat, causing another stream of cum to pulse from deep in my balls. As I pull out, her mouth is so full that some spills down her chin. She swallows and chases my tip with her tongue as I withdraw, trying to get every last drop that trails from me. I decide to let her polish my cock clean, then pull her up toward me.

She's falling forward onto me on the couch as I bring her up, unsteady in my arms as I lick her salty cheeks clean. I love the taste of her tears from my assault. Just when she thinks I'm going to release her, my mouth finds hers. She falls into the kiss, and I hold her up completely as I dip my tongue into her mouth. I taste every corner, nibbling on her bottom lip and kissing her until I imagine her lips will be as swollen as her eyes and throat.

I finally break the kiss, pressing my forehead to hers, and whisper to her, "What a good fucking girl you are for me, Dandy." I brush another kiss to her lips, "So fucking good."

She initiates another kiss, peppering my lips with sweet little pecks until she allows her lips to mold onto mine. I pull up her legs and allow her to sit in my lap, holding her comfortably to me until she's satisfied with the kiss. She breathes deeply and tucks her head between my jaw and shoulder, resting in my arms. I hold her, rubbing her back lightly as I savor the moment between us.

Logan is breathing deeply on my chest, and I can't tell if she's asleep or just in a post-sex haze. Either way, being able to feel her breath across my chest, her bare skin under my hands, it's exactly what I needed from her. I wish I could take off my shirt without moving her. I'd love to feel her skin against my skin, but for now I'll settle with the content look on her face as I hold her. Her makeup has mostly washed off from the tears and I can see the scattering of freckles across her face. She looks so innocent, though I know she's far from it, but it feels like a dream to have her to myself like this.

S. Belle

Her eyelids flutter open, and a broad smile comes across her face as she looks up at me. I can't resist the urge to smile back at her. "What are you smiling at?"

"Oh, just that I got to be your first kiss; nothing major." She giggles at herself as she closes her eyes and snuggles back into my chest. I chuckle softly, watching as the movement vibrates against her. It's cute that she's as excited about it as I am. I wasn't planning on revealing that information to her, but I guess if that's what she needed to let me back in fully, then I'm glad she knows.

I hunch over, pulling her off my chest slightly so I can kiss the tip of her nose. She looks up at me as I tell her another naked truth, "This is the way I've always wanted it to be with us."

Her pupils contract and her eyes fall to my lips. I meet her halfway for another kiss. It starts off innocent enough, just me trying to express how much she means to me and how in love with this moment I am. Slowly though, she begins to deepen it and turns in my lap so she's now straddling me. As if he hasn't had hours of attention already, my dick hardens, ready to see what the inside of her feels like. She starts grinding her hips, craving more from me. I gently set my hands on her waist and hold her still, breaking the kiss.

"As much as I want to continue, if I end up in you tonight, there's no way I'll survive the withdrawals tomorrow."

She gives me a sultry grin as she responds, "I can stay the night. Then you can have as much of me as you want now and in the morning."

I can smell her arousal, and I wish I could do what she's asking me to do. "I have plans tomorrow, with Royce."

140

As if someone just doused her with ice water, she goes still and her face falls flat. She doesn't say a word as she shifts off me to sit next to me on the couch. She still leans into my shoulder, but I feel it. One mention of her brother, and all the progress we made today disappears. I wrap my arm around her, grazing my fingers up her side. I see the goosebumps flare across her body as she winces, as if it pains her to feel the way she feels right now. She shifts away from me, and I accept that our perfect bubble has burst.

Not much longer, she tells me she should probably get going and starts getting dressed. I don't argue with her, but I watch her as she dresses with urgency. The silence lingers as she puts on her shoes, until I finally break it. "I'll call you an Uber."

I could drive her home, but I'm not in the mood to force small talk with her right now. We both know what just happened, even if neither of us say it out loud.

"It's okay, I can walk," as if she can't get out of here fast enough. It's miles back to her place, and she has a stalker. That's not happening, even if it means she has to suffer being in my presence longer.

"No, you can wait here for an Uber."

Instead of arguing with me, she just shifts on the couch and we both stare at the TV until her Uber gets here. She stands up from the couch, stepping away from me after she rises. I look up at her.

"Okay, well, bye," she stammers uncomfortably.

She turns toward the door before I even say a word. I should probably stand up and hug her, or kiss her, or at least walk her to the door, but I don't. No pleasant exchanges of 'this was fun' or 'I'll see you soon,' just a goodbye. When she walks out the door, I look away, trying to numb the ache in my chest from her leaving.

I wake up the next morning, a throbbing in my head and banging on my door. I switched to bourbon after Logan left, and I don't remember eating dinner as I drowned my emotions in it. The banging continues, and when it stops briefly, I see my phone light up with a text from her.

I throw on a pair of gray sweatpants to attempt to hide my morning wood and grab the hat on the dresser, pulling the bill toward the back of my neck as I head to the front door. I'm unlocking my phone to see what her message said when I pull open the door and see her standing in front of me. She's dripping sweat that I can see through her shirt, and her hair is tied back in a tight ponytail. Fuck, I glance down at my phone and realize it's not even 6 a.m. yet, well aware that she ran here. The memory of me telling her to change her route to finish here flashes through my brain, but after how we left things yesterday, I was not expecting her to do it. I didn't even go back to the store to pick up the lingerie I bought her.

Her bright voice rattles around in my hungover brain as it tries to make sense of her words, "I'm here for my underwear, as directed."

She's more chipper about the situation than I would've expected. I guess I shouldn't complain about it and should just hope her reaction yesterday was a fluke. She's still running in place, as if this is just a pit stop en route. "Were you planning on running back with it?"

"Yeah, I wanted to get a long run in."

"Well, you get a pass today. I didn't have a chance to make it back to the store after you left."

"Oh, okay." Her face looks a little disappointed and she turns to leave.

I reach out and grab her sweaty hand. "No, you're not leaving. Your run is over." I tug her into the apartment, curl a hand around her throat, and push her into the wall beside the door. I crash my lips into hers and kiss her with aggression.

She moans into my mouth and relaxes into the kiss. She tilts her body into mine, deepening the kiss. I pull my mouth away momentarily, still holding her to the wall by the throat, "Do you regret yesterday at all?"

She doesn't answer me, just pushes against my hand trying to get back to my mouth.

"Logan, I asked you a question."

I watch as her eyes move up from my mouth and I see it. The avoidance in her look. I feel my chest rising and falling harshly as I wait for her to speak. "I just feel like we're betraying Royce."

"Betraying Royce?" I'm fuming. She fucking crawled for me yesterday, and she's worried what her brother would think of us?

"Yeah, what if he doesn't approve? What if something happens and we force him to take sides? I can't risk losing him, or him losing you." But not her losing me, that she's willing to risk.

I release her and step back, my voice sterile when I speak, "Fine, if that's the way you feel, you should leave. Don't bother coming back. I won't say anything about what happened yesterday, but it will not be happening again."

She tries to grab my wrist as she pleads my name, "Blake, that's not what I want."

I shake her off, speaking harshly as I glare at her, "I will not be something you regret."

I turn to walk away, and she starts to follow me. "Blake, please don't be like this, I don't regret you."

I whip my head back to her. "But you're fine pushing me away? Losing me so you don't lose your brother and he doesn't lose me? You're not getting it, Logan. Until you do, get the fuck out."

I storm off to the bedroom, slamming and locking the door behind me, making it clear to her I don't want to be followed. I don't know how long she stays, because I force myself back to sleep, trying to pretend the girl I've wanted for a decade didn't just break my heart twice in the past twenty-four hours.

CHAPTER 14

Logan

My alarm goes off, and I roll over reluctantly. 4:15 a.m.—enough time to run before I need to head into work. But where am I supposed to run? I should go back to one of my old routes. Showing up at Blake's yesterday went horribly wrong. Why did he have to ask if I regret it? I don't, but I can't help but feel that what we're doing is risky. Snoozing my alarm, I contemplate just lying in bed for a few hours before it's time to go. I know moping won't help the situation, but the thought of leaving this bed and having to decide what to do with Blake is terrifying. If I don't show, it'll be over for good with no chance of going back. I can't imagine not being able to touch him now; never being able to feel his lips on mine again. That look of pure adoration after I've given him whatever he needs, it's everything. He makes me feel high when he touches me; I can't lose that. The thought of letting him go and him ending up with another girl runs through my brain, and my stomach heaves. No, I can't do it. I can't let him go. He needs to forgive me. Even if I can't tell Royce, I need him to know how much I love him. He was the first boy to enter my heart, and I've never let anyone else in the same way since. But what if he doesn't want me anymore? What if I've ruined it?

My thoughts continue to swirl as I get ready. I know he'll make me beg. He'll demand my tears and my body, and I still may not get what I want, but I can't not try. I need him now more than I've ever needed him before. I head out the door, running so slow it takes me twice as long as it should to get there. If a light starts changing, I slow down to wait for the next one instead of trying to beat it. When I finally get to his complex, I take the long walk up the dozens of stairs instead of the elevator. Dragging out this confrontation as long as possible before there's nothing left to do but knock on his door.

Unlike yesterday, I don't knock incessantly. I give a couple firm knocks and wait. I can hear shuffling on the other side of the door before Blake opens it, barely wide enough to see half of his body. His hair is disheveled, he hasn't shaved, and he looks exhausted. Did I do that to him? His voice comes out exasperated. "What do you want, Logan?"

"You. Please." I'm as direct as possible, hoping it makes a difference.

Without a word, he turns and walks away, the door drifting further open when he releases it. I follow him into the apartment and see him walking toward the kitchen. He walks to the refrigerator, grabs a carton of orange juice, and places it on the counter before reaching for a glass. I see a bag from the lingerie store we were at, and when I walk over to peek inside, I see it's the set he let me pick out.

146

Well, at least he had them out waiting for me. That's something right? He still doesn't speak as we stare at each other across the kitchen island. I pick up the bag, give a smile as sad as I feel, and turn to head out. I'll push a little more tomorrow. He let me in and had my gift ready for me; I shouldn't be greedy and try to ask for more from him. I have my hand on the handle ready to walk out, but I can't open it. God, what is wrong with me? I should just walk out. Instead, I walk back into the kitchen, drop the bag back on the island, and walk straight up to him, placing both hands on the side of his head as I pull him toward me for a kiss. He bends so I can reach him, allowing me to kiss him, but he gives me nothing back. I keep trying but I get no reaction from him, so I stop.

I pull an inch away from his face so my eyes can find his. "Do you still want me, or did I ruin it?" The second half comes out broken, fear gripping my voice.

He looks at me silently for a moment, and I can't read his emotions. His eyes roam my face, studying my mouth before returning to mine with a piercing glare. Darkness coats his voice when he speaks, "Get on your knees."

I don't argue and I don't question him. Dropping down in front of him, I crane my neck back to see him towering over me.

"What exactly do you want here, Dandy?"

Dandy. Air fills my lungs. There may be venom in his words, but I haven't lost him yet. So, I beg. "I want you. I want you to fuck my face, to use me however you need. I want to be yours." I don't try to hide the desperation in my voice.

I don't move an inch as he pulls his sweatpants down with no underwear underneath to hide his erection. He steps toward me, trapping me between the island and him.

I shut my eyes and take it as he thrusts into my open mouth roughly. He wraps a hand around my ponytail and pulls, setting the pace with his hand and hips. I can't keep up, and I start gagging. He doesn't slow down for me, and I end up with slobber all over my face as he pulls in and out relentlessly. Tears stream down my face, though, I'm not upset by how he's taking everything out on me. If he wants to fuck out his anger, that's fine, as long as he never stops touching me. I welcome it when he presses deep into my mouth, pulsing down my throat. I breathe through my nose as he holds his dick there, pushing the back of my head into the island as he falls forward, resting his hands on the countertop. I feel him slowly softening in my mouth, making it easier to breathe around him. When he pulls out, he extends a hand to help me stand.

He licks down my jaw to my chin, tasting the salt before his lips find mine. Relief washes over me with the kiss, and I relish every second of it before he pulls away. When his lips abandon mine, I turn to my bag on the counter and start trying to leave.

"Where do you think you're going?" His voice is still deep but lighter than when he told me to get on my knees. I look back at him when he tells me, "You don't get to leave yet."

"Oh?"

He stalks over to where I had escaped to, trapping me between his arms. "You're not going anywhere until you know, without a shadow of a doubt, you cannot breathe properly if I'm not fucking you. You're going to learn that you need my dick to survive."

He pushes up my tank top and bra, pulling my tits out the bottom. Holding it up, he spins me and shoves me down so the cold granite is against my chest. He removes my shorts and underwear aggressively, pulling them down to my knees but not letting me take them off before two fingers slam into me.

He fingers me against the countertop, shoving in and out of me roughly. He uses his other hand to toy with my clit as he works a third finger in, and I'm squirming underneath him. Whimpers spill from my mouth, and the coldness on my nipples has me on edge easily. I beg him, "Please, I need to come."

"You want to come on my fingers for me? Show me how tight you'll squeeze my dick when I make you come with it next?"

"Yes, please." I'm rocking back and forth against his hand, the countertop pulling at my breasts as I chase the relief, when suddenly, his hands are gone. I cry out in frustration, but he's unfazed as he throws me over his shoulder and carries me through his bedroom to the shower.

He walks in the shower with me and places me on my feet. I don't fight him as he pulls my shirt and sports bra off over my head, and I allow him to pull my shorts off the rest of the way before he steps out of the shower to toss them in a pile on the floor.

He stands near the open shower door as he pulls off his pants. "Sit on the bench."

I do, continuing to watch as he takes off his shirt. Seeing him naked for the first time leaves me gawking. His legs are chiseled and there are tattoos I've never had the chance to appreciate on his upper thigh. I catalog the different artwork across his body, and when he turns to pull down the detachable shower head, I notice a dandelion tattooed on his side. Just above his hip bone, the seeds blowing off it toward his back.

"Is that a dandelion above your hip?"

His eyebrows raise, knowing I was just opening the door for a conversation. "Do you want to talk about the tattoo, or do you want to get fucked?"

I reach out to trace it with my fingers, and he hesitates, watching me as I do. My voice is small when I ask, "Is it for me?"

I can't bring myself to look up as he answers, "It's not for Olivia."

He turns on the water, playing with the settings on the shower head as he directs me. "Keep your ass as close to the edge as possible, then put your feet on the edge and spread them as wide as you can."

I have to hold myself up as I put myself in the position he's requested. The position causes my lower half to tilt upward, spreading my lips apart and putting me on full display for him. When he turns the shower head on me, a hard stream of ice-cold water rinses over my head, across my face, then down each arm. From a distance, the pressure on my arms and face isn't too rough, but he steps closer, allowing the stream to become more forceful as he moves back to pelting each of my cheeks just below my eyes.

"You look a little thirsty from your run. Open your mouth for me."

I do, and I feel as he moves the stream to hit my tongue. I let the cold water wash over my mouth.

"Drink." He commands while I try to catch some water with my tongue, curling it and throwing it back in my mouth repeatedly. Then he tilts the stream so it hits the back of my throat and I struggle to keep up with drinking the water. I start coughing up water, but he doesn't ease up right away. When he finally does, I'm gasping through the coughs. "God, I love the sound of you choking."

I continue trying to cough up the water that entered my lungs as he moves the stream down my body, running it over each nipple until they're rock hard. It's trailed down my side, over my hip, then put even closer as he blasts my clit. He bends down on one knee onto the tile in front of me, holding the shower head only a couple inches away from my clit. As I squirm under the stream, rocking back and forth, trying to keep it in the right spot, he fondles my breasts and pinches my hard nipples. Again, I'm close to the edge, and he keeps slightly shifting the stream just enough, forcing me to chase it with my hips. I beg as the cold water feels even harsher on my red-hot clit, "please, oh God, please let me come."

He places a soft kiss on my trembling jaw, tilting the shower head toward the floor. "Later." Sobs rack my body as he releases me, standing to put the shower head back on the holder and turning the water warm.

"Are you crying because you couldn't come?"

I nod through the tears.

"Well then, I guess I'll have to deny you every time. You know how pretty I think you look covered in tears."

"Please, Blake, I need to come." I cry harder, unable to even move to place myself upright.

"I know you do, but I need you to hold on a little longer. You're doing so well for me. I know you don't want to disappoint me, do you?"

I sniffle. "No."

"Good, then this is another lesson for you." He cups my face lovingly. "You'll only come if you beg, but I decide if you deserve to come or not. If you come without permission, you will be punished. Your orgasms are for my enjoyment, and you will say thank you when I give you one."

I'm trembling in his arms, "Blake…"

"Shh… you're so strong, Logan, can you do this for me? Let me use you until you break. Make me proud. Can you do that?"

I close my eyes, trying to soothe myself and stop crying as I nod.

He kisses my forehead and reaches behind me for the shampoo on the bench. He washes my hair, and I press my face into his chest as he massages my scalp. We swap positions so he can rinse out my hair for me, and then he coats my hair in conditioner. He washes his own hair while my conditioner soaks, allowing me to have the water while he stands in the cold. Rinsing his hair clean, he pulls me to him and steps backward so the water runs over my head, cleaning out the conditioner. He takes his time as he washes and massages every inch of my body. The relaxing motions erasing the pain from the scene before. He finishes cleaning me, and quickly washes himself. When I give him the water to rinse off, he reaches a hand out to me, sliding two fingers into me and curling them to pull me into him.

His other hand guides my head to rest forward against his chest as he slowly rubs back and forth on my clit with his thumb. His fingers move gently, as if my pussy is his own personal fidget toy to play with. I'm so swollen and sensitive from the kitchen and the cold water, it's not long before I'm pleading for more.

"Please, harder."

"Shh, this is enough."

My eyes burn, ready to cry again. "No, please. I need more. I need you to make me come."

"You're doing so good, Logan. You don't need to come yet."

"I do, please." I draw out the last word.

"Is my girl feeling desperate to come?"

Exasperated, I groan out, "God, yes. I need it."

"Tell me you need my dick in you."

"I need you to fuck me, Blake."

"Say you need it more than you need air."

"I need your cock inside me more than I need air, please."

He smiles. "You're so perfect when you beg." His hand slides out of me, and he turns us so I'm facing the shower head. He gently bends me over, and I press my hands into the wall. Trembling, I feel his head at my entrance, and he slides in painfully slow, giving me time to accommodate his full length.

The gentleness disappears as he begins pounding into me. I press back against him, trying to hold my ground against his huge body, but it's no use. The force rocks me forward with every slam, and my arms quickly tire from absorbing the force. His balls slam against my clit and I'm so close to coming, I almost forget to beg. I cry out to him, "Blake, I'm so close, please."

"You want to come?" He retorts.

"God, yes."

"More than air?" He slows down when he feels my walls shaking and I swear I'm going to explode.

"Fuck, yes, Blake. I need to come on your dick more than I need air."

He pulls my head back by my hair, holding me under the water stream. He wraps his other arm fully around my waist and slams into me repeatedly.

"Hold it a little longer. You can do it."

The water pelts my face; I'm inhaling it every time I take in air. I end up coughing against it, and all I can focus on is the cock impaling me.

"I can't—" I try to speak through the water. "I need to—" I try to breathe through my nose while talking, accidentally inhaling more water.

"Tell me you need to come more than you need air."

Through gasps I beg, "Please, Blake, please. I need to—"

His hand wraps around to my throat as I hear his whisper in my ear cutting me off, "Come for me."

I cry out as my upper body falls forward out of the water stream and my whole body spasming through the orgasm. He holds onto me with his arm squeezed tightly around my waist, his hand tightening around my throat. He continues fucking me as I spasm around him.

"That's it, Logan. Fall apart for me." His voice has me clenching his dick harder. "Don't stop crying," I realize tears are streaming down my face from how hard my body was just rocked. His arm around my waist drops to rub my clit, pressing so hard I try to pull away. The orgasm finishes, and I beg him to stop.

He pulls out of me unexpectedly and releases me. I turn to face him, and he presses the top of my head down. "Kneel, spread your legs, and get your pussy as close to the floor as you can."

As I'm getting in position, I feel the water getting cold again as it runs on the floor around me. He bends over and slides the shower head onto the floor beneath me, the firm stream back against my clit. I jolt away from it, my body still hypersensitive from everything before.

"You'll sit there and let the water tease your clit until I come. Understood?"

I swallow and nod, unable to stop trembling.

His dick finds my mouth, and I try to focus on the taste of his precum against my tongue instead of the torture on my clit. My legs are shaking, barely able to stay folded underneath me from the exhaustion, and I moan in relief when I feel a warm stream filling my mouth. The taste is my favorite praise, proof of a job well done.

When he steps back, I shift forward, the stream pounding my stretched opening, though offering some relief from the pressure on my clit.

"Sorry beautiful, you're going to have to take it a little longer." The relief vanishes as he informs me he wants me back against the water.

"But you said—"

"I know, but you're going to sit there until I give you permission to get up, which is not yet."

Defeat overwhelms me as my head drops, tears again flowing down my shaking body as he steps around me to get out of the shower. I sob audibly as he disappears to the bedroom, leaving me overstimulated and struggling to keep it together on his shower floor. I'm so close to calling out "peaches" when I hear his footsteps returning.

Through blurry eyes, I try to make out what he has in his hand. I can see a chain, but nothing else, as he moves to drop it on the counter near the sink. He walks over to me with a towel in hand. "You can get up now, baby."

I try to stand, but my legs fail me. I crawl forward to the bench seat and pull myself up, still trembling when I get upright. Steadying myself with a hand on each wall of the shower. I wobble toward Blake. He wraps me up in the towel and dries me off, then grabs a second towel to help wrap up my hair. He is being so tender with me. If he wasn't so kind to me outside of sex, I would swear he hates me, but I think he just loves the torture. He loves seeing how far I'm willing to go for him.

When I'm dry and warm, he walks back over to the counter holding three clamps attached to a central ring in his palm.

"You're going to wear this under the lingerie for me today, okay?"

"All day?"

"Yes." He grazes a thumb over my nipple, and even through the towel, it aches. "Does that hurt when I touch it?"

"A little."

"I want the ache to last all day so you're still sensitive tonight. I had to overstimulate you a lot to make them hurt this much, and I don't want to have to do it all over again when you get back."

"Why does it need to hurt?"

"Because, just like in life, the pain makes the pleasure better. You're the one who taught me that."

On wobbly ankles, I force my body upward toward him and pull him to me for a kiss. He lets me take my time before I stop to say, "Okay, I can do it I think."

He removes the towel from my body and places the first clamp on my nipple. There are rubber covers over the tips so the metal doesn't cut me. He loosens a screw on the clamp, causing it to pinch tighter. I watch my nipple but I can feel him watching my face. He continues tightening the clamp slowly. "Does it hurt yet?"

"It's uncomfortable, but it doesn't hurt." He tightens it further.

"How about now?"

"Yeah, now it hurts." He tightens it a bit more, and I wince.

"That's how much it should hurt. If it gets too comfortable, you can tighten it for me. If you tighten it all the way and it's still comfortable, open and close it three times."

"Why?"

"That will allow blood flow and swelling," he answers casually as he moves to the other side, tightening it slightly past a comfortable pain. Lastly, he squats and pulls back the hood of my clit to place the clamp directly on it. It hurts at its loosest, and he tightens it until I'm fighting a scream.

"The wetter you get throughout the day, the easier that's going to fall off. If you can't feel it, I need it tighter. Okay?"

Nodding, the movement rattles the chains and the ring that hits just above my bellybutton. He goes to grab the lingerie and helps me put it on delicately over the clamps.

"If one of those clamps comes off, you're going to text me, okay?"

"Okay. I assume I'm supposed to put it back on?"

"Yes, you'll text me saying how it came off, what you were doing, and then send me a video of you immediately putting it back on and tightening it so it doesn't slip off again. I don't care if you're in the middle of a meeting. You will record the video for me and send it right then and there. Okay?"

"Okay." Thank God I don't have anything important to do at work today. I can tell he's serious, and with how much this is going to affect with my blood flow, he'd be able to notice if I let time pass before fixing it.

I follow him out of the bathroom, and I realize how much this underwear will pull on the clamps, even just walking. He slips one of his hoodies over my head, falling nearly to my knees with our size difference.

"I'm going to check on you throughout the day, okay?"

"What if it's too much?"

"Just tell me. Call me, and I'll try to talk you through it. But if you can't make it, we'll stop. I believe in you. After what you just did for me, this is nothing."

I feel his affirmation in my bones. If he really thinks I can do this, and it's not just to be cruel, I'm going to try. I follow him to his car, and he drives me home so I can get ready for work.

When I get to the Camellia Club, I drop my stuff off at my office and notice Ana folding towels near the weight room. Laundry is definitely not in her job description. I could let it go, but she's watching someone intently in the weight room, so curiosity gets the better of me, and I head over to her down the hallway toward her. I'm realizing the hallway is much longer than I previously thought.

"Hey Ana, what are you doing?" I try to say it without judgement. We're close friends, but I'm still her boss at work and I don't want her feeling scolded.

She looks down at the towel she's folding briefly, then turns toward me. "Oh, I didn't have anything better to do, so I figured I'd help out."

I lean over the laundry cart, trying to get into the same line of sight as her. In doing so, I extend my body too far, and the clamp on my clit pulls off. I immediately feel it throbbing without the pressure of the clamp restricting the blood flow. The rush back into my sensitive bud makes me swallow a yelp, hoping Ana doesn't notice.

When I look over at her face, she's eyeing me warily. "Sorry, give me one second." I say as I step around the corner headed toward the hall entrance to the locker rooms, hoping no one comes out in the next thirty seconds.

I flip to my phone's camera, clicking record. The video starts with a shot down my legs of my dress and wedges. I pull up the hem, holding it my mouth as I shimmy the black lace panties down my thighs slightly. The clamp falls, swaying freely and pulling on my nipples. A soft groan escapes my lips as I shift the camera in position to see me replacing the clamp properly and tightening it further. The amount of swelling from the past minute already makes the initial tightness more painful than before, and this extra twist puts me in agony. I drop my dress and end the video, subtly fixing the underwear in case anyone walks by.

I quickly text Blake, explaining I leaned over a cart to see something while talking to Ana, and the clamp came off. Attaching the video, I hit send and walk back around the corner toward my friend.

"Sorry about that, something was pinching me, and I needed to fix it."

Believing my not-exactly-a-lie that she probably assumes was about the underwire of my bra, she just nods still staring into the weight room. I'm pretty sure she's looking at Boston McLeod, and I decide not to question it yet. When she still doesn't speak, I ask her, "Are you sure you're good?"

"Yeah, I'm fine! Just keeping my hands busy while I wait for my next client."

"Alright, well, if you need more to do, I'm sure I can come up with a few things to add to your plate."

She laughs. "It's okay, I'm good here." I walk back to my office, worried I'm going to soak my dress through my underwear by the end of the day. Halfway there, I get a text from Blake telling me how beautiful my pussy looks when it's swollen. I feel a jolt of desire and a throb against the clamp, and I have to fight another groan of pain-pleasure. Today is going to be so fucking long.

He checks on me throughout the day, and after having to tighten the clamp on my clit all the way because it keeps falling off while I move around in my chair, I'm holding back tears. If I was home with him, I'd be crying but I don't want streaks in my makeup at work, so I bite my lip so hard I draw blood, fighting the urge.

I call Blake, and he answers on the second ring, "Everything okay?"

"I don't think I can do it." I admit through heavy breaths.

"Yes, you can. Just breathe with me. Breathe in," he breathes loudly on the other end of the phone, sucking in air. I play along, "breathe out." He helps me settle my breath. "Now tell me what's wrong, is it too tight?"

He's been getting videos all morning of me tightening the clamp from it falling off, so he knows exactly where I'm at. "Yes, it hurts so much. And it keeps falling off no matter what I do."

"Okay, do you want to try something a little different?"

"What is it?"

"Why don't you try as I walk you through it, and if it doesn't work, we'll be done. Is that okay?"

"Yeah, yes. Just tell me what to do."

"Are you in your office?"

"Yeah, door is shut."

"Go lock it."

I get up, walking over to the door and when I sit back down, the motion pulls the clamp off again. "Fuck, Blake, it came off again."

"It's okay," my phone vibrates in my hand, and I see he's FaceTiming me. I answer it and hold the phone out in front of my face. "Hey pretty girl. Prop your phone up on your desk for me and scoot your chair back toward the wall."

"Okay," I use the keyboard to hold up the phone against my monitor, then slide back until he tells me to stop.

"Go ahead and lift up the dress and pull down your underwear so I can see you." He's in his office, I think, the lights dim as he watches me intently through the phone. "Hell, you're so wet, Dandy. I think that's the problem."

"I don't know what to do. I'm so turned on but every time it comes off I swell more and it hurts worse to put back on."

"And that makes you even wetter and easier for it to come off, right?" I nod in response. "Alright, take the rubber tips off the clamp and put them aside." Racing thoughts attack my brain about how badly this clamp will hurt without the padding. "I can see your face, it won't really hurt that much more, there's just a little more risk of you getting cut if you pull them off too hard."

"I don't know if this is a good idea."

"Do you trust me?" I respond by pulling off the rubber tips and putting them on the desk. "Good, now tighten the screw all the way so it's as loose as possible." I do it, feeling better since he plans to let me wear it looser. "Go ahead and put it on and tighten it as much as you can handle."

I do, and I can feel the grip isn't as affected by the lubricant all over my crotch right now. I tighten it once, and it hurts, but I know better than to think he'll let me stop there, so I give it another turn until I'm wincing.

"Good girl, you can stop there. Roll your hips around in the chair a little bit." When I move, it holds better than it was before even at its tightest.

"I think this might work."

"Good, but you need to be extremely careful. I don't want you cutting yourself, okay?"

"Okay," I put my underwear back in place and roll up to the phone. "Is that your office?"

"Yeah, it is."

"Can you show me it?"

"You can come see it for yourself when you're ready." I know he's alluding to the fact that I don't want people knowing about us, but I don't want to start a fight.

"You are no fun. Well, I should go so I can get out of here early for dinner tonight."

"Alright, I'll see you soon. You sure you're okay?"

"Yeah, thank you." He smiles at me and gives a quick nod before hanging up.

When I walk into Ikeda, I give the hostess Blake's name. She informs me that he's already been seated and walks me back to our table. We're sitting next to the chef's station but have a personal two-person booth.

"I wasn't sure if you'd prefer a booth or sitting at the workstation, so I picked a booth and left you the side where you can watch if you'd like."

"This is good. Thank you." I settle into my seat, placing my purse beside me. "How was your day? Anything interesting happen?"

"I was able to get a deal for two of my clients, and both agreed to take them, so that was a relief."

"Were they challenging cases?"

"There was no way we were going to win if we went to trial. I got a great deal for one, and the other one was just okay, but they had so much evidence he knew it was better than risking a more severe sentence that was probably coming."

"Well, that's good. You never did tell me why you picked criminal defense. I would've guessed you'd be more of a prosecutor type."

"I think everyone deserves justice, but that goes for those on trial too. A lot of times, people get railroaded, or the full story doesn't make it out. A lot of my clients are willing to admit their wrongdoings if they can just explain the why, which usually helps with their sentences. It's tricky trying to balance it while making a deal, but I feel like I get to help make things fair on this side, instead of just prosecuting and trying to keep my conviction rate up."

"What about estate law, divorces, or something?"

"Pass." He scoffs at the idea. "I could not put up with a lot of that. Honestly, criminal cases were the only thing I ever really thought about doing."

"Is that because…?"

"Yeah, that's what made me want to go to law school in the first place."

I nod, trying not to think about what happened with Royce. Blake and I have moved past it, but I can't help getting angry at the memory and I don't want to ruin tonight. Luckily, Blake moves the conversation to a new topic.

"Anything interesting happen at work today?"

"I caught Ana watching one of our members."

"What do you mean watching?"

"I mean she was folding towels so she could gawk at him while he was lifting."

"Wait," He smiles as food comes out.

"Did you order for us?"

"I didn't want you to have to wait too long, and I know what you usually like. Is it okay?"

I look to see an assortment of sushi rolls in the center of the table to split and a pile of chicken, shrimp, and scallop hibachi with fried rice and vegetables on a plate in front of me.

"Yeah, this is perfect." I reach out and grab a Rainbow roll from the center plate, moaning at how good it is. When I open my eyes, I see him watching me eat, and I blush.

"Anyway, you were talking about Ana. Do you know who she was watching?"

"I think so, but I want to see if it happens again before I tell you who it is."

We eat comfortably, continuing to chat about our days. He finishes faster than I do, and he seems absolutely fascinated by my mouth as I continue eating.

"Does this make the list of places to come back to?"

"Absolutely, it's so good."

"What if I only let you come back after wearing the clamps all day, still worth it?"

Heat rises to my cheeks, thinking about how hard my nipples are against the lacy bra. I wore an extra layer to work, but I took it off when I changed for our date, knowing he'd want to see my hard nipples through my dress. The bra holds the clamps flat enough you can't see them distinctly, but the way his eyes are grazing over my body right now, I know he's looking for evidence of them.

"They're still on, I promise."

"Good, I'll be checking as soon as we get home."

The thought riles me up. "And to answer your question, yes. I'd still come back if I had to wear them all day."

"Did you like how it made you feel?"

"They feel good, even when they hurt, if that's what you mean."

"No, I'm wondering if you liked feeling like a needy little slut, wearing clamps at work and ready to be used whenever I wanted you."

Heat flashes through his green eyes, and I remember just how wet I've been all day. "Yes, I liked being ready for you all day. I can't wait to get home."

"What would you do if I told you that you're going to sleep in them, and you can't come until they come off?"

"You mean I can't come until tomorrow?"

"Would that make you cry?"

I panic, knowing how much he loves both me begging and my tears. Would he really do that to me? Or is he just fishing, trying to get me to beg for an orgasm at the dinner table?

"Blake, if you're trying to get me to beg in public..."

"Would you?" He asks.

Heat rises up my neck. "Royce would kill you if he knew how much you were torturing me right now."

I didn't mean to bring him up; he's just always been part of our banter. When I say his name though, Blake detaches visibly. "He knows how much I like to torture my women." He says coldly, looking around for the waiter.

I know he meant for that to sting, comparing me to the girls before. "Luckily for both of us, he won't know and y'all won't fight about it." I say it, hoping it'll remind him why we're not telling him in the first place. Unfortunately, it just angers him further. I see his grip on his wallet tighten. He asks the waiter for the check and a box for me, not acknowledging my statement.

Instead of making it worse, I sit quietly, picking at my food until the waiter returns with the check and a box. Blake grabs my plate from under me, my fork in motion to pick up a bite, and he dumps everything in the box,

S. Belle

stacking the rolls on top. He closes it, throws cash on the bill, then stands up to walk out, assuming I'm following behind him.

The car ride home is uncomfortable. He's clearly upset, but when I try to ask about it, he says that he's fine. I don't know what else to do, so I just drop it. We make it upstairs, and he heads toward the kitchen to put away my food.

"Go to the bedroom and take off your dress then wait for me on the bed."

When he comes in to find me, he immediately frowns. "Why are your heels off?"

"Oh, I... you said my dress, so I just assumed." I move to put them back on, and he bends down in front of me, swatting my hands away as he does it himself. He rubs his hands up my legs, massaging my calves before standing back up and giving me a quick kiss in passing. He goes to the bathroom and comes back with a pile of supplies. He wraps leather cuffs around my ankles and wrists and pulls them tight. Then he sits down beside me and begins braiding my hair. The act helps me find the right headspace to be ready for whatever he needs from me.

When he's done, he lightly massages between my shoulder blades with his thumbs. I know I should be scared if he's being this affectionate with me right now, but I can't help but melt into his touch. Eventually the massage stops, and he pulls my hands behind me, clipping the cuffs together.

He pulls a leather belt from the pile on the bed and slides it under the chain from my clamps, tightening it across my stomach. "Suck in as far as you can."

Nervous for what's coming, I do, and he pulls tighter, locking it in place. It restricts my diaphragm, and I can only breathe shallowly through my lungs, my shoulders rising

166

and falling with every breath. I feel a tug at the back of the belt, knocking the little air I have out of me. "I'm going to use this handle to hold you steady while I fuck you senseless later."

Excitement courses down to my toes at the thought. I want to curl them but can't in my strappy heels. It doesn't fade when he presents me with a thick black collar, a large ring hanging off it.

"You can always use your safe word," he reminds me as he straps the collar in place, spinning the ring to the back underneath my hair. He moves behind me, and I feel him threading rope through the O-ring. I listen carefully as he stays behind me, tying the rope off to something else. He brings the tied-off object with him as he moves back in front of me. The object isn't something I've seen before. It's an oversized thick hook, with a large, tapered ball on the end.

While my brain is still trying to register what I'm looking at, Blake helps answer my question. "Suck on the anal hook. It's the only lube you're going to get."

My eyes widen as I quickly wrap my mouth around it, trying to collect spit on the metal before he pulls it from me. He pulls my hands up slightly to ensure the rope runs beneath them, and pulls my underwear out of the way as he slips the hook under the waistline, slowly pressing it into my ass.

"*Blake...*" I groan as he presses it in. I feel it tugging upward, adding extra strain as he pulls the rope tighter. I arch my back slightly, and he continues to tightens it further. He knots the rope at my collar, and I'm stuck where I can either feel the pull on my neck or my ass, or both, but can't arch enough to get relief for both at once. I'm pulled to the edge of the bed unexpectedly, and my panties are pulled down. A string of fluid stretches as they're lowered, clear evidence of how needy I've been all day. I watch as he slips a vibrator into the panties before pulling them back up. He puts the remote in front of my face as he presses the on button, a slow vibration shaking the chains attached to my clit.

He slips the remote in his pocket, watching me. "Would you like to come tonight?"

"Yes, please." I don't hesitate to beg. I know it's my only chance.

"Then you have two options. I'm going to call your brother." Fuck. "Option 1: you can beg me to make you come with him on speakerphone." Pause. "Option 2: you don't, and I invite him over. You will sit in this bedroom, tied up and on edge until he leaves. After he leaves, you'll be allowed to come."

"You won't make me wait until tomorrow?"

"If you come without me, I'll torture you and deny you for the next week straight. Otherwise, no. You'll get to come tonight. How long you wait, that's up to you."

I take inventory of my body. There's no way I can wait for Royce to come over, hang out, and leave before I orgasm. I've been on edge since 6:00 a.m. this morning since the last time he fucked me. But I can't beg for an orgasm from my brother's best friend while he's on the phone. "Blake, please just fuck me now. I'll hold out until you're done using me, but please, don't make me wait or tell Royce. Just let me come."

"Those are your only two options." He plants a kiss on my lips as we listen to the phone ring.

The sound of Royce's voice fills the room. "Hey man, what's up?"

"Hey, how's your day?"

"Oh, it's fine. Nothing too crazy popping off. How about you?"

"It's been a good day," he watches me, waiting for me to speak. "Do you have any plans for tonight?"

"Absolutely nothing. What about you?"

He raises his eyebrows, waiting a beat, giving me one last chance, but I can't do it. "I was just planning on having a couple beers and playing Halo. You want to come over for a bit?"

"Sure, that sounds good. I can be there in twenty."

"Perfect. Do you think Logan has plans? Would she want to join us?"

He turns the vibrator up to full blast and I bite my lip, fighting the urge to beg.

"I don't know man, she goes to bed so early, by the time I get over there she'll probably be in her pajamas."

"Alright, we'll drag her out another time then. I'll see you soon."

The boys hang up, and Blake looks disappointed. "Looks like you made your decision."

He turns the vibrator back down to one of the lower settings. It'll never be enough to make me come, but I won't be able to tune it out either. My ankles are pulled to the foot of the bed and tied to the corners of the footboard. "If you can be a good girl for me tonight, I promise I'll reward you." He licks one side of a ball gag, then spins it so that same side is pressed into my mouth. He secures it behind my head, then pulls out his phone. I see my own phone light up on the dresser beside him. Answering his own call, he puts both phones on speaker. "Go ahead and lie back for me." When I do, I'm forced to lie on my restrained arms, which push the rope tying my neck to my ass even tighter.

S. Belle

I watch with a turned head as he places my phone near my face, about a foot away.

"Try and say my name."

I try several times, figuring out how to make it coherent around the gag. When I get close enough, he adds to it, "Now say 'Blake, please.'" It comes out slurry, but I'm able to do it.

"Good, my phone will be on the coffee table on speaker, flipped over all night. If you want to come, all you have to do is ask." I'm facing the door and can see that he pulls it closed, but not latched, a sliver of light making its way through.

CHAPTER 15

Blake

My phone is upside down on the coffee table next to the large pizza box that only holds one remaining slice. I place my beer on top of the case and turn to look at Royce. We switched from Halo to Madden about an hour ago, and I ended up helping Royce eat some of the pizza he brought after the first two hours of gaming had passed. Logan has been in my room alone for over three hours, and I've spent most of the time with Royce positioning myself so he couldn't see the raging boner I've had all night. A few times while we were playing, I'm pretty sure I could hear her sobbing, not clear enough for her brother to notice, unfortunately. She's been exceptionally good at being quiet.

When I face Royce, he looks exhausted, and there are worry lines in the corners of his eyes. He bottoms out his fourth beer, clunking it on the table.

"How do you still look so stressed out?"

Letting go of his beer, he shifts backwards and drops his elbows on his knees, lightly folding his hands between them. His head hangs in a way that makes his loose brown curls fall forward, "I think I'm fucked."

"What do you mean?" I try to keep my voice level, but my heartrate spikes at the confession.

"I have a large shipment coming in, and I know it's being watched."

"What do you mean watched?"

"One of my guys found a tracker in the barrel of an AR."

"How the hell did they get that close to your product?"

"I have no clue. It makes me worried about an undercover in our mix or in the suppliers, but honestly, I haven't even had a chance to think through that yet."

"I assume he got rid of the bug?"

"No, it was already at the old warehouse. That's why I needed to get a new building for homebase and move everything so quickly. If we destroyed the bug, they'd know we know and there'd be a raid at my building. I don't want that anywhere near me."

"That's actually a smart move. Are you sure it's the ATF and not a competitor or a client trying to steal?"

"Yeah, I'm sure. It's the ATF. My tech guy traced the signal. Even though it was smart not to destroy it, it's got me edgy. I haven't decided what the hell I'm going to do about the deal either. The shipment is too big to not deliver it myself. If I send someone else, they'll know I knew something's up, and I'll have the cartel gunning for my ass."

I cannot believe he's contemplating going. "Royce, you *cannot* be there. I cannot get you out of that. You will go to prison." I normally don't push him, but I need him to hear me on this.

"You think I don't know that?" His voice is harsh as he snarls at me. "Fuck, I'm sorry. I'm not mad at you. I'm mad at how fucked this is."

"Does anyone else know yet?"

"My tech guy and the driver who found it."

"If the driver found it, he's probably not the one placed it."

"I know, that's why I'm less worried about a leak. I've got Eddie watching his shit though just to be safe."

"I don't see why you can't send someone else."

"And let one of my guys go down for this shit? It's bad enough there's no way I'm getting my driver out of this. I can't let someone else go down too."

"What if you move the truck early and have him meet someone there so they can both get out of there?" I hate that I'm helping him pre-emptively avoid arrest, but this is Royce we're talking about. I nearly forget about Logan in the other room, who can definitely hear this conversation. She'll probably find a way out of those restraints just to beat my ass if I can't talk some sense into Royce before this is over.

"That's… not a terrible idea. It'll be a tight line to walk between being too early and suspicious to the ATF, and too late that we accidentally cross paths with the cartel's scouts."

"That would be my vote. Have them drop the truck off, get them the hell out of there, and you go absolutely nowhere near it."

"The cartel's going to know I knew though. Fuck, man."

S. Belle

"I know taking your chances with the cartel risks you ending up dead, but you're better off trying to work out a deal and losing your ass financially than risking it with the ATF. I'm telling you as your friend and your lawyer, there is no way in hell I can get you out of there if you walk in. You are the top dog, there's nobody to flip on; nothing you can give them they'll care enough about to let you walk. Even your supplier, if they've got a guy on the inside, won't be enough to walk. Maybe a reduced sentence, but it'll be game over. You'll be away for life."

"At least I'd still be alive."

"You could still be alive this way if you make a good deal after the fact. But you know who won't survive with you in prison on a life sentence? Fucking Logan. You have to try to find a way out, man, and that means living to see another day outside of prison."

His eyes close and he groans in frustration. Hopefully, pulling the Logan guilt card is enough to convince him not to be an idiot. When he gets done running his hand through his hair, he stands up.

"I should probably get going. It's late and I've got to decide what I'm going to do." He looks me in the eye. "I appreciate you being here."

I don't stutter when I respond, "Always for you, man."

"You might want to get some extra security for yourself for the next week or two. I can supply it and fund it if you want. When you were gone, I never really had to worry about you; you were out of reach and most people weren't aware how close we are. That's gone now."

I just nod in agreement. "Guess I should probably turn notifications for the security cameras around the building back on, huh?"

"I know there's so damn many of them, but yeah, I would. Do you still have all the passwords and access codes?"

"Yup, I've got them."

"Alright, well I'll see you later. Be safe."

"You too, Royce."

We give each other a pat on the back, and when I'm sure he's not going to walk back through my front door for a forgotten wallet or keys, I pick up my phone and whisper into the microphone, "You ready for me?"

She screams behind her gag in response. Instead of going to the bedroom right away, I slowly clean up the living room, taunting her through the phone the whole time. I can hear her sobs through the phone, and she confesses as well as she can that she's soaked my sheets— I'm sure with both her tears and her pussy—while she was waiting for me. When I tell her she can wait a little longer the murderous scream that comes from her is a little unnerving. When I'm convinced her emotions are at an all-time high, I kick the door open with my foot, still talking to her through the phone, "Hey, baby. Miss me?"

I end the call on my phone and take in the sight of my girl spread out on my bed. I can see her glistening from the doorway and her eyes look wild as they beg me to come touch her. Seeing her need me like this, it's perfection. I walk to the head of the bed, and she tries to follow me with her eyes. She looks backwards, adding extra pressure to her shoulders and arms, and she winces quickly before looking back at me with glassy eyes. I take a sip of my beer, switching the vibrator to a pulse. I've flipped the settings all night, mostly leaving her on the setting that crescendos upward, then cuts to nothing just shy of being powerful enough to do anything. Now watching the strong pulses hit her, I see her flinch, trying to run away from it, probably from how sensitive she feels after her clit has been touched continuously by something for the last 15 hours. After a minute, I switch it to the highest setting, and she looks away, scream-sobbing behind her gag.

"Have you been able to come at all?"

She shakes her head, flinging tears and snot everywhere. "Poor, poor baby. Would you like my help with that?"

She tries to self-soothe, and through a few hiccups she speaks with a full mouth, "Please."

I lean over and kiss her lips around the gag. "You look so beautiful like this. Covered in drool like a thirsty little whore." I run my hand over her face and smear everything together. "If I could come home to you tied up and waiting like this every day, I'd probably get fired for leaving work early every night."

I squeeze her shoulders and she gasps, flinching from the sensation. "You just sit here in so much pain, praying I'll come take care of you. Tell me," I slide my hands over her shoulders and around the sides of her breasts, rubbing gently against the welts I left on her just two days ago, "Do you love the pain? Do you crave it?"

She shakes her head, no, vigorously. "Oh, then why…" I lean over and run my tongue over the outside of her soaked underwear, "…can I taste you through your panties?"

She groans at my behavior, her eyes rolling back. "Admit you love the pain I give you. Admit you relish sitting her waiting for me to turn it all to pleasure. Admit you need me."

She locks eyes with me, then lets them hood over as she nods lightly.

"Good fucking girl, Dandy."

Quickly, I drag her down off the edge of the bed, her feet hitting the floor harshly. She falls forward then sideways as the rope tied behind her won't let her bend forward the way she tried to when catching herself. I help stabilize her, then twist her so she's facing the bed. The ropes at her ankles are tied to the corners of the bed and are too short, forcing her to cross her legs at the ankles. She's unsteady in her heels and looks fucking amazing. Her arms are an ugly purplish red and I watch as the blood starts to flow back into them. Grazing my fingers over them, she shoots away from my touch as much as possible. "Is it like a million needles as the blood flows back in?"

She nods, and I don't push her as she works through the sensation, but I do keep rubbing my hands up and down her arms, forcing the feeling to drag on and drawing more tears from her. I give her ass a quick squeeze before grabbing my favorite toy with her, a paddle. She doesn't watch me when I walk back to see what I grabbed, so I run it lightly across her face. She feels it and groans.

"I can't wait to leave marks all over your ass the way I did your beautiful tits."

On my way down, I give a quick flick of the paddle over the underside of her right boob, catching several welts lightly. She falls forward slightly, figuring out how to curl her back properly in her restraints.

"Stay just like that." Her back is arched deeply, hovering over the bed. I can see her asshole twitching at the throbbing pain from the pull. I slap a hard hit across her backside and her entire body twitches. "Look at your asshole work, I can't wait to sink inside it and feel how tight you are." I continue to paddle her ass, varying force but consistently increasing the tempo. Her breath picks up, and

I can tell the pain is getting her close to the edge. "That's my girl, tell me you're ready to come."

She begs around the gag another simple please. I press lightly on the rope near her ass, pulling her collar tighter. "I'm going to need more than that."

Continuing a fast rhythm, she begs harder, more desperately to come until the words are uncoherent around the gag and she's shaking. I pull tightly on the rope so I can bring my hand to the side and grab the chain connecting her clamps all in one hand. The pull of the rope causes a harsh cry from her, and I loosen it as much as possible, holding the pressure in my left thumb as I hold the chain in my pinky. The cry caused her to stop begging.

"Oh, you don't need to come anymore?"

She gasps for air as she begs, and with one last firm whip, I pull my pinky into my thumb, ripping all three clamps off her simultaneously. Her screams are beautiful as she thrashes in pain, pushing her into her orgasm. She convulses through it and I drop the paddle to the floor, kneading her bright red ass in my palms.

When the wave has passed and she calms down, I uncuff her wrists. I can tell she thinks she's done when she looks back to watch me, but I instead hold her left wrist as I walk around the side and tie it to the headboard. I put out my hand and she willingly gives me her other wrist, telling me she's prepared to continue.

The pull in her arms is different, and likely tugs at her sore muscles, but she doesn't appear too uncomfortable. I walk back behind her and kneel below her, pulling off her panties and switching off the vibrator. If only she could see the way I admire her, wondering how I got so lucky to be just a few seconds away from slipping my tongue into her soaking wet cunt. I easily work two fingers into her and lick up her inner thigh, savoring every drop of her that is trying to reach the floor. As I work my way up, I leave more bite marks to match the ones that are starting to fade. I mark all over her inner thighs and leave a few on the back of her thighs and the crease of where they reach her ass as well. She tries to kick on one bite and nearly falls over, I quickly steady her by the hips and sink my teeth into the spot responsible, trying to leave my darkest mark there.

I make my way to her clit, so swollen and sensitive. I bite it first, smiling as she pulls away initially, then thrusts her hips toward my mouth. "Such a desperate little cunt you have," I speak with my lips brushing against her folds. My tongue darts out, and I start massaging her as my fingers work faster. It's not long before she's coming all over my hand and face and I cherish every drop she gives me.

Without changing her position, I pull my fingers out and pull off my pants. She looks back over her shoulder and whimpers, shaking her head at me. I can tell it's borderline too much.

"Can you say your safe word around that gag?"

She nods. "Then use it or take this cock I'm going to give you like the needy little slut you really are."

Unable to bear the strain on her neck and ass anymore, she turns her head back around, sniffling but making no words. I slam into her and fuck her relentlessly, pulling on the handle around her waist. Between her waistbelt and the collar tugging at her, her breath grows rapid and shaky, and the lack of oxygen drags a third orgasm out of her around my dick. It's enough to send me over the edge and I pull out at the last second to coat her ass with my cum. When I pull out and the first stream hits her ass almost immediately, she whimpers. I finish pulsing all over her, then move to remove her gag. Squatting in front of her head, I ask her, "Are you disappointed I didn't come in you?"

Her big eyes look up at me, almost regretting her answer before she says it, "Yes." I chuckle a bit in response, then nearly lose my breath when she pleads, "Please don't pull out next time. I'm on birth control, I promise."

If I thought she could handle it, I'd fuck her again right now just so I could give her what she wants. Instead, I let a smile find its place and rub her cheek gently, "you've gotten so good at begging. Doing it even when you don't need to." I place a kiss on her lips. "I love it. Beg me for anything you want and it's yours, sweetheart."

I unclip her hands and wrists from the bed and scoop her in my arms, carrying her to the bathroom. I place her on the toilet, allowing her to use the restroom as I grab a towel to clean her up. When she stands, she moves toward the shower and her fingers work to start taking over her collar. Placing my hand over hers, I press them both flat stopping her ability to take it off. "What exactly do you think you're doing?"

"Oh, I—"

"I know what you thought, but I'm nowhere near done with you."

CHAPTER 16

Logan

My eyes open to the sound of my alarm on my phone I left in the kitchen last night, and I spring out of bed to turn it off before it wakes up Blake. Rubbing the sleep out of my eyes, I crawl back into the bedroom with intentions of going back to sleep, I register there's a pile of clean gym clothes on the dresser. It's the outfit I left here the other day. I feel like I got hit by a truck thanks to my boyfriend. Boyfriend? Wait, I don't know if I should be calling him that; boyfriend is something I'd have to tell Royce about. Regardless, no matter how rough I feel, this train of thought just proves I need a run.

I quickly dress and slip out the front door, mapping a route on my phone to get a few miles in before making it back to the apartment. I took Blake's key so I could lock the door on my way out, and I almost text him about it before deciding he'll figure it out.

I end up walking part of my run, my body refusing to ignore the delicious abuse it was put through last night.

When I make it back in the front door, Blake is already pacing toward me with long strides and an angry expression.

"Did you go on a run?"

"Yeah, why do you sound mad about that?"

"You left without saying anything." Under the anger is a hint of fear.

"It was just a run. I had everything I needed, and I didn't want to wake you."

"Well wake me up next time."

"No, because you would've just tried to convince me to stay in bed." I try to joke and get a smile out of him, but it doesn't work.

"Logan, I'm serious. You can't just disappear like that on me." His anger is subsiding, and his voice is almost normal. "Are you changing your routes when you run? With what Royce does and your stalker, you can't run the same routes all the time. You can't even run in the same areas too much; it'd make it too easy."

He looks everywhere but at me as he rants, and I understand. I'd make it too easy for someone to make me disappear, and he'd feel responsible for another person in his life going missing. I probably triggered something awful in him when he woke up this morning and I wasn't there. Instead of being upset about his overreaction, I wrap my arms around him and lean in for a kiss.

"I'm okay, Blake. I'm right here. I always vary my running routes, you know that. I don't think my stalker is going to be expecting me to leave your place at 5 a.m., but even still, I made a new route this morning."

I tell him what he needs to hear, and I can feel his shoulders relax as his arms tighten around me. He lands another kiss on my lips before telling me, "Let's go take a shower."

We both shower quickly, sharing the space comfortably as we hurry to get cleaned up and out the door. I almost believe we're going to get through the whole experience without Blake trying to get inside me when I feel his lips find mine under the water as I'm rinsing off. His kiss is tender, and I relish in the feeling of his skillful mouth—knowing he saved this piece of himself just for me. I don't complain, despite my body's exhaustion, as his hands bring my body against his, or as he gently lifts me up and slips inside me. He's overly affectionate as he gets us both off in record time, then slips out of the shower to grab our towels. I dry off, run a brush through my hair, and cover myself in Blake's oversized hoodie for the car ride home.

He pulls open a door in his wardrobe to reveal three shelves lined with small bags from the lingerie store. I reach for one impulsively and resist the urge to peek as we leave. Lost in my excitement while walking out to his Audi, he throws an arm around me and pulls me against his hip.

"I don't think I'll ever get enough of you," he shares reverently.

The admission tugs at my heart as I realize I agree. No amount of time with him will ever be enough, and I spend the rest of the car ride home wondering what the hell I'm going to do about that realization.

When I make it home, I go upstairs to the bedroom and remove the tissue paper in my bag to find a dusty blue lace thong and matching bra. It's one of the sets I was debating between when we went together. Ripping off the tags, I quickly throw it on under the hoodie and head to the closet to pick an outfit for work. While standing there debating what to wear, I can't stop thinking about Blake even though he left less than five minutes ago. I find myself pulling up his hoodie and taking a below-the-neck selfie of the new set with a glimpse of his hoodie still on my body, captioning the message:

Me: *I miss you already*

Is it possible to be this infatuated with someone you've known nearly your entire life? I don't think it should be, but somehow, I still feel like a kid who's discovered a secret treasure with their best friend, and I don't know what I'm going to do with myself when this feeling fades away.

I sigh, dragging myself out of my daydreams of Blake and force myself to finish, getting ready and heading to my car. I try calling Dallas on the way in, but she doesn't answer. I've got a spare half hour, so I take a detour en route and make a pit stop at the hospital. The charge nurse at the nurses' station recognizes me and we chat casually while I wait for Dallas to fly past us.

"Dallas!" I call out when she breezes by, not even registering my presence.

"Oh shit, sorry Logan, I didn't even notice you there. Can you wait a minute? I need to check on this patient then I'll be right back."

Knowing that a minute never means just a minute in the ER with her, I head down the hall to the cafeteria and grab us both a breakfast sandwich and her a fresh coffee. When I come back, I see her talking to the nurse.

The nurse nods toward me and Dallas' eyes light up at the aluminum-wrapped sandwich in my hand, "God bless you, you angel child."

I laugh as I hand her the sandwich, and she rips the coffee from my hand.

"Long shift today?"

"Yeah, and I'm just getting started."

"When do you work until?"

"7:00. Why, you going to bring me dinner too?"

"Or..." I drag the word out playfully, "You could come by after your shift and we could do a dinner-date night?"

"Why? What's going on?" She eyes me suspiciously, knowing my impulse drop-in has more meaning behind it.

"What? Can't a girl just want to have dinner with her best friend?"

"Sure, but you could've just texted me. You showing up and bribing me with breakfast means something's up."

"Pfft," I wave her away. "You're silly. I just want dinner. Oh! Look at the time, I've got to get going to work." I laugh, "So, see you tonight?"

"Yup, and I can't wait to hear what's actually going on in that brain of yours!" She laughs along with me.

Later that night, Dallas and I are hanging out at my townhouse enjoying our short evening before we both have to head to bed and start the day over early tomorrow.

"So, we've both finished eating and I still don't know why I'm actually here."

"I still don't know what you're talking about," I say, waving my empty fork around in the air.

"You clearly want to talk about it, or else I wouldn't be here, so spill."

I huff and drop my fork. "I'm seeing someone I shouldn't be seeing, okay?"

"I knew it! Who is it?" She nearly pounces at me across the table.

"I'm so not going to tell you that."

"Why not?" She starts to pout.

"Because he's someone Royce wouldn't approve of, I don't think, and I don't want to put you in a situation where you'd have to potentially lie."

"That's the lamest excuse ever." She pauses for a minute and asks, "Wait, is he Cartel? Or Bratva? Or Mob? Or—"

"Dallas! No, he's not part of an illegal gang."

"Well then I don't see the problem."

"He just…" I look up at the ceiling, trying to find the right words, "Royce wouldn't be a fan of us together." Dallas gives me a questioning look. "They know each other and, I just, I know Royce wouldn't like it."

She starts connecting dots in her head, "Oh, my… GOD!" She screams, "It's Blake, isn't it? It's totally Blake! Holy shit, Logan!"

I chuckle nervously, "I…uhm…. Fuck. Yeah, it's Blake."

"Get out of here!" She squeals at me and launches up so she's now practically squatting on her chair. "Why are you not more excited about this?"

"Are you forgetting the part where Royce isn't going to like it?"

"It's his best friend, he literally already likes Blake. I don't see the problem."

"He likes Blake as a friend, not as a guy I'm sleeping with!"

"Logan, this is great news. You've been obsessed with him since we were kids, and now you're together? We should be celebrating. We need more wine!"

"Are you not hearing me right now?" I say laughing, but I feel an ounce of annoyance that she's not understanding why I'm so bothered by this.

"No, I hear you. I just think you're maybe being a bit '*Logan*' about this situation." She tries to soften the insult.

"What exactly do you mean by that?"

Her excitement dies, and she settles into her chair as she sighs. "I think maybe you're looking for problems in this situation here. Sure, Royce may not be thrilled you're are together, but he's protective of you so that's to be expected. He knows Blake isn't a serial killer or anything crazy, so it's just something he has to get used to."

"But what if things go south and Royce gets stuck in the middle?"

"Then he'll choose you. He'll always choose you."

"But I don't want him to need to; I don't want there to be any possibility he loses Blake because of me."

She reaches across the table and grabs my hand. "I hear you, and you're being a good sister. But he'd want you to be happy, right? If shit hits the fan, then you and Blake need to make it so Royce doesn't have to take sides. That's on the two of you, and you have control of that."

I recognize she has a point, but I'm not sure I'm ready to fully agree with her yet. I think I still need time to come to terms with everything, and maybe just some time to ensure the infatuation doesn't wear off before we tell him. "Okay, you may be right. But I just still need more time."

"Okay, but maybe you should really talk to Blake about it. If the feelings are real on both sides, maybe you tell Royce sooner rather than later, so he doesn't feel lied to by you both." I give her a quick nod of acceptance. "So can we be excited now, outside of the Royce thing?"

"Yes, we're very happy outside of the Royce thing." Warmth washes over me. "He is so much better than I could've even imagined when I was sixteen. Everything is so natural with us."

"Agh! I'm so excited for you." She can't stop smiling at me, and I allow myself to show some of the bliss I feel with him before changing the subject.

"You know, you've been awfully quiet about your love life lately. What's up with that?"

"Well, there is this guy I met at the ER that's been in my head a lot lately."

"Oh?"

"Yeah, he's so hot but clearly trouble and I just think it's a bad idea to get involved."

"Tell me more."

"Well, he came into the ER for a bullet wound to the chest, if that tells you anything."

"Definitely trouble. But at least it's the hot kind."

"Dude, it's crazy. He demanded that I be his doctor while he was recovering. So, I had to keep going to the ICU to check on him. He literally injured himself one time when I refused to come."

"That's a little psychotic."

"It's completely psychotic. But I don't know, he has no issue putting it out there that he's interested in me, and I can't get him out of my head. I've hardly looked at anyone else since I met him. It's absolutely ridiculous."

"Have you gone out with him at all?"

"No, and I don't know if I'm going to ever. Anyway, I feel like maybe we should do something fun with the girls to distract us all from our boy drama. What do you think?"

"I'm in, what do you want to do?"

"Well, I think Ana and Ari were wanting to do another river float before the summer was over. Do you want to see if everyone's free Saturday?"

"Yeah, I'll text the group. Are we inviting TJ?"

"Of course! He's the new honorary member of the girl gang."

We end up making plans with everyone for a float this weekend, and Dallas heads out for the night, leaving me alone with my thoughts and several empty bottles of wine.

CHAPTER 17

Logan

A few days later, I'm jittery as I stride confidently into O'Brion's, excited to see the two most important men in my life. Worrying about keeping my behavior toward Blake in check around Royce, I try not to let my anxiety take over. The sight of them sitting together in the booth brings a smile to my face subconsciously. Blake is in the side of the booth facing me and notices me approaching. He gives me a warm smile as I walk up, his perpetually stern face softening at the sight of me.

I slide into the booth next to Royce and greet him with a hug.

"Hey Logie, what's new?" Royce's relaxed smile distracts me momentarily from the pull I have to the man across the table.

"Oh, not much really. I had dinner with Dallas on Tuesday, and I think we're going to have a girls river float on Saturday."

"That's it? Nothing else new and exciting happening?" The weight of Blake's smooth voice reaching down in my stomach as he tempts me to tell Royce about us.

"Yep, that's it really. What about you two, anything exciting happening with you this week?" I don't look over as I redirect the attention from me.

Royce takes a sip of his Corona before answering, "Nope," without any further elaboration. Blake opens his mouth to say something, but our waitress cuts him off.

"Hey, can I get you something to drink?"

"Just a water with lemon, thanks."

She nods, "Are we ready to order?"

Everyone orders quickly, and Blake orders a basket of pretzel bites for the table at the end. "Those are Logan's favorites here, they're pretty good," Royce tells Blake as our waitress walks away with our order.

"Yeah, we split some last week when you couldn't make it," he says smoothly, eyeing me as if he's remembering that night.

"Good, I'm sorry I never made it."

"Don't worry about it, we had a good time catching up, didn't we Dandy?" I feel him grazing his leg against mine under the table.

"Yeah, it was really no big deal Royce." I give Blake a sharp glance to drop the topic of conversation. "Did everything go okay with that deal you were working on?"

"It hasn't happened yet." He shares a look with Blake that makes me nervous when he answers. "But I'm hoping everything will go as smooth as possible."

I want to ask what exactly is going on, but I get the sense that I'm not going to like the answer, even if I was allowed to know the information. I nervously bite on my lip, seeing the concerned expression on Blake's face makes me wonder exactly how much he knows now that he's back in town.

"I'm sure it'll be fine!" Trying my best to sound like I believe the words coming out of my mouth. Royce just nods as he swallows another sip of beer. I feel my phone buzz on the table, and I see *B* light up on my phone with the message:

B: *You should tell him about us tonight.*

I quickly pull the phone off the tabletop and respond in my lap.

Me: *No.*

Small talk floats around the table when another message from Blake lights up in my lap:

B: *I want you sitting beside me so I can finger you under the table while we wait for food. Then I'll be able to taste you on my burger when I eat it.*

My eyes dart up to him. He's focused on Royce without a trace of evidence that he just texted his best friend's sister that he wants to be able to taste her on his dinner. Registering I'm sitting next to him, I check on Royce out of the corner of my eye as I lock my phone screen, not bothering to respond.

"Who's B?" Royce asks me suspiciously.

"What do you mean?" I dodge the question, trying to figure out how much he saw on my phone.

"You just got a text from '*B*'. Who is that?"

"It's not my stalker, he likes to text from unknown numbers instead of introducing himself," I say, trying to deflect with humor.

"It better not be Dad." His pupils pulse as a wave of emotion runs wild under his cool exterior.

"No, it's not Dad. He hasn't reached out for a while."

"I guess his luck must be pretty good this month then. You know you can't help him right? It only enables him to keep gambling. It'll never stop if we keep bailing him out."

I sigh. Our father is a mess with his gambling addiction; it's why he was hardly around when we were kids. When he was up, he was enjoying his winnings and when he was down, he was doing God-knows-what to earn enough money to get back into the game.

"I know, Royce, I haven't helped him in a long time." Irritated with the situation, I slide out of the booth, "I'm going to go to the bathroom before our food gets here. Excuse me."

"That's a good idea, I'm right behind you." Blake states practically into my ear as I walk past him. He's tight on my heels, and when I take a few steps past the Men's bathroom to get to the Women's, I feel his arm reach over me and push the door open.

"What are you—" His lips crash into mine as his body pushes me into the bathroom. I hear the swish and thud of the deadbolt as Blake locks the door behind us. He holds my face against his as I'm backed up into the wall of the bathroom. We're moving so fast, my body slamming into the wall is audible, and draws a groan from my throat.

"You looked sexy reading my text at the table, and I didn't want to make you wait. Let me take care of you."

"Right now?" It comes out breathy as he bends to slide his hands under the hem of my dress.

"Yes. I know you need it. I could smell your desperation across the table."

Before I can answer, his tongue forces its way into my mouth. He kisses me roughly, only giving me a reprieve to forcefully pull my dress over my head. The kiss overwhelms me, and I accept everything he takes from me as he nips down my jaw and neck while stripping off my bra and underwear. His teeth tug on my nipple as my ears register the sound of his belt opening and his zipper going down. He pulls away, but he doesn't release me from his mouth as he stands. I muffle a cry with my own hand as he stretches my breast too far, and it pulls roughly out of his teeth.

His large palm grabs my elbow and removes my hand from my face, pinning it against my waist as he pushes me sideways. I spin and am pressed roughly into the wall at the center of my back, my cheek and sensitive nipples scratching against the splintering wood slats of the wall.

His smooth bass warms my ear, "You'll look perfect getting fucked into a bathroom wall, don't you agree?"

His dick slams into me without warning, sliding me up the rough wall as I rise onto my tiptoes. He fucks me unapologetically, pressing me up with both his body and his hands on my hips. "You're going to be licking my cum off this wall when I'm done with you."

I wish my stomach rolled at the idea of it, but instead, my walls twitch and Blake notices. "Yeah? You like that idea."

I envision his cum on the wall and clench him tighter, imagining the taste of him.

"Lick the wall for me right now and show me what a good filthy slut you are for me."

S. Belle

I'm not sure what comes over me, but I stick my tongue out and taste the Sharpie-covered wood, trying not to scratch my tongue as I continue to lick.

"Good fucking girl." His hand moves from my hip to the side of my face as he presses me harder into the wall. His thrusting picks up speed and force, and I feel my own orgasm building. He pulls out and I feel spurts of hot cum grazing my inner thigh as he covers the wall between my legs. When no more heat is spraying between my legs, my head is shoved down. I try to bend at the force, pressing my ass against him, but as I continue to be pushed down with nowhere to go, I stumble to my knees. Fingers curl into my scalp and my head is tugged forward against the wall. He rubs my face up the wall, coating my cheek and nose in cum and scratching the tip as he forces it side to side to cover my face. Instinctively, I flick my tongue toward my nose and over my lips, lapping up the streaks near my mouth. He tips my head and presses my lips against the wall. "Eat it."

Desperate to please him, I start licking the wall. His hand relaxes in my hair, not releasing me but allowing freedom as I slobber across the wall, trying to wet the drying cum and get every last drop. I sense him squatting behind me and his fingertip finds my clit, circling me generously as I continue to lick him off the wall. His other hand presses lightly into my inner hip, and I gasp against the wall.

"That's it, baby. Show me how needy you are to taste me."

He shifts onto his knees behind me, and I feel his head pressing against me again. Leaning backward, I plead with my body for him to re-enter me. He does, and slowly thrusts into me as I lick the wall spotless.

Remaining inside me, he stands us up. His hands move from my waist up to my breasts and tug them upward to a painful height. I try to stand as tall as possible, getting on my toes and he just keeps tugging higher. A useless whimper escapes my lips, doing nothing to relieve his grasp. He just holds me there as he rocks slowly in and out of me.

"Do you want to come?"

I nod viciously, "Yes, please."

He leads me by rough tugs on my breasts toward the sink, pressing my hips into the counter. I'm bent over, and he holds my head up, making eye contact with me through the mirror. When my eyes begin to drift shut from pleasure, I'm punished with a forceful slap across my ass. A loud yelp sneaks out.

"We need to be quiet, remember?" He says playfully. Watching me through the mirror, he pulls out his belt and wraps it around my head. He tightens it into a gag, then pushes one of my knees up onto the counter. The new position has my clit hitting the edge of the counter, and the pooled water beside the sink gives me no traction to resist the force of the impact. He holds me up by my hair with one hand and spanks me repeatedly with the other. I can feel blood rushing to my thigh as it bangs into the counter, and the hand spanking me takes a break to start abusing my nipples.

"Look at yourself. Look how natural you look, covered in cum, getting fucked in a public bathroom. What a beautiful fucking slut my girl is." His degrading praise has my body trembling. "That's it, fall apart for me. Come all over my cock, my pretty little whore." We lock eyes through the mirror and it's over, I shatter around him, and feel him pulsing into me in response.

As we both come down, his hold on me relaxes, and eventually he pulls out of me. I slip down off the counter and take the wettened paper towel he hands me to work on getting the cum off my face as best I can without destroying my makeup. In the reflection, I see him tuck my underwear into his pocket and bring me back only my dress.

"Get dressed, we need to go back out." Sliding the dress over my head, I try to walk around him toward the toilet.

"Blake, I need to go to the bathroom."

"No, you don't. You're fine."

"Okay, then I need my underwear. Your cum is dripping down my leg."

Unexpectedly, his hand is under my dress, and he scoops up the cum on my thigh, using two fingers to shove it forcefully back inside me. He pulls out and lands a quick pat across my swollen center. "Keep dripping for me. Maybe you'll drip on the floor in front of Royce, and we can explain to him together how I just used you like my own personal whore in the bathroom."

My mouth opens in shock, and he uses the opportunity to slip his two coated fingers in my mouth. Like a possessed woman, I lick them clean, and he rewards me with a deep kiss before unlocking the bathroom door and walking out. I debate going to the bathroom, but Blake would probably notice the extra time it takes me to get back to the table and I'd end up punished for it later.

Sliding into the booth next to Royce, I move carefully to fight leaking down my leg. The cool leather of the booth is a shock against my warm, exposed skin, and I can't help but feel another rush of stimulation. If there isn't a wet spot when I stand up to leave it will be an absolute miracle. I shift to tuck the back of my dress underneath me and pray that will be enough.

The guys are already digging into their food on the table. "Wow, that came out fast."

Blake wipes his hands on his napkin as he types out a text. My phone buzzes on the seat between Royce and me with his message.

B: *I'd come fast too if you crawled under this table right now to give me head.*

Praying Royce didn't see the message, I flip my phone over and try to focus on my food and the banter circling the table. I pretend the message was from Ari. "Ari wants me to pick up my bridesmaid dress tomorrow since it's done, and she needs the space."

"I can do it for you if you need me to. My day is pretty light."

"Oh, you don't have to do that. I'm sure I can make it by after work before she heads out."

"It's really no big deal. Her store is close to my office building, I'll just swing by and grab it."

"Are you sure?"

Blake sends three more texts over the course of the next ten minutes, and with the two-minute reminder vibrations, it feels like my phone has been going off nonstop. I can't resist anymore and see that the last text is about how he can't wait to tie me to his bed tonight and watch me beg him to paddle me until I come.

Royce chuckles. "This guy really wants your attention, Logan. You sure you don't want to tell me who it is?"

"Yeah Dandy, who is *B*?" Blake says nonchalantly across the table.

S. Belle

"Can we please just drop it?"

"You know if I want to find out who he is, I will." Royce states without any bite to it. I know he's just trying to encourage me to share, but—

"I'm just not ready yet. Can we table it for later?"

Royce starts to agree, but Blake won't drop it. "Oh, come on, we just want to know who he is."

"I'm sure you do, and if he's anyone worth telling you about, I'll share." I say it playfully, but the sting lands and plasters across his face. Royce is focused on his phone, and I'm not sure he's even listening anymore.

"Ouch, I can't imagine a man wants to be talked about like that," Blake says, still trying to keep up the guise that we're talking about someone else.

"Well, if he wants to stick around, he should respect my boundaries. He knows where I am right now."

"Maybe he's just hoping he'll come up if he keeps texting you, and you'll tell us about him."

I am beyond pissed at Blake for not letting this go. He knows exactly how I feel about telling Royce, and instead of having a conversation about it, he corners me, trying to force my hand. Royce is still typing a response on his phone, so I direct my gaze back to Blake and speak under my breath.

"Peaches." I leave my food half-eaten on the table and abruptly head out of the restaurant.

My anger fuels my walk initially, but I slow down after the first fifty yards. The streets were lined with cars when I parked a little over an hour ago, forcing me to walk about five minutes from my Bronco to O'Brion's. It looks like many of the happy hour patrons have made their way home, as most of the street parking spots are now vacant. The empty corporate buildings create a haunting feel on the sidewalk, and I wrap my arms around myself as I focus on making it another few blocks to my car.

Waiting to cross the street, I feel a presence behind me. Expecting to see Royce or Blake, I turn around and find no one there. My vision roaming side to side, I inspect the long path back to O'Brion's, but I only see strangers at the outdoor seating off in the distance. I swear I catch a shadow move near the alley between buildings a few strides away, but when my ears strain to find any evidence of life, I hear nothing. I turn back around and see the crosswalk countdown at four seconds. It's not enough time to make it across four one-way lanes. I huff and wait for the next light, checking over my shoulder every few seconds, still sensing someone behind me.

When the walk sign lights up, I cross the road quickly, watching over my shoulder to ensure nobody is following me. A sense of relief watches over me as I take the next block, but when I round the corner onto the street I left my car on, I swear I hear footfalls close behind me. I check again, but this street is poorly lit with only a parking garage on either side of me. The distance of the garages and a now-empty strip mall parking lot, abandoned with the stores closing, stand between me and my car. I pick up the pace, telling myself the feelings and sounds in my head are just my imagination and forcing myself not to break into a run.

My shadow is long beside me, and I watch it intensely as it crosses the path of other objects: a trash can, the light pole, and random boxes left on the street. I hear a can clink at the bottom of the trash can I passed about five seconds ago, and I whirl around to see nobody. My breath catches and I notice the alley directly beside the can, sure somebody is hiding there. I backpedal away, uneven breaths wreaking havoc on my ability to move. When I make it to the edge of the strip mall parking lot, I turn and burst into a sprint. My throat burns worse than my legs and I feel wobbly, unable to run in a perfectly straight line.

When I make it to my car, I fumble with the keys and nervously drop them. My lungs burn as I squat to pick them up, then turn my back to the car to stand. Vision blurring and hands shaking, I can't find the damn unlock button for my car in my unsteady state. Quickly giving up, I turn and type in my code on the door's keyless entry and slam it behind me, hitting the lock button repeatedly the second I'm inside. I try to take deep breaths to even out my breathing, but it turns into hyperventilating when I realize whoever was following may have seen the passcode for my car. What if he did, and he uses it to hide in the car to wait and attack me? What if he figures out that it is the same code I use for my security system at home? The blurry edges of my vision take over and everything goes black as I fail to get enough oxygen in my system.

I can't focus on anything, and my chest tightens. If he approached the car right now, he'd see me in a full-blown panic attack. I'd be such an easy victim. The thought worsens everything, knowing I'd be helpless to defend myself right now. Feeling lightheaded, I know I'll pass out soon if I don't get my breathing under control. I force my trembling hands up to find the steering wheel and run my thumb slowly over the stitching on the leather. One. Two. Three. Four. I count a third of the way up the wheel before I feel my breathing evening out. The world comes back into focus, and I try to convince myself to sit here for a minute before driving away. When the fear starts edging back up, I know I'm better off pulling out and taking a long route home instead of sitting here any longer and risking another panic attack. I check my mirrors incessantly looking for any sign of a car following me, and once I'm convinced nobody's there, I head toward home.

When I make it inside, I debate texting Royce about what happened, but I don't want to have to admit I had a panic attack over it. He'll demand I get personal security, and I don't want that for so many reasons. I could talk to Blake about it, but the idea of texting him right now and needing him is completely off the table after how he acted tonight. I leave every light in the house on as I walk around getting ready for bed, and they all stay that way as I patiently wait for sleep to overtake me, curled up in bed.

B: *My trial is over. Can I come pick you up?*

That's the message Blake sent me at 2:37 p.m. while I was in the middle of working with our kitchen staff on a revamped dining menu. I'm exhausted from sleeping terribly last night, and my ability to focus on that meeting after receiving that text is non-existent. I agree to menu changes that I'm not sure of, just so I can get out of there, then stare at my phone in my office for too long before responding.

Me: *When?*

The response is immediate.

B: *I can head over there now.*

Me: *I'm still working.*

My heart is heavy in my chest trying to tell him no.

B: *I have somewhere I want to take you.*
Can you leave early?

                                    Me: *I guess. Can it wait?*

B: *I'll be there in 20 minutes.*

I guess that's a "no, it can't wait." I do my best to focus on work and wrap up a few things before he gets here. When the text comes, I pack up my bag slowly and head out front to where Blake is waiting, leaning against his passenger door.

He opens it when he notices me, and I climb in silently. There isn't any tension in the air, but neither of us speaks as he drives down the winding road leading away from the Camellia Club. Music plays softly in the car, filling the quiet drive, until I realize where we are.

"Why are we here?"

He parks before answering me, "We have always communicated best here, and we need to talk."

I know he's right, but that sentence never sits well. Reluctantly, I get out of the car and try not to look up at the playground as I walk over to a picnic table next to the lake we grew up by. He sits beside me, and we both stare out over the water for a few moments.

"I understand why you left yesterday, but I need to clarify something."

It's the first time in a long time I've noticed nerves in his voice. It catches me off guard. "What do you need to know?"

"Did I push you too far in the bathroom, or was it just after we got back to the table?"

I realize the nerves are from the fear he took it too far. He's afraid it was too much.

"No. That was, a lot, in the bathroom, but I…" How do I describe how much I trust this man to abuse my body in a way that leaves me desperate to do anything he needs? "It was disgusting, but in the best way. I can take whatever you give me, you know that."

He nods and doesn't say anything else.

"I'm serious, Blake. I enjoyed myself in the bathroom. I just wish you could respect how I feel about telling Royce."

"I can't stand being around you and not being able to touch you." He stops looking at the ripples in the water and focuses on me instead. "How do you not care? How does it not drive you crazy to sit across from me and pretend I mean nothing to you?"

"I just need time."

"Time for what exactly?"

"To be sure of us. I don't want to put him in the middle of our relationship if it falls apart."

He looks away again, shaking his head. "You're just waiting for this to fail so you don't have to tell him."

"No, I don't want that."

"Are you sure about that?"

"Yes, I'm sure. I, I've been in love with you since we were kids. Why would I want us to fail?"

He doesn't even turn to face me over my admission, he just closes his eyes, restraining his voice when he speaks. "I'm not sure. But I do know if you truly loved me, you wouldn't be afraid for Royce to find out. You'd believe in this." When his jade-green eyes meet mine, they're frigid. "But you don't. You don't trust this to work. I don't know what else I can do."

I want to give him the answer. I want to be able to tell him exactly what to do to quiet my brain and believe in our happily ever after, but I don't know what that thing is.

"I'm sorry." I whisper.

"Me too."

I lay my head on his shoulder, but he doesn't wrap his arm around me. We stay there and watch the sun begin to set, listening to the sound of the birds and the water lapping on the rocks until my stomach growls, disturbing the peace.

"I should take you back to the club so you can get your car."

"Your apartment is closer. You can just take me to get it in the morning." I'm hesitant to suggest the idea, and apparently for good reason.

"I don't know if it's a good idea for us to do that tonight." He stands and waits for me to follow suit before walking us back to the car. The only thing that eases my heartbreak is the way he laces his fingers with mine as we walk.

The ride back is quiet again, but he keeps a comfortable hand on my knee as he drives. I admire the trees lining the drive as we pull back into work. Heading back to the employee lot, he parks beside my Bronco.

His hand squeezes my knee lightly. "I want to keep seeing you, Logan, but not if you're going to be ashamed of being with me."

"I'm not ashamed of us." I panic, trying to dispel the thought from his brain.

"I'm not so sure of that. When you decide what you really want, you know where to find me." He lightly strokes my face before climbing out of the car and opening my door.

I want to say something, anything to convince him he matters to me, but I know the only thing that will fix this is telling Royce about us. I can't promise him that I'm ready to do that, so I get out of the car and hug him goodbye.

"Nope!" Dallas states as she jumps back up from her float, her backside wet with ice-cold water.

"Oh, it's not that bad! You're just in a cold spot," Ari tells her, holding herself still against the current with her foot on a rock.

"It's pretty cold," Ana adds in.

"We can share a raft if it'll help keep you warm," suggests TJ.

I walk across the small rocks on the riverbed and drop my float in the water. The river flows fast enough that it never gets too warm, but it'll feel good after a few minutes of baking under the 94-degree sun.

"You knew it was going to be cold, Dallas. Just get in."

She grumbles before sitting back down. "Can someone at least toss me a beer?"

The cooler is tied to Ari's raft already, and she slips a Natti Lemonade into a koozie before tossing it to her. Ana ties up loosely to Ari's raft, and Ari works on attaching everyone else's rafts with a lot of slack as they float by.

"Why do we tie everyone off again?"

"It'd probably be better if we did it in pairs, but it'll keep everyone moving at roughly the same speed and on the same side of the river." Ari launches herself off into the water and suddenly we're all drifting down river much faster.

"Okay, who needs a beer?" The light rapids about forty yards ahead mark the end of shallow water, and we all settle in with our drinks before we reach them. Sunscreen gets passed around and two floating bags are tied to the cooler float with everyone's phone and keys in them.

"Everyone ready for the hill?" Ari calls out, our floats having spun so she's one of the only ones facing forward. The first rapids are light but have a bit of a drop off to deeper water on the other side. A few squeals escape everyone, and somehow Ana ends up drenched from the hill.

"How did that happen?"

"TJ soaked me when he caught the last rapid," she mumbles, trying to brush the cold water off her arms.

"Yeah, I did," he drawls, making Ana splash water in his direction with a laugh.

"Speaking of, Logan, anything you'd like to share with the group?" Dallas waggles her eyebrows at me.

"Anything *you* want to share with the group?"

"A really hot guy showed up in the ER, got obsessed with me, and then disappeared. Next!"

She quickly throws it back at me, but Ari jumps in, "I'm sorry, what? We're just now hearing about this?"

"There's not much to hear. Logan, on the other hand, has lots to share!"

The whole group looks at me, and I accept I'm going to have to give them something. "I was hooking up with Blake."

"Oh shit!" TJ launches out of his raft, splashing into the water with excitement at the drama and dragging a hearty laugh out of Ana and Ari.

"Was?" Dallas catches.

"He wants me to tell Royce about us."

"I don't see the problem," Ari says confused.

"That's exactly what I said!"

"It doesn't matter because it's basically over."

"What are you talking about?" Ana tries to push me gently for more information.

"Well, we kind of got into it on Thursday over how he was acting at dinner with Royce, and then, yesterday he essentially told me he doesn't want to keep seeing me unless we tell him."

"So he wants your brother to know about y'all; I think that means he's serious about your relationship. What exactly is the problem here?" Ari questions me, echoing Dallas' sentiments from the other day.

"What if it falls apart?"

"Well, right now it's falling apart because you're being stupid."

"Ari!" Ana scolds her. While she wasn't exactly nice in her delivery, she's saying the same thing everyone else has been, which makes me wonder if I really am just being ridiculous.

"I think if you wait him out, he'll cave. Guys always cave for sex."

"Not helpful TJ!" Dallas scolds him.

"Hey, I'm just saying. If you don't want a relationship with him, I'm sure he'll come around to being friends with benefits."

"No, I do want him."

"Doesn't seem like it." Ari sips on her beer.

I glare at her. "If it wasn't littering, I'd throw my can at you right now."

"Maybe, what everyone's trying to say is that if you really want him, you should take the risk and tell Royce," Dallas is always trying to be the gentle voice of reason.

"Maybe I don't want to be having this conversation right now."

"I'll drop it if everyone jumps off the rope swing right now." Ari leverages my discomfort to bully us all into taking a dip into the freezing cold river.

I beg the rest of the girls to join me so we can move on, and they're all nice enough to play into Ari's game. TJ is the first one swimming over, more than ready to play along. Everyone is freezing when they climb back into their rafts, but the sun dries us quickly and we move on to talking about everyone else's lives, Ari keeping her promise to not bring the conversation back up.

The rest of the float goes smoothly, but I have a constant nagging in my brain, asking me what the hell I'm going to do about Blake. The thought hovers in my mind the rest of the day, and I can't push it out during my run the next morning either. I don't go by Blake's place. I don't expect him to want to see me if I don't have any answers for him, but as the day drags on without hearing from him, I feel a pang in my chest, registering that this is what it would feel like to lose him. I push through the next few days, feeling lost and hollow without talking to the one person I want to be around most.

When I wake up Wednesday morning, I ignore the route I mapped on my phone the night before and decide to run a previous route that ends at Blake's apartment. When I get to his front door, I knock lightly a few times. A shirtless Blake opens the door in his grey sweats, clearly having just crawled out of bed.

"I'm sorry, I didn't mean to wake you."

"It's fine." He steps back and lets me in. I can see into the kitchen behind him and see a line of bags out on the counter that I hadn't picked up. When I count, there are four there; if he had been expecting me today, there should've been five. My heart sinks knowing today was the day he gave up.

"You can go pick one out," his sleepy voice says, breaking my train of thought.

He remains standing by the door, eyeing me as I walk over and peek into a couple of the bags before grabbing one in my favorite shade of lavender.

"Do you want me to drive you home?"

"No, it's okay. The sun is coming up, so I'm just going to walk back."

"You sure? That's a long walk."

"Yeah, I'll be fine. But is it okay if I come back over tonight so we can talk about everything?"

He's wary, trying to dissect what I mean. "Sure, if that's what you want."

"It is." I walk over to him and tug on his arm, pulling him down so I can plant a kiss on his cheek. "Go back to sleep." He doesn't resist my affection and I'm hopeful after our conversation tonight we'll be in the best place we've ever been.

CHAPTER 18

Blake

My cross-examination of this witness is horrific. I'm not drawing any sympathy with the jury because I'm so damn tired from my hangover and unexpected wakeup call from Logan this morning. When I heard that light tapping on my door, I was convinced it was my imagination playing tricks on me. Seeing her through the peephole, sweaty and swaying back and forth, unsure of herself, I felt as off-balance as she looked. Whatever she's hoping to say tonight, she should've just said this morning. I'm going to lose this case for my client since all I've been able to do is work through every possible scenario of what she might say tonight and how I could leverage her to get what I want instead of focusing on my actual job.

During our recess I check my phone, hoping for a message from her, and I see a text from Royce asking me to call him immediately.

"Hey, I have to be back in the courtroom in five. What's going on?" I get straight to the point when I hear him answer.

"Things went exactly as I expected them to last night," he tells me cautiously. I can tell he regrets whatever happened, but I can't ask him for details over the phone.

"What do you need from me?"

"Mostly, I need you to watch your back. We've been hanging out a lot over the last few weeks, and if anyone was paying attention, including people on my own team, they'll know you're a weak spot. Just be careful, okay?"

"Okay, thanks for giving me a heads up. You know to call me immediately if anyone comes sniffing around, right?"

"I know, and I might have to soon. Just, be careful."

"I will be. I've got plans tonight, but do you want to get to dinner early tomorrow so we can catch up before Logan gets there?"

"Yeah, I think that's a great idea."

I'm getting ready to hang up before another thought hits me: "Should we change the location? We always go there."

"We always go there because it's a friend's place."

I nod to myself. I want to ask him about Logan's protection and if he's putting a detail on her, but it's not my place. If he called me, I'm sure he's already got something in motion for her. She may not let him have a bodyguard on her, but he's not leaving her completely unsupervised, I'm sure of that.

"Alright, then I'll see you tomorrow. Be safe, man."

The clock reads 9:45 p.m., and she's still not here. She texted earlier that she'd be over after dinner at Dallas', and she said she was leaving dinner just before 9:00 p.m.; Dallas doesn't live that far. When she wasn't here by 9:20 p.m., I sent her a text that she never read, asking if she was close. Dallas could've coaxed her into another glass of wine, so I sent her a second message, asking if she's still coming. After another half hour, I wonder if she's just blowing me off. I'd expect her to at least make up an excuse if that was the case, and knowing the situation with her stalker sends my protective side into overdrive. She's going to be furious with me, but I decide to text Dallas directly. She can hate me all she wants; I just need to know she's safe. Not sure if she still has my number saved, since we haven't spoken in several years, I preface my text:

Me: *Hey, it's Blake. Is Logan still with you?*

Dallas: *No, she's not with you? She said she was headed straight over.*

There's a glimmer of joy in my system that Logan told Dallas about us, or at least that she was coming over, but that's outweighed by the ache in my bones triggered by not knowing where she is.

Me: *No, she's not here. She didn't say she was stopping anywhere on the way or going home first?*

Dallas: *No, she was itching to see you.*

Fuck.

Dialing Logan's number, the line rings repeatedly before going to voicemail. Trying another time, when I get voicemail again, I hang up and storm into my office. Logging in to the security cameras, I move through the system to find the footage from the cameras at the front entrance of my apartment complex. I watch the video in rewind looking for any sign of Logan. I can hear my pulse pounding in my ears when I catch sight of her on the screen. My stomach churns as the scene replays in reverse, but I force myself to rewind to the beginning to get the full picture.

She's walking along the sidewalk, presumably from where she parked down the road. An SUV pulls over near the side of the road and calls out to her, probably asking her for directions. She approaches the car while talking, and someone runs from beside the building and wraps her up from behind. *Damnit, Logan.* He covers her mouth and a third person inside the SUV flings the back door open, and she's gone off the street in a matter of seconds. The camera doesn't catch a view of the license plate, and I immediately dial Royce, rewatching the scene as I wait for him to answer.

My ears don't hear the line trilling as I watch her dark brown curls fan out around her kidnapper's head. The way he wraps his arms around her and covers her mouth makes my blood boil. Underneath the anger, though, is the fear we'll never find her; that she'll be gone forever. I repress the thought when I hear Royce's relaxed voice on the other side of the phone.

"Hey, what's up?"

"Check the security footage from my apartment at 9:11 p.m." There's ice in my voice, and the tone clearly spooks him.

"Shit, what happened?" I can hear him fumbling with his phone as he works to pull up the footage.

"Just watch." My voice cracks, and my eyes blur watching the screen.

18 years prior...

I'm standing at the edge of the water, chatting with Royce when Olivia interrupts us. "I'm bored, I'm going to play on the hill."

"This is way more fun, but that's fine." I turn to Royce, "Is Logan coming?"

"No, but maybe Dallas will stop by and entertain her, so she stops bothering us."

"You know she's going to want to go on the swings soon, and we'll have to go over there with her."

"I just wish we could come out here without them some days, not have to play big brother all the time. Maybe hang with some of the girls our own age."

"You're telling me," I scoff, "But honestly where is Logan? You normally don't like leaving her home alone."

"She didn't want to come, and I can't make her. If she wants to risk being home alone when Dad gets back, that's on her."

I skip the last of the rocks in my hand and start picking around for a few more. When I look over my shoulder, I see Olivia near the top of the hill plucking dandelions.

"What's the most you've been able to skip today?"

"Four, you?"

"Same, the wind has the water kind of rough today."

"If that's your excuse," he laughs as we both try to get a smooth throw for five skips on the water. When I think to look back for Olivia, I don't see her. When I turn around, Royce looks at the hill with me.

"You think she went up to the swings?"

"Probably, but she knows she's supposed to say something."

We walk up the hill, and when we get close enough to see she's not anywhere on the playground, I start to get really annoyed.

S. Belle

"I swear if she went home without me, I'm never going to hear the end of it from my parents."

I ask a few of the kids on the playground if they've seen Olivia, and they all say no. A couple of the younger kids' parents hear us looking for her, and I can feel the panic radiating off them. I run toward the woods and start calling for her, my own fear taking over. Before long, the whole park is frantically searching for my lost sister. Someone calls my parents, the police arrive, and I get pulled away from looking for her to be questioned. I fight with the officers, telling them I should be helping look because she'll listen to me, but they won't let me go. They tell me she's probably just lost and try to reassure me that we'll find her. When the flashlights turn off and the dogs go home for the night unable to find her, my twelve-year-old brain is certain if I could've been out looking for her, I could've found her. It's my fault when the weeks turn to months and years of never finding her; I wasn't paying enough attention, and I don't even know which direction she went. After several years, the police tell us she's presumed dead, but my parents don't hold a funeral; hoping she's still out there. I know though, I know she's gone and it's my fault.

I know Royce carries that day with him too; he treated Logan differently after that, never complaining about the responsibility of being an older brother. When I failed at it, he realized just how important it was. I'm going to fail Logan, too; I can feel it. She was at my fucking door when she was taken, and I was so engrossed in throwing a pity party for myself and assuming the worst of her I didn't even look for over an hour.

"Blake, are you listening to me?" There's a sharpness to his tone that cuts through my thoughts.

"What did you say?"

"Are you okay?"

"What the hell do you think? Of course I'm not fucking okay. This was over an hour ago, and I just fucking saw it. What the fuck is wrong with me? Why do I let this happen to everyone around me?"

"Get over to the new building I showed you. We'll find her."

"Do you think it was her stalker?"

"No, I think that's one guy; this was a team. I think this is related to my call earlier. Just get over here as soon as you can and I'll start working on it, okay?"

"Are you already there?"

"No, but I'll beat you there. Be safe." He hangs up, and I realize I'm already in my living room grabbing my keys, feeling detached from the moment as I pray to whatever God is out there that we find her in time.

One of Royce's guys meets me at the back door and walks me into the main space where a dozen or so others are posted up trying to find Logan. Royce hears us coming down the metal stairs and watches me with a grim expression as I descend.

He turns his back to me when I get close, looking at a large screen, and starts speaking stoically. "The men who took her are confirmed members of the Cartel. From what we know, there's a few places they could be holding her around the city. We haven't heard from them directly yet, but the fact that they took her instead of shooting her on the street is a good sign they're not planning on killing her, right away at least." He takes a drawn-out breath, "I've got a few men scoping out some of the possibilities of where she may be, so until we hear from them, it's a bit of a waiting game and trying to come up with other possibilities if she's not at any of those locations."

"We're supposed to just wait here? She's already been gone for hours Royce. We can't just wait."

"If we drive in the wrong direction, it may take us even longer to get to her. We're in the middle of the city. The second my guys know something, we'll hear about it."

I hate the idea of waiting around. I start to pace in the space, but try not to unleash my anger. My skin is crawling, itching to do something, anything, but I force myself to keep the simmering rage in check. Royce might cut me out if he thinks I can't handle my emotions right now. His need for control looks different than mine, but if he feels like I'm slipping, I won't even realize I'm being left in the dark.

With his back still to me and watching one of his men click through images slowly on the screen, he speaks again. "While we're waiting, want to explain to me what my sister was doing coming over to your apartment at 9:00 p.m. on a weeknight?"

His tone is steady, but underneath it is a cool wrath waiting for an excuse. I pace behind the monitor to draw his attention from the screen and greet him with a harsh glare. "Seriously? What do you think the answer to that question is?"

"I'm hoping it's not that my best friend is hooking up with my damn sister behind my back." I don't say anything. "Because that's a really shitty thing to keep from me, especially since I know how you normally treat women."

The fact that he thinks I would treat Dandy like the other women I've been with is absolutely appalling.

"Fuck you. I love her." His facial expression tells me he wasn't expecting that. "I've loved her since I was thirteen years old, maybe even before that. She is not just some woman, and I cannot lose her." My voice cracks, and I clear my throat. "If you are the reason I lose both my sister and the love of my life, you will wish for a death that won't be coming because you will not even deserve that mercy from me."

The dig about Olivia breaks his exterior, and his flash of vulnerability cracks open my anger into an unrelenting force, hardening my tone. "I can't lose her, Royce. I can't fail both of them. And if we never find her, God, I can't not know again. I won't—" I have to stop to swallow down the emotions. I won't survive not knowing what happened to her and spending the rest of my life wondering like I do about Olivia. Logan is the only one that keeps me stable, and if I don't have her, it won't be worth it anymore.

Royce steps toward me and opens his mouth to speak when one of his men comes in from a back room. "I think we've got her," he announces.

"Where?" There's a fierceness in Royce's voice I'm not sure I've ever heard before.

"The old train station."

"Alright, pull in my SUV and let's get loaded up."

The amount of firepower thrown into the back of Royce's Levante is impressive, and honestly slightly concerning as his attorney. His men have the car loaded in a few quick minutes, and several break off to pile into the car while the rest stay behind. I take one of the last seats available in the back. There's absolutely no way Royce is going to find Logan without me.

I'm caught off guard when one of Royce's guys jumps in the driver's seat instead of him. Looking through the window, I see him walking toward the front of the building with his motorcycle helmet in hand. That fucker. He's going to try to beat us there. I swear, if he goes in without me and they both end up hurt...

S. Belle

When we pull out of the building, Royce is already long gone. The drive is silent and painfully slow as the SUV speeds just enough to avoid giving any cops an excuse to pull us over. If it was me, I'd lead an entire battalion of officers to wherever we're heading and gladly take my punishment for "running" from them if it meant getting to her faster. But Royce's guys are methodical, and they're not going to risk getting caught. I have no choice but to wait impatiently for the ride to be over and catch up to Royce, hating that he intentionally left me behind.

CHAPTER 19

Logan

There's an open street parking spot about a block away from Blake's apartment that I pull into before practically skipping out of the car. As the day went on, my confidence continued to grow about letting Blake know that I want to tell Royce about us. Hopefully, being ready will be enough to make him forgive me. He may need to fuck me thoroughly first, but I'm more than happy to take a punishment from him. Hell, maybe I'll even ask for one. My smiling reflection looks back at me in a window as I approach the apartment complex front door.

There's a car pulling over beside me, and a man a decade or so older than me leans out of the window. "Hi, miss. My daughter just moved into this apartment complex and I'm trying to find the best place to park. Is there a garage nearby?"

I face him and start to approach the vehicle as I answer. "Yeah, if you take a left at the next light, there's one about—" I feel a strong arm wrap around my waist, and I naively look over my shoulder expecting to see Blake. Instead, I'm greeted by a twenty-something Hispanic man with an angry expression. His hand covers my mouth and nose before I have a chance to scream. Standing upright, he pulls me off the ground and runs toward the SUV occupied by the man I was just speaking to. The back door flings open, and I'm thrown in harshly, the guy who grabbed me jumping in right after.

I hear the slide of a barrel and feel the hard metal pressing into the side of my head by the man who flung open the door. "You're alive right now because we have a plan for you. If you give us trouble though, we are more than willing to adjust our plans. Royce won't even know you're missing before your brains are splattered all over the window. Is that clear?"

I don't even look over as I nod. Tears well in my eyes, and when I shut them, they begin streaming down my face. I fight back the sobs as best as I can, knowing that crying hysterically is not what they would consider behaving.

While the one continues to press the pistol into my head, the other works quickly—tying my hands behind my back, binding my ankles together, then roughly forcing my mouth open to shove a towel inside before wrapping duct tape around my head. The one who grabbed me off the street rubs my cheek through the duct tape sensually, "I'm going to see if Luis will let us record a video to show everyone just how well-behaved you are."

The one driving chimes in, "I hope she's got a little fight in her, I'd love an excuse to blacken that face."

"You know he won't let you do that before he gets the pictures."

"If she gives us enough reason he will."

"If she gives too much reason, she'll be dead. You want to rape a corpse?"

"Of course not, corpses don't fight back."

The gun slides down the side of my face and under my chin. The man holding it uses it to turn my face to him. "Are you going to fight us? Or are you going to spread those legs on command and accept that we can do whatever the hell we want with you?"

I close my eyes and shake with an inaudible sob, the sound trapped by the gag. Throughout the entire car ride, they continue to vulgarly describe what they plan to do to me, along with several other men who are apparently waiting for our arrival. Trying to see through my tears, I do my best to look through the tinted windows of the SUV. There's not much I can discern until I notice a heavy tree line replacing streetlights and buildings.

We come to a stop, and the youngest of the group gets out and throws me over his shoulder. I can't see where we're walking, but I see one worn paved road that is surrounded by heavy woods. They carry me inside what I realize is an old, abandoned train station, and a large one at that. There are groups of two to three men patrolling, and a small group surrounding a few desks with computers along with a makeshift living space of several couches and chairs.

I'm thrown onto a twin-size mattress covered in a layer of dirt, sitting directly on the floor. A middle-aged man rises from the couch and walks over to greet the men who dragged me here.

"Any complications?"

"It was a public pickup, but nothing unexpected."

"I don't think anyone saw us," the youngest adds to the driver's report.

"Good." He squats in front of me. "Do you want to know why you're here tonight?"

I think I already know, but I nod anyway. "Your brother ratted us out. My *son* is in prison right now thanks to him, and it's time he learns he's not as untouchable as he thinks he is."

He rises and walks away, throwing a nonchalant order over his shoulder, "Strip her."

The man who originally had his gun trained on me takes far too much pleasure cutting my clothes open with a pocketknife. His hands linger, and I swallow bile rising up my throat when he shoves an unwanted hand under my bra and gives a forceful squeeze. I try to pull away and scream through the gag, which simply triggers his laughter.

"Carlos, leave her alone. We need her cooperative for the pictures."

"Don't worry, Luis. I'll make sure she's good and ready for her photo shoot."

The driver steps in. "No, you won't. You'll just make her look good and used." He shoves Carlos out of the way and removes the gun from his waistband. "I'll take care of this."

"Fuck off, Sebastian."

The driver, whom I now know is named Sebastian, ignores Carlos' comment. "Ale, can you come help me with this?"

The young kidnapper steps forward and pulls me up to my knees by my arm. "Stay just like that." I watch him walk over to the desk, grab a digital camera, and stroll back over. I look up at him as he gets close, and a bright flash goes off as he snaps a picture. Instinctively, I turn my head away, which causes him to reach out and grab my face.

"You will look at the camera, and you will stop with the damn tears. They won't save you."

His harsh tone simply makes me cry harder, the taste of salt leaking through the duct tape and beginning to saturate the slobbery towel in my mouth. He shoves me back onto the mattress by my shoulders and pushes me until I'm flat on my back. More pictures are taken as he kneels above me, then when he tries to pull my knees apart, I scream through the gag. My chest heaves and my back arches off the mattress as I panic.

"That actually looked pretty hot, keep doing that and I might bid on you myself." Sebastian spews out from above me. I sob harder and continue trying to resist Alejandro from prying my knees apart. I feel a harsh slap across my face. "Open your fucking legs."

I cry as my knees drop apart, and he snaps a picture of my lower half. He stands up and takes more pictures from various angles, eventually flipping me onto my stomach and propping my ass in the air for pictures of my backside. The shutter of the camera finally stops, and I sob heavily through my gag.

"God, stop with the fucking crying." I'm not sure which one hits me since my eyes are closed. Still face-down on the mattress, a gentle hand touches my shoulder and chills run up my arm. Nervously, I open my eyes and see Luis squatting in front of me, the back of the camera turned to face me. He clicks through the pictures of me, lying in my underwear on the dirty mattress. Seeing myself like this makes me flash back to Blake and the way he's restrained me before. Is this what he sees when he looks at me? I look terrified. But I never feel terrified with him. I trust him with my life; these men have full intentions of ruining everything about our relationship, and they don't even know it.

"You're quite beautiful, aren't you? We need a couple more with those eyes open, though. They're so... unique. Auctioning you is going to make us a lot of money." He strokes my face delicately, and I try to pull away.

"It's okay, you can try to resist if you want. But tomorrow night, you'll have a new owner who paid a lot of money for you, and the ones who want someone docile are usually much gentler than the people who buy fighters. You may want to think about how you want to look in your pictures."

He turns the camera around to take a picture, and I look at the floor submissively.

"Good girl." He pats my cheek and takes several more pictures before sitting me upright.

"You understand that we're planning on auctioning you off, yeah?"

My eyes fall shut, and I nod once.

"Good. There's not a single thing your coward brother can do to stop it. You'll be gone without a trace before he ever finds this place."

Out of energy, the anxiety takes over. My brain races, trying to find a way out, wondering what will happen to me, if I'll end up in another country, trapped in a cage... The tears return harder, and my whole body shakes. The gag restricts my breathing, and my panic attack is winning. Sebastian must've been the one who hit me earlier, because my tears warrant another slap from him. I can't stop it, and the searing pain only makes my shaking worse. This time, the blow comes from the blunt end of his pistol across my jaw, and I fall hard. My head lands off the mattress, directly onto the concrete, and I feel instantly dizzy. My weeping slows as blackness finds the edge of my vision. Woozy, I try to shift myself back onto the mattress, but Sebastian has now made a game of letting me try to work my way onto it, only for him to kick me harshly back off. Somewhere in the cycle, I start to black out, my last thought being of Royce— hoping he notices soon.

I think I'm hallucinating when I hear Royce's voice. My vision is blurry, and I can feel the immense pressure in my head as I try to lift it. I swear I see Royce standing near Luis, smoking a blunt as he studies a monitor displaying photos, a countdown, and a "latest bid," indicating someone has offered $2.31 million for me.

I focus on the sound of Royce's voice. "I'm telling you, the bust wasn't my fault. One of my guys tailing the truck tipped me off that they had company, and I bailed at the last minute. I swear I didn't know it was a raid before that." I can tell by Royce's too-steady voice that this is a rehearsed story, but I'm hoping Luis doesn't know his tells like I do.

"Why didn't you call us, then?"

"I wasn't going to risk incriminating us if they tapped our phones. Are you for real? I lost a shit-ton of money in product in that raid, too. Why would I do that to myself?"

"I don't know what your angle is, boy. But I don't believe in coincidences."

"You don't have to believe me. I really don't give a shit. This is about the money, right? I'll split the cost of the loss with you, which hurts like hell since I don't have that product to move anymore. But I'll do it if it means you agree to let Logan go. I'll forget you took her, eat part of your cost, and we can move on with this relationship."

S. Belle

There's no way Royce would ever let this go, but he sounds believable. Maybe that's just the concussion talking, though.

I'm pulled back to the conversation when Luis scoffs at Royce's offer. "You really don't know how bad this is for you, do you? My son was there. Manuel's son was there." Royce freezes, his blunt halfway to his mouth. That is not a good sign. Who the hell is Manuel? "Even if I genuinely believed your story, there is absolutely nothing you can do to earn Logan's freedom. She's worth far more than you could ever offer us, and this is your punishment for your unsatisfactory business deal with us. I suggest you accept it before you make it worse for both of you."

Luis sounds arrogant, and Royce isn't responding, which means he's out of moves and trying to come up with another. Silent tears roll down my cheeks, wondering how the hell we're getting out of this.

CHAPTER 20

Blake

A worn blacktop leads us to the abandoned parking lot of a train terminal. It's a massive station that likely handled dozens of trains coming and going daily. The brick façade is faded, and the rustling of the surrounding woods demonstrates clearly why this is where the cartel brought her. Plenty of escape routes if they get cornered, but nowhere for her to run to easily for help.

When I recognize the SUV from the surveillance footage earlier, I fling open the back door. The Levante comes to a harsh halt.

"What the fuck are you doing?"

The driver scolds me as the man sitting beside me latches onto my arm and forces me to stay in the car. We continue moving forward slowly, keeping a safe distance from the building, and meet up with Royce in the shadows of the tree line. He's leaning against his bike, arms crossed, inspecting the station.

"What the fuck are we doing sitting here, Royce? That's the SUV. Why aren't we going in?"

"Do you see any other cars here?"

"No?"

"Do you think there's really just three of them here holding her? I didn't recognize any of the guys in that footage. Meaning they're all just foot soldiers. They brought her to someone higher up. I don't see any other vehicles though, which means they're probably hidden in the building."

He pauses, inspecting my heavy breathing. "That means we don't actually know what's going on in there. We could be walking into an ambush. They could've left that SUV out here hoping I race in there and blow it all up. There could be men manning every exit, waiting for us to approach. We are not storming in there blind. If we do, there's a very good chance we get all of us, and possibly Logan, killed. Is that what you want?"

The rasp in his voice is harsher than normal as he scolds me like an ignorant child. As much as I want to blatantly ignore him right now, he's right. This is out of my league. I huff out some of the frustration building inside me and trot back over to the hood of the SUV to lean against it.

An eternity passes while Royce continues to stare at the building. Finally, he looks away and digs his phone out of his front pocket. Leisurely scrolling through his contacts, he makes a selection and holds the phone to his ear, walking away from the group as he follows the tree line toward the building. His shoulder presses up against the trunk of a tree as he relaxes against it. I strain to hear his side of the conversation.

"Listen, I know you took Logan. Just get to the point and tell me where and when we're meeting."

He shifts upright, pushing off the tree. "Like hell I am. You haven't even justified why you took her yet. Unless you plan on giving me an explanation and a heartfelt apology, this is going to be a very bad business decision to continue this charade." His eyes raise from the ground to the building. "Fuck that, Luis. We already found her and I'm already here. I'm coming in."

He shoves his phone back in his pocket, walking over to his bike. He speaks generally to the group, looking at no one in particular as he starts climbing on the Diavel. "You are all going to wait here. As far as they know, I came alone. I'll be out with Logan, or out alone, but they don't want me dead." He tosses his helmet on but doesn't bother to clip it, visor raised. "Once I've scoped out inside, we'll make a move quickly so they don't have time to anticipate it." He directs a firm glare at me. "Nobody moves until I get back. Got it?"

All his men mumble their affirmatives, but he doesn't take off until I give him a curt nod. He peels out of the trees and rides up the stairs directly to the door of the train station. He takes his time before we see the door to the building open for him to slip inside.

My eyes burn holes into the side of the building. My girl and best friend are in there with one gun between the two of them. We have a whole damn armory out here and Royce wants to handle this by himself? It's fucking ridiculous. I doubt it's been a full ten minutes since he went in there, and there's no way I can convince these guys to go in yet. I alternate between watching the building and watching the guys. A couple of them are getting antsy, and after about half an hour, I speak.

"This is ridiculous. If he could get out of there, he'd be out by now. With or without Logan."

"He gave us our orders."

"Those orders don't mean shit if he dies."

A guy smoking a cigarette against the tailgate throws it on the ground, stepping it out. "Listen, Blake. We do this far more than you want to know as our lawyer. Trust me when I say Royce knows what he's doing. If he doesn't want us in there, he doesn't want us in there."

"Remind me who you are again?" I mean it as rudely as he takes it.

"Noah," he spits out with a straight face.

"Right, Noah. See how you knew my name and I didn't know yours? That means I outrank you, because Royce couldn't even be bothered to explain to me who you are."

"I know who you are because Royce had us watching your ass in case you got caught up in shit. When he's gone, I'm in charge. You're more of a liability than a help right now."

"Who do you think Royce learned to shoot with? Who do you think he got into trouble with before you were around?"

"I wouldn't guess the lawyer who wore light gray sweats to a rescue."

"What's wrong with my sweats?"

"They reflect light, and you can see blood on them. You trying to get caught by the cartel, the cops, or both?"

I loathe conceding, but this pissing match isn't getting me where I want. I switch tactics subtly. "Look, maybe I don't know what I'm doing operationally, but I'm not a liability. Regardless of how you feel about my presence, you know he should've been out by now. That's why he told us he'd come out without Logan. If he's not out here, it's because he can't be."

He scowls at me, then turns to open the back of the truck. He starts handing out various ARs and pistols. Most of the men are given both, but he only hands me a Glock 21.

"Can I get one of those?" I point to the two remaining ARs in the trunk.

"Have you ever shot one before?"

"No."

"Then, no. We don't need any stray bullets from you or to worry about being in your line of fire." He taps the pistol in my hand. "It's a .45 caliber; it'll do the job." He hands me a couple spare magazines to tuck into my pockets. "Don't make shit worse."

I grab a knife from the truck and clip it to the waistband of my underwear, feeling more secure with a back-up weapon. We stand around the back of the SUV and discuss strategy; Noah leading the conversation.

"We need to decide what entrance we want to breach. Eddie, were you ever able to find blueprints of the building?"

"Sure, from when the terminal was still active decades ago. I have no clue if they've renovated it at all."

"Show me what you've got."

The man who was sitting next to me, Eddie, pulls up some images on his phone. Noah looks over them, then passes them around to the two guys to his right.

"I think coming in on this track," he points to a spot on his phone I can't see, "is going to be our best entrance. It's all the way on the backside of the building but drops into the main terminal and connects with two of the three tracks. Thoughts?"

"I like this track better, less risk for exposure."

"Sure, but if they're not in the main hall we'll have to regroup and risk doing that where they have home-court advantage."

The three of them continue debating back and forth, and I wait for someone to ask my opinion. I look over to Eddie, who's watching me out of the corner of my eye. "You're Eddie, right? Royce's tech guy?"

"Yeah, but I'm pretty good in combat too."

He can tell I was wondering why the tech guy is out here. "Does he normally take you out on missions?"

"Not anymore, but I was one of the first people truly loyal to him. He trusts me with the big stuff."

"He didn't want you back at HQ if he needed something?"

"Guess not."

He nods over to the other three who have gone quiet. I ask, "We come up with a plan?"

"Yep. We're going to go in on the lone track. Less exposure, but if we don't find them, we'll clear the building methodically from there. You follow my lead in there, got it?"

"Until we find Royce and Logan, you got it."

He doesn't like that answer, but one look at me makes it clear to him anything else would be a lie. He accepts my honesty, and we slowly work our way through the trees to the backside of the building. I had assumed sweats and sneakers would be good for movement, less restricting than jeans and boots. Now I understand why that's the attire of choice.

When we're able to see the back of the building, there's a pause in our movement as two heavily armed men stand post under the cover of the overground tunnel originally designed to shelter waiting trains.

I speak softly, "There's no way we make it across the clearing unnoticed without killing them first."

"Hopefully nobody is close by to see them drop," Noah says, stepping up beside me to take two distant headshots, killing both men before they realize what was happening. We follow the tracks across the large opening, moving quickly while trying to see into the dimly lit tunnel. We continue moving meticulously down the tracks, checking various offshoots as we work our way deeper into the building.

As we near what is supposed to be the main terminal, the ground begins to drop off and we climb up to the walking ledge several feet in the air. Forced to approach one-by-one, Noah leads, and I insert myself between him and Eddie as we move single-file. The ledge gives way to the platform, and we're able to take a stronger formation as Noah peers around the wall to see into the large empty terminal.

The majority of people inside the building are currently at the far side of the terminal, closer to the main entrance and the other tunnel we debated entering through. I can hear Royce arguing with a large Hispanic man in the middle of the room, and that's when I see her. She's lying off the side of a mattress in her underwear, and I can't tell if she's conscious. She's bound, gagged, and wearing bruises I didn't give her. Ringing fills my ears, and I hastily charge forward.

It's Eddie who grabs me from behind and spins me, I start to try to shove him off when he spits out at me, "Do you want to get her killed, or can you get your shit together?"

He holds my face close to his, watching me angrily until I regain my composure. We split into two groups, and slowly work our way closer to the other side of the main terminal, hiding behind structural columns and door frames along the edge of the room as we approach.

There's a younger man standing over Logan, and Royce has a gun aimed at him across the room. The heavy-set one he was speaking to before draws Royce's attention and coaxes him to hand over his gun. Fuck. Now he's unarmed. He's not going to be able to protect Logan when we move in, and we're going to have to find a way to cover them both until they can get out of the middle of the damn firing zone. Royce doesn't even look concerned that he just handed over his gun, his back is turned to Logan. How is he not livid right now? How dare he take his eyes off her. Wait, did I just hear the word lawyer?

My ears strain to make sense of their conversation, but I catch enough to fill in the blanks. He promises to sell Logan to the highest bidder, then tells Royce, "If you plan on walking out of here alive, you will give us your blessing regarding your sister, and ensure your new lawyer friend will be taking on our men as new clients free-of-charge. You know, since it's your fault they're in jail to begin with."

"And what exactly are your plans if I don't agree?"

"If you don't agree, you won't walk out of this building at all. And if your friend puts up anything less than a stellar defense resulting in every last one of our men walking free, I will hold you both responsible."

"Fucking hell, man." I breathe out the swear, making eye contact with Noah and stashing my pistol. "Move on Logan's mark," I direct him with a loud whisper, hoping the sound makes it to him across a large portion of the room. I quickly move up two more pillars, then step into the broad opening. One of the men on the far side of the room apparently monitoring the space notices me first. As he raises his gun toward me, I call out, "Did someone say they needed a lawyer?"

For show, I throw my hands out to the side, looking around perplexed. Several more men fix their guns on me, but nobody fires.

"What the hell?" He looks angrily at Royce.

I hear the smirk in Royce's tone, "Luis, meet Blake Weber, your new attorney."

Royce turns to look back at me, and I see his gaze drift past my shoulder. I continue walking toward Luis, trying to distract him from where Royce is looking. "I would say it's a pleasure, but it looks like I've caught you in the middle of quite the mess."

"What do you think you're doing here?"

"I have my ways." Focusing on Luis, I instruct him sternly. "Don't doubt me."

"If you get any funny ideas, my—"

"There's no need to finish that sentence. I'm sure you've heard of attorney-client privilege before."

"That doesn't apply if you're present during a crime, I'm not an idiot."

"You're correct. But I do care about my own life, so you'll have to trust I care more about self-preservation than justice in this scenario." I scan the eyes of the men watching me. "As far as everyone is concerned, I wasn't here today, and anything I know about this situation was relayed to me after the fact and therefore protected."

The auction is still pulled up on the screen, and I direct my gaze toward Logan to hide the fury in my eyes. "You're planning on auctioning her, yeah?"

The man hovering near her responds warily, "That's the plan."

"Well, why don't we sample the merchandise? Then you can guarantee the buyers the quality they'll be receiving." Everyone watches me suspiciously. "What? I'd be happy to start the show if you need proof to believe I'm as 'invested' in your case as you all are."

As I move toward Logan, the younger man steps aside, and I focus my energy on her. She looks terrified as she stares up at me, her tears racing down her cheeks. I do my best to block out the look of horror on her face and convince myself this is something I've done to her. She's willingly allowed me to tie her up, gag her, and is eagerly awaiting the pain I'll inflict on her to heighten her pleasure. Her voice through her gag breaks the fantasy I'm building for myself to try to separate from this awful situation.

"Blake, please. Please, don't." I'm not sure if anyone else can make sense of her gibberish, but I'm so familiar with her sounds now that I catch every desperate word. She scoots backwards onto the mattress and backs away as much as she can. I bend over to break the gag, and she coughs out a towel. Fuck. Every last one of these men is going to pay for how they treated my girl. But I maintain my image and continue the show.

Standing above her, I pull her up by her hair to her knees. She screams in pain as I slap her harshly across the face. "Beg all you want; I'm not going to stop." A red mark begins to appear where I hit her, and I hate the way it looks on her already swollen face. I force a hand into her bra, and roughly paw at her breast. She sobs louder with the pain. "It's okay, I know you like it rough."

Pulling her further toward me, I force her to bend forward slightly. Reaching past her, I spank her hard enough to make her flinch, then the second harsher hit causes a blood-curling scream to escape her lungs. "I bet those panties are soaking. Aren't you excited to show everyone what a good little whore you are?"

"Pl—, plea—, please, Blake." Her full lips tremble as she begs me to stop. "I, I can't, p-p-peach—" I slam her mouth shut. This isn't a scene she can stop, and this is unfortunately the only way I'll get her through this alive. She may never allow me to touch her again after this, but I'll do anything to keep her breathing.

I lick the streak of salty tears from her collarbone, up her neck and past her jawline, stopping mid-cheek. As I pull my own head back from her face, I whisper so low only she can hear, "Trust me, baby." I go back in and bite her neck so hard she screams. "Please. I've got you."

When I stand to my full height, she looks up at me and though still terrified, the tears seem to ease off slightly. God, I hope she knows I hate this as much as she does. When I begin to pull down my sweats to pull out my cock through my underwear, her eyes widen again, and she panics looking around the room.

Begging again for me to stop, I ignore her as I shove my dick into her open mouth. She continues to beg around my cock like I've trained her to do, and I hear Royce losing his shit in the background.

"Blake! What the hell do you think you're doing? That's my fucking sister."

I glance over my shoulder briefly and see two of the men who were close by have stashed their weapons to restrain Royce. One of them speaks, "Don't worry, he's just warming her up for us. She's about to be sold anyway, time to get used to the idea. At least she gets to start with a cock she knows abusing her before it's five strangers at once." They laugh as he continues to curse at me and them.

Pressing her face fully down my cock, she makes gurgling sounds as I hold her there to reach behind her and release her hands. I allow her to pull back but grab both hands to wrap around my dick. Giving her a brief second to catch her breath, I press back down her throat and allow one hand to work part of my length while dragging the other up onto my pelvis. She tries to pull the hand away, but I press it harder to me until I'm confident she feels the knife tucked inside the elastic waistband of my Calvin's. I feel her hand twitch, and she begins to willingly suck my dick as we focus on shifting the knife from my waistband into her palm.

Thank God, she gets it. She gets what I'm trying to do. Hopefully she understands this was my only option.

To maintain the image, I coo mockingly at her, "See? I knew you loved sucking dick. This is all sluts like you are good for."

I keep my hand over hers to help hide the knife in her small hand, then call out to the guys holding Royce. "So tell me, what are your names?" I say it as if my girl isn't nearly naked, sucking my dick, in a room full of strangers I intend to murder shortly.

"What do you care?" The older of the two asks.

"Well, I was going to come invite you to feel how incredible her mouth is, but I only share women with men whose names I know. Luis, do you want to come try it out while I fuck her?"

Arrogantly, he strolls over toward us, and Logan freezes. I force her to continue slowly, and squeeze her hand with the knife, silently encouraging her as best I can. When Luis gets close, her panic takes over again, so I force her motions. Pulling her hand off me, I wrap her fingers around the base of the knife and remove it from my waistband, then shove her down face first toward the ground. The knife is slightly exposed in her hand as she falls, and I use my leg to shield the sight from view. The swiftness of the gesture breaks her out of her own mind, and she recovers quickly, using her forearm to hide the tip of the knife that extends beyond her wrist.

Instead of moving myself, I spin her so that her ass is in front of me, and I shield her body from most of the room. The only ones who can see her are Royce's men, who have moved into strategic positions around the space. Luis walks around me to her face, and I begin toying with her lightly through her underwear. The slight stimulation appears to ground her, and she keeps her grip on the knife as Luis pulls her up by her hair.

He's so enthralled with her as he pulls down his pants, he doesn't notice her lifting her arm upward to thrust the knife through the backside of his balls straight into his shaft. I wince myself at the sight of the pointed tip sticking through the top of his hard penis. With Luis hunched over in pain, I forcefully drag her to me with one hand as my other grabs the gun in the back of my waistband and puts a bullet through the top of his skull.

Stunned and frozen between my legs, Logan's lifeless eyes stare at Luis' body toppled over in front of her. I reach over her to remove the knife from his body, and shove it into her chest for her to take possession of it once more. Dazed, she takes it from me, and I tilt her face up toward mine. "Do not hesitate to use it again. You did so well, sweetheart."

I kiss her hastily before spinning to see most of the men around me are already down, and Noah is moving with one other guy toward an entrance lighting up with fire. A few moments later, the echo of gunshots has ended. Royce barks orders at his men to separate and post-up around the space, watching for anyone else lingering. He and Noah go to clear the rest of the building. When I trust they've got us covered, I focus on the woman beneath me.

I drop to my knees and pull my shirt off, situating myself in my pants and forcing her body into the shirt before wrapping her in my arms. "I'm so sorry baby, I hate that I had to do that to you. You were perfect. You're safe now, I promise."

She heaves violent cries into my chest, and I do my best to hold her through it. Her breathing and sobs become erratic, and I help her shift to her side as she upheaves straight onto the concrete beside us. When she turns back toward me, the cries have stopped, and her breathing is labored. I use this as an opportunity to reach down and untie her ankles, but her registering her restraints sends her back into a teary frenzy.

Exhausted, her heavy eyes find mine, "Blake," she whispers.

"Shh, you don't need to say anything. I've got you." I rub her head softly, leaning back so I'm sitting directly on the floor and cradling her in my lap. She passes out against my chest, and a few silent tears escape through my eyelashes buried in her hair.

I'm not sure how much time passes before Royce makes his way over to us. As he approaches, I stir Logan slightly in my arms. Her eyes flutter open, and there's a brief lightness to them as they look at me, before reality sets back in and they grow distant, looking through me in an instant.

"Logan, I was so worried about you." He tries to lighten his tone. "I'm happy you're okay."

"Okay? You think I'm okay?" Her voice is abrasive with dismay. "You got me kidnapped, Royce. I am so far from okay, and it's your fault."

"Logan, I'm sorry. I thought your safety measures were enough."

"Well, you were wrong. How did you let this happen to me? You're supposed to protect me!"

He flinches at her yelling. "I'm sorry, I know I fucked up, okay?"

When he gets no response from her, he turns to me. "What the hell was that 'show' you put on back there? Have you lost your fucking mind?"

"Don't you dare. I got her untied, armed, and got Luis taken out without getting any of us killed. Don't you dare try to yell at me for cleaning up your fucking mess." He starts to speak, but I cut him off. "No, I don't care what you think you have to say. If you hadn't fucked us all, she wouldn't have had to go through any of that. It's your fault, and you know it."

He scoffs at me. "I don't think you needed to assault her in front of me."

"If I didn't, someone else would've, and I wouldn't have been there to protect her." There is no comeback to that because he knows I'm right. "Now get your team to clean this shitshow up so we can get Logan home."

"I can take her home on my bike right now. She doesn't need to be here for this."

"No!" Logan's arms wrap tightly around my waist, and I hold her securely against me. "I want to stay with Blake."

"I can take you home if you want me to." I offer, knowing I could take the SUV and be back before Royce's guys are done with this blood bath.

"No, I don't want to be alone. Please, let me stay?"

I kiss the top of her head, and Royce makes an appalled face. "This is ridiculous, Logan should be going home." He speaks to me as if she's not sitting right there.

"I think you're done making decisions for her for a while."

"Seriously? If I had gotten to make decisions for her, she would've had a bodyguard, and this wouldn't have happened."

"Don't you dare blame her for this."

He lets out a frustrated huff and rasps out, "Fuck this," as he storms away.

When he's gone, I speak softly to Logan. "I'm going to go get the SUV and pull it closer, do you want to walk with me?"

She nods, and we get up slowly. I track down Noah for the keys, and we walk out the front door toward the car. She stays tucked under my arm, holding on to me tightly as we walk. A stick breaks beneath my foot, and I realize she's barefoot. Without a word, I scoop her into my arms and carry her the rest of the way to the SUV. When I place her into the passenger seat, I stand there waiting for her to release me, which she never does.

"Logan, baby, you have to let me go so I can drive."

Bloodshot eyes find mine, and my heart breaks with how she looks at me. There are ghosts dancing across her eyes, and her expression pleads with me to save her, as if I could. Guilt courses through me as I blame myself for letting her be abducted at my doorstep. She shouldn't be looking at me like that. I failed her.

I pry her arms off me and kiss the top of her head. "I'm going to go get in the car now, okay?"

She nods, and I reluctantly shut her in the car before walking around and climbing in beside her. I drive us up to the building and park beside Royce's motorcycle. She's dazed, looking out the window.

"Dandy?"

When she looks at me, I'm not sure there's anything behind her eyes anymore.

"Do you want to wait in the car?"

"I..." When she first trails off, I think she's debating it. As the silence drags on, I think she ends up lost in her own mind again.

I reach my hand over to hers. "I don't think you need to go back in there."

"Will you wait out here with me?" It wasn't a request so much as it was curiosity.

"I can if you want me to, but if I go in there and help, we can probably get you home sooner. I'd rather get you back to somewhere familiar, but that means you need to be okay out here by yourself."

"Can someone else come sit with me?"

"No, I'll stay if you want someone to stay with you."

"No, you should go help Royce." At this point, I don't think she's thinking clearly. I'm certain that response was autopilot, from somewhere deep in her subconscious.

"I'm much more worried about you than Royce right now." She's still staring at the brick wall in front of us. "I'm going to stay here with you. We'll leave when they're done. It will be fine."

"No, no. Go in. I'll lock the doors and I'll be fine. Go help so we can go home." She looks over at me finally, and there's focus in her gaze. "I want to go home."

Hesitantly, I ask her, "Are you sure you're going to be okay out here alone?"

She nods, closing her eyes softly as she does.

"I'm going to need you to use your words if you want me to believe you."

The gentle command stirs her, and she locks onto me once more. "Yes, I'm sure. Go, so we can leave. Please."

I lean over the console and kiss her forehead. She doesn't flinch from my touch. Pulling the phone from my pocket, I slide it over to her. "Call Royce if you need anything. The passcode is your birthday." I give her a gentle smile and leave to go find Royce.

When I open the door, I see two men loading bodies into cars driven in by the cartel guys. The rest are working on policing all the brass in the building, ours and theirs, and cleaning up the pools of blood. The auction is still counting down, but I see Royce hovering over Eddie's shoulder as he tries to take everything down.

"He's erasing those pictures, right?"

Royce watches me approach. "Yeah, he's getting everything down and going to make sure they're not popping up anywhere else. He's got the camera too so he can destroy the chip with a magnet and hammer later."

I nod, satisfied with the answer. "How much longer do you think this is going to take?"

"Well, we can probably get going soon. Eddie is the only one coming back with us."

"What's the plan?"

"They're going to wait until nightfall and then drive the two cars full of bodies into Maiden Lake. Then they'll ditch the third car somewhere it'll get towed quickly and disperse from there."

"Noah overseeing everything?"

"Yeah, he's solid. I trust him. There's no reason to keep Logan here any longer. Though, there may be one thing you want to see before we go."

He gestures for me to follow him, and we take a path down a long hallway to a smaller boarding platform. Off the platform is an office space with newly reinforced steel doors. He pushes it open, and I see why he brought me down here.

There are close to a dozen twin mattresses shoved together around the perimeter of the room, with steel hooks on the wall about six inches above the center of each one. In the corner are a few haphazardly stacked boxes full of various items left behind. Jewelry, emptied purses, stuffed animals, and blankets.

"They were taking women and kids."

"Looks like it. As my lawyer, I know you won't like this, but I want to take an inventory of what's here. I'm hoping Eddie can find a way to share the contents online in a way local families can see it. If people recognize something, maybe that will give them some peace—some direction as to what happened."

"You're right, I don't like the idea at all." I pause thoughtfully for a moment before continuing. "Let's just leave all this here for now, and we can revisit this later."

I continue to pick through the top box, feeling a heaviness in my chest as I see what was left behind. When I go to put back a worn toy rabbit, I knock the top box over and the entire pile falls. I spend the next few minutes slowly putting things back in the box, feeling the weight of each object as I go. When I straighten up the bottom box, I notice a discolored silver charm bracelet at the bottom of the box. There's a pair of ballet slippers dangling off it, along with a pearl charm and a script font "O" with fake diamonds lining the letter.

I pull it out of the box and run it between my fingers. Made for a child, the bracelet is dirty and corroding with age, but I recognize it.

"She was here." I turn and show the bracelet to Royce. He doesn't say anything, but I don't need him to. "I have to know where they took her."

"Blake..."

"It's hers, Royce. I know it."

"I believe you. But after this long, what else do you think we're going to be able to find out? We're lucky we even found this much."

"But we know so much more than we did five minutes ago. We know who took her. We need to investigate. We have to figure out what else we can learn."

He nods solemnly. "I'll see what I can find out; see if Eddie can find anything on the computer. Though, I don't think individual auctions are what they usually do based on what this room looks like. And I doubt they keep records that old."

"Yeah. But maybe if we just know who they sold her to... Fuck, Royce. Having even this piece of information, it's—" I don't have words to describe how I'm feeling. I've spent eighteen years wondering what happened to her, and now on some level I know. I don't expect we find her alive after all this time, but knowing what she went through, where she was when she died—it matters. "I need to know as much as we can. I need to know what happened to her."

A darkness finds me that I thought I buried a long time ago. Royce recognizes it immediately though. "I can't promise how much more we'll be able to find out, Blake.

But I'll do everything in my power to get you answers. Okay?"

"Do not let Logan get in the middle of it again." I hate the harshness in my tone as I clarify with my best friend that I don't want him doing anything for me that could risk Logan getting hurt. He's offended but doesn't let it show.

"I won't. Are you sure you want to know? The information we find may make things worse for you."

"I think it's pretty clear she was sold into sex trafficking, Royce. I owe it to her to know the truth, to live with it. Someone should know her story."

He nods, accepting my determination. "Okay, let's get going." I slip my bracelet into my pocket as we head toward the car. Logan is asleep in the passenger seat when we get there, and I can hear her gasp through the door when Royce clicks to unlock the car. I open her door and help her into the backseat, before climbing in beside her. Royce drives and Eddie takes the passenger seat.

Royce shifts the Maserati into reverse, but I stop him. "I think I should show her this before we leave." I hold up my closed fist to where he can see, and he nods, putting the car back in park.

"I found something important when I was in there with Royce," I tell her, dancing around with my words. "It's going to be hard to hear, but I don't want to hide it from you. Do you want to know now, or do you want to wait until you're in a better headspace?"

"No, whatever it is, just tell me now."

I reach out for her hand and lay it flat, dropping the bracelet into it. Momentarily motionless, she shakes her head, then looks back at the bracelet in her hand as if she doesn't believe her own eyes. When she looks up at me, I see the tears pooling in her eyes.

"It's Olivia's."

"Yeah, it is."

"How? Wait. Where did you find this?" She struggles to decide what she wants to ask first.

I glance over at Royce, uncertain if she really needs to hear this today. "It looks like the same people who took you, took her all those years ago. I found it in a box of stuff in one of the back rooms. A lot of other people's stuff was there too. Personal items that were… left behind."

She understands my meaning and begins to sob, falling headfirst into my lap. I resist the urge to join her and brush my hand through her tangled hair.

"I'm going to find out what happened to her, for both of us. I promise."

CHAPTER 21

Logan

The light cream fabric of the couch is soft against my bare legs as I curl into Blake. His arm is wrapped around me and my upper body is so far into him I might as well be sitting in his lap. He watches me intently, and I feel safe enveloped by him. Royce is in the kitchen, and I can hear cabinets opening and closing as he searches for food. Its near dinnertime, and between the long night and day without food, we're all starving.

"Do you want me to get you some water?" Blake offers.

I nod. "Yes, please."

I shift off him to allow him to get up from the couch and watch as he makes his way toward the kitchen. From my position, I lose sight of him when he joins Royce, but I can still hear them clearly. I slouch against the back of the couch and snuggle into a blanket as I listen. The sound of items shuffling has stopped, and I can hear the guys talking.

"I think we should call Dallas to have her check out Logan."

"Are you insane? She works for the fucking cartel. You know, the people who just kidnapped her?"

Royce keeps his tone steady despite the verbal lash Blake just gave him. "Dallas is her best friend, and an ER doctor. She's not going to hurt Logan."

"No, but if they want to retaliate for the massacre that just happened, we'll be leading them right to her."

"Blake, we're in her apartment. My SUV is out front. It's not that hard to figure out where we are. Dallas isn't going to change that."

"I don't like it. Why don't we just take her to the hospital?"

"So Dallas can check her out there, and then she has an obligation to report?"

I mentally agree with Royce that having Dallas evaluate me is a good idea. I could go in there and interrupt their bickering, but it takes so much effort just to get my phone off the end table, I decide I'll just call Dallas myself and they'll get the point.

"Hey, how are you?"

I choke on a sob as I ask her, "Can you come over?"

Her tone shifts immediately. "Of course. What happened?"

"I—" I pause to calm my harsh breathing. "I was kidnapped. I need you to come check me out and make sure..." The tears fight to break through, and I have to stop again.

"It's okay, we'll talk about it when I get there. Let me round up a few things and I'll be there in about fifteen minutes, okay?"

I sniffle. "Okay."

"Are you alone?"

"No, Blake and Royce are here."

"Good. I'll be there soon, okay?" She speaks to me gently.

"Okay."

"I love you, babe." I can hear the sympathy in her voice. I tell her I love her too and hang up the phone. A worried Blake stands beside a nervous Royce, and I shift to imply I want Blake to come sit beside me again. Royce's phone rings a moment later, and he disappears back to the kitchen.

Blake tilts my head to face him while he speaks. "Logan, I'm so sorry I let this happen to you."

"You didn't—"

"Yes, I did. I thought you were blowing me off, and I took too long to look for you. I knew about Royce's deal hitting the fan and about your stalker. I should've walked you from your car. You shouldn't have been alone for that to happen; it's my fault."

"Blake," I place my hand on his arm and wait until he looks at me. "It wasn't your fault. You don't need my forgiveness because I'm not mad at you." I blink away tears as I whisper, "You saved me."

His head drops again. "I hurt you. And now Royce knows about us, which I know I wanted but you didn't, and it's just not fair to you that—"

"I wanted him to know." I cut him off again but speak gently when I do.

"What?" He looks at me as if he doesn't believe me.

"That's what I was coming over to tell you. I wanted to tell Royce about us. I was excited about it. I just hate how he had to find out, but I'm glad he knows."

"You're glad he knows? He wasn't very happy about it when he found out."

"Well, he probably thinks we're just hooking up, right?"

He replies cautiously, "That was his assumption, yes."

"Well, maybe when he realizes we're together, he'll be less upset."

"I think right now you could have whatever you want from either of us."

That makes me smile slightly. "How bad was it?"

"Probably exactly how you'd expect." His eyes drift sideways, and he smiles to himself at the memory. "But I made it abundantly clear to him that you, Dandy, are the most important thing in my life. Nothing is getting in my way of having you, not even him." He kisses me gently. "He got the point."

I smile and lie against him. I think I drift off briefly, because the next thing I know, Royce is letting Dallas into the townhouse.

I must look as awful as I feel because Dallas struggles to hide her surprise at the sight of me. Royce speaks first: "I filled her in on the big picture, but not all the details, since I don't know everything."

He's speaking to me. Should I be mad at him for telling her? I'm sure he was just trying to be helpful, but I'm still so furious with him over the entire situation that it's hard to be kind to him right now.

I focus on Dallas, ignoring Royce's comment. "Thank you for coming."

"I'm glad you called. Why don't we go upstairs to your bedroom? It might be more comfortable for you."

I start to stand, but Blake grabs me. "Just do it on the couch."

She's not speaking to him like a lifelong friend, but like a doctor to a concerned family member. "I think she may be more comfortable on the bed while I look at her." She glances at my bare legs. "And she should probably change into something else after I'm done examining her."

"Why?"

She directs a question at me. "Did you come home in those clothes?"

I nod.

She looks from me to Blake. "I assume that's your shirt. I'd guess it would be good for her psychologically to change out of the clothes she left that place in—even if it is your clothing."

Understanding washes over Blake's face. "Okay, but I'm coming up there with you."

"Logan, are you okay with that?"

"Yeah, it's okay."

This time, when I stand up, Blake rises with me. He helps me up the stairs, my legs heavy as we walk. I sit on the edge of the bed, and Dallas looks over my body, inspecting the cuts and bruises while peppering me with questions.

"Some of the bruises on your back look pretty bad, Logan. They're going to hurt for a while. The good news, though, is that they're not near anything important that I think you need imaging for. How does your head feel?"

"I have a headache and I'm tired."

"On a scale of one to ten, how bad?"

"Around a two for the headache. I'm mostly just exhausted."

She runs her hand lightly over the marks on my jaw and temple. "Did you black out at all?"

"Yeah, I think so."

"For how long?"

"I'm not sure."

"Okay, I'm sure you have a concussion. It's probably mild, but for tonight, we're going to be extra cautious, okay?"

"What does that mean?"

"Blake, I want you to stay awake while she sleeps if you can. Also, no more than two hours of sleep at a time. Wake her up for at least twenty minutes before she goes back to sleep. You can take naps between her sleep periods if you need."

"Okay, we can handle that," Blake answers for us.

"Try to ask her some simple questions too. Test long-term and short-term recall. If she shows any signs of amnesia, call me, but I'll probably have you bring her into the hospital for a head CT."

"Okay. Anything else?"

"I'd ice as many of those bruises as you can. Even an ice bath maybe for all the areas on your legs and back. It'll suck, but it'll help everything heal faster and hurt less."

"How long do you think these will take to go away?" I lightly touch my face.

"I don't know. It could be a couple of weeks before they're fully gone, but hopefully only a couple days before a good makeup job can hide them."

Blake pushes off the bed beside me. "I'm going to go get some ice for your face, okay?"

"No, just wait until we're done, and we'll all go back down together. Can you grab me some pajama pants and a hoodie, though?"

"Sure." He kisses my cheek then starts working through my drawers to find the clothes I requested.

While he's digging around, Dallas lightly rubs my knee and squats in front of me. "Okay, I need to ask you one more question."

"Why does that sound bad?"

She glances over at Blake before asking me, "While you were there, did you experience any sexual contact with anyone against your will or while you were unable to consent?"

She holds her breath while waiting for my answer, and I notice Blake go still in my periphery. "No." When she finally lets out her breath, I attempt to crack a joke. "Well, no one besides Blake, anyway."

Her eyes widen, and she throws a harsh glare at him. "What the fuck?"

He rushes back over to the bed, dropping the clothes in his hand on the top of the dresser. "Shit. I—, it was the only way I could get her a weapon. Fuck, Dandy, I'm so damn sorry."

"What the hell are you talking about?" Dallas snaps at Blake, clearly pissed.

A hysterical laugh bubbles up in me, and all of a sudden I'm laughing so hard that I'm on my side on the bed. Blake and Dallas are both looking at me like I've completely lost it, and maybe I have, but watching Blake panic and Dallas rage over my joke is hilarious.

When I finally get my laughing fit under control, I try to speak. "Dallas, I was joking. Well, kind of. Blake made me give him head in front of everyone so he could sneak me a knife."

"It was a little more than that. I—"

I cut him off, not wanting Dallas to know the worst of it. "No, it wasn't. You did what you had to do to make it believable, but you kept anyone else from touching me, untied me, and armed me—all with everyone watching us. Other than being absolutely mortified, I was okay."

Dallas is still wary until a realization hits her. "Wait, you said in front of everyone. Was Royce...?"

"Yeah. Which is why it was completely mortifying."

"I'm sorry, I couldn't think of anything else in the moment. I didn't mean to embarrass you like that or say the shit I said to you. I hate that I put you through that."

"Blake, truly, it's okay. I know you didn't want to do anything you did. We made it through. That's what matters. But I have to start laughing about it, or I'm never going to stop crying."

There's worry sewn into Blake's expression, but Dallas fills the silence. "If you're in a laughing mood, we can all go to karaoke. Next week or so, since I need you on brain rest for a couple days and karaoke is not that."

For the first time in the last twenty-four hours, my chest warms. The idea of breaking eardrums with my best friends sounds like the type of utterly normal activity I need to distract myself from everything I've been through.

"That sounds like a great idea."

"I don't think so," Blake challenges.

"Why?"

"There are too many reasons to count."

"Please? I think this could be really good for me."

"It doesn't have to be a girls' night; you could come too." Dallas tries to sweeten the idea to Blake.

"Do you really think that's a good idea?"

"Yeah, I think it'll help me feel normal."

"Okay, then. We can try it. But not until next weekend at the earliest. Deal?" He's reluctant to agree, but I know that once we get there, he'll see how much this is going to help me move forward.

"Great. Dallas, can you text everyone and let them know?"

We head downstairs as Dallas coordinates our plan, and Blake finally grabs ice for my face. We're sitting on the couch chatting, Royce nowhere to be found, when there's a knock at the door.

Dallas looks at me. "Were you expecting anyone else?"

"No."

Royce rushes from the back of the place to the front door and meets Blake there. They shoulder each other trying to see through the peephole, and Blake finally opens the door. Two men come inside, armed with boxes and packing tape.

"What's going on?"

"It's the movers I hired. It's fine." He directs them to my bedroom and tells them to pack everything.

"The movers you hired?" Royce questions.

Two more movers appear, and Blake directs them upstairs as well. "Yeah, Logan is moving in with me."

"I am?"

"If you think I'm letting you out of my sight after this, you're delusional."

"That's a little bold of you to assume."

"Baby, this wasn't a fight I was going to let you win. I need you to agree. You know you want to, so please don't push me on this."

After a brief pause, I say, "Alright, but only because I would've said yes." He leans in to kiss me, and Dallas squeals with excitement for us.

Unfortunately for both me and Blake, and intrusive thought enters my brain, and I'm too tired to fight it. "Wait, what happens when we fight and break up, then you kick me out and I have nowhere to live because I gave up my townhouse?" Blake looks caught off guard by the question. "Nope, never mind. I'm going to stay here."

Blake shakes his head, laughing. "Dandy, that's never going to happen."

"It could!"

"It's not, but if it makes you feel better," he pauses briefly, "let's get married. It'd be harder for me to just 'get rid' of you if you'd get half in the divorce."

I pull the ice pack off my face in shock. "I'm sorry, what? You can't be serious."

"I am." He checks his watch. "The courts are closed, but I could probably pull some strings."

"As much as I love that offer, maybe we just get my name added to the lease so you can't kick me out, and we just date for a while? You know, not in secret?"

"Alright, that can be the plan, for now."

The whole room bursts into laughter, and Royce slips out while Dallas helps direct the movers as they pack up all of my stuff. She helps me sort through what needs to come and what can be boxed up for sale or donation, then volunteers to help get rid of it. I convince Blake that a few lighter pieces of furniture are needed to make his apartment feel like home for me. He agrees to bringing one of my cream couches to replace his, along with a few other pieces. The excitement of moving in with my boyfriend dulls the pain in my body.

The movers finish loading everything into the truck, and we all agree that unloading it and settling into Blake's apartment feels like a tomorrow problem. Dallas says her goodbyes shortly after the movers leave, and Blake and I are left cuddling on the couch in a peaceful silence.

He has his legs stretched across the couch with his back against the armrest, and I sit on my hip between his thighs.

He lightly massages my shoulders and upper arms as I lean against him, and his lips press against my forehead.

"I'm so grateful you're safe." I feel his grip around me tighten as he continues. "When I realized you were gone, I felt like I was twelve years old all over again. The fear. The guilt. The unknown. Everything that happened with Olivia felt like it was trying to recur with you." His face buries into my hair, and the last part comes out as a whisper. "I'm just glad history didn't repeat itself."

I let him hold me, knowing he needs the grounding feeling of me in his arms, but I shift so I can look at him. "You'll never lose me, Blake. I'm not going anywhere."

"You can't promise that. And knowing it was out of my control was the worst part of it all. I can't live without you, Logan. After Olivia, you were the only one who could ever make me smile; make me forget what I did. You keep me from losing myself in her death."

"There were years we didn't even speak, and you did just fine." I try to reassure him.

"You weren't there. School and work were great distractions, but without you I felt empty. I lived for stories from Royce and watching your social media. Even without you, those little glimpses were what kept me going to get back here. To get back to you."

"Blake," I say breathlessly. There are no words that can convey to him what I feel right now, so I lean in for a kiss. He kisses me tenderly, and I push it deeper, begging him to give me more. His kisses are languid, and I savor the feeling of his lips on mine. When his hand cups my cheek, I wince instinctively from the pain. He pulls back immediately.

"Shit, I'm so sorry. You're too hurt for this. We should stop."

"No, please. Keep going."

"It's okay. We have all the time in the world for this."

"I need you. It's the only thing that will make me feel safe and whole again. Please, Blake."

I pull his hand back to my face, encouraging him to touch me. "I know how to make you stop. Please."

Hesitantly, he starts kissing me again, but when I encourage stronger pressure against my body, he deepens the kiss once more. He cradles my head as he slowly leans me backward on the couch, positioning himself above me. His hands slowly slide up the hem of my shirt until it's above my breasts, and he lightly caresses me. I break the kiss to pull my top off, then try to pull his off as well. He helps, but when I start to pull down his sweats, he stops me.

"Are you sure? We don't have to do this tonight."

"God, yes. I'm sure. Please stop asking and fuck me already." I sound desperate as I beg him to continue. He pulls off his pants and underwear and continues to kiss me as he rubs circles on my clit, gently working two fingers into me. He trails kisses down my neck and collarbone as I wrap my fingers around his long shaft, finding comfort in the familiarity of the sensation. I can feel myself dripping down my thighs and onto the couch as he continues to work me up. Finally, he removes his fingers and eases himself inside me. He locks eyes with me as he thrusts rhythmically in and out of me. His thumb finds my clit, and he bites lightly on my neck. I feel my legs begin to shake.

"It's okay. You can come." He coos gently.

I fight the urge. Between breaths, I say, "I want you to come with me. Come in me, please."

My plea causes his restraint to break, and his speed and force pick up. I cry out, continuing to fight the orgasm as I feel him getting closer. When I can't resist anymore, I fall over the edge and feel his cum coating my insides as he follows quickly behind, heightening my pleasure.

He kisses me tenderly as we ride out our combined orgasm and pulls out delicately when it's over. Never breaking the kiss, he sits upright on the couch and pulls me into his lap.

"You are so incredible, Dandy. So strong, and beautiful, and perfect. With everything you've been through, everything I put you through, to be intimate with me is amazing." He kisses me again so passionately that I get dizzy. "I love you, Dandy. It's impossible not to."

As much as I already knew it and already felt it from him, to hear him say those words sets off an avalanche of emotions in my heart. "I love you too, Blake."

"I've loved you so long. You're mine now, and I'm never letting you go."

After basking blissfully in our post-confession bubble for probably a bit too long, Blake helps me get cleaned up, gets me some new ice packs, and relocates us to the bedroom. His wake-up calls always start with him finding different ways to make me orgasm, and end with fresh ice packs, water, and gentle massages to help me back to sleep. He doesn't let his own exhaustion show as he helps me recover, and by early afternoon, I'm begging him to call the movers and let us get started on our life together.

CHAPTER 22

Logan

It's been five days since I was abducted, rescued, and moved in with Blake. Sitting on the couch, I'm enjoying being able to read again since I'm slowly coming off brain rest when I get a text from Blake.

B: *How's your day going?*

> **Me:** *Less boring since I can start thinking again.*

B: *If I get you an Uber, do you want to come have lunch with me?*

Blake and I both agree it's probably still a bit too soon for me to be driving, and I haven't been back to work yet, but I will be soon. Ana has been keeping me updated on anything important and delegated my responsibilities while I'm out. A lunch date with Blake sounds like a perfect way to appreciate this day off, even if it's just for recovery.

> **Me:** *That sounds great. Give me 30*
> *minutes so I can cover these bruises*
> *before you call it?*

He loves the message, and I head upstairs to change and cover up my face. I don't want anyone questioning me or Blake about where the bruises came from. Thanks to Dallas' advice, they're fading quicker than I expected, and hiding them isn't too difficult. I throw on a navy summer dress with an elastic ruched top and off-the-shoulder sleeves, along with a pair of sandals, before heading out. Blake texts me the Uber driver's information, and I confirm everything before getting in the car.

Assuming we were meeting at the restaurant for lunch, I'm a little surprised when we arrive at the firm. I follow the building signs to the correct floor, and a receptionist escorts me to Blake's office.

"Hey, are you ready to—" My words trail off when I notice the scene.

The wood-paneled walls are illuminated in warm candlelight, and the rich, dark-brown leather couch has been shoved up in front of the desk. Blake looks up at me from arranging the sushi containers on the desk around two glasses of ice water, sauce, and utensils.

"Hey, I hope sushi is alright?"

He knows it's my favorite. "Of course it is. I didn't realize we were eating here."

"I wasn't sure if you were up for going to a restaurant yet."

I move to the couch, and he sits beside me, pulling me into a hug. With an arm slung around me, he grabs a spicy tuna roll off the plate with his chopsticks and feeds it to me.

I cover my mouth while I finish chewing. "Thank you for doing this."

"Don't thank me yet," he says with a smirk.

"What exactly does that mean?"

"Finish eating, and you'll find out."

I devour my food, antsy to find out what he has in store. Unfortunately for me, when I finish, he still has half his plate left and takes his time eating it. He tries to distract me with small talk, but I can tell he's intentionally drawing this out to aggravate me. When he nears the end of his food, his hand curled around my waist slides upward, his thumb stroking the side of my breast slowly.

My breathing picks up, and I lean into the touch. He finishes his last bite, then turns to look at me. "I love this dress on you, but I need you to take it off."

"Yeah?" Since the abduction, he's been noticeably hesitant to touch me, and I've had to initiate almost everything. But him requesting that I strip in his office right now feels like things are truly headed back to normal. I stand up to pull off the dress and wait patiently in just my thong as he moves the food containers out of the way, leaving the candles scattered around the table.

He turns toward me and cups my face in his hands. "Remember I love you, because I'm about to treat you like I don't." He plants a soft kiss on my lips before giving me his command, "Lay down on your back."

He helps guide me to lie in the space between the candles before kissing me sensually. Eventually, he pulls away, rolling up the cuffs of his shirt and then pushing my legs open further. He watches my chest rise and fall against the desk, and I feel my skin redden from the weight of his attention.

"The walls here are relatively soundproof for privacy, but I can't have you yelling through this. Do you think you can handle that?"

S. Belle

I chuckle nervously. "I guess it depends on what 'this' is?"

Without warning, he picks up a candle to my right, turns it over, and runs it across my chest, allowing the wax to splash all over my breasts. I gasp before I realize there's no burn, just a comfortable warmth from the oily liquid.

He puts his hands on me and massages the oil into my boobs, pressing firmly and kneading them just to the edge of pain. "Did that hurt at all?"

"No, I was just surprised."

"Good. That candle is a massage oil candle. Its melting point is about 100^{OF}. We're going to see how hot you can handle."

His left hand moves to circle my clit through my underwear, and I relax at the familiar touch. He uses the same candle to trail lines down each of my legs, massaging down my thighs and calves. He repeats the process over each of my arms, then removes my thong before putting the candle down. Warmth caresses my body, and I feel hazy and relaxed, barely registering him picking up a different candle.

"Sit up on your elbows."

I shift my weight and watch as he pours the wax of the new candle into the crevice where my collarbone meets my shoulder. It stings slightly, and I instinctively suck in air as the sharp heat fills the space, rolling down my chest and onto my nipple.

"That one hurt more," I tell him.

"It's soy. Melting temperature around 120—130^{OF}."

I watch as it cools and hardens on my skin. "Will it hurt to pull off?"

He smirks at me and quickly peels off the hardened streak. It tugs like a sticker but doesn't really cause any pain. "Oh, okay. That wasn't bad."

He runs a few more streaks from that candle down my chest, and the initial sting becomes more comfortable. When he barely gets a reaction from a drop on my neck, he announces, "Looks like you're ready to move on."

I swallow nervously as he grabs two blue candles, one in each hand.

"Close your eyes for me and tilt your chin down a bit."

I tuck my chin to my chest, and flinch when I feel a burn hit my cheekbones and run down my face to my jaw. Heavy streams lengthen the burn as it pools on my collarbone, and continues running.

My eyes warm with the beginning of tears at the duration of the pour, him finishing with a heavy streak up my cheekbones allowing several separate lines to burn down each side of my face.

"You can open your eyes now," he offers to me. "I know that one hurt, but I wanted to see your tears in color."

I steady my breath as the pain subsides, and I feel the wetness between my legs growing. I catch myself looking down at the erection straining in his pants, and he smiles at me.

"Not quite yet. Do you think you can handle a bit more?"

I nod at him, and he leaves trails of blue down my stomach, inner thighs, and hips, running dangerously close to my lower lips. As the sting becomes more familiar, I start to crave it, leaning into the heat, and my gasps getting breathier.

"Good girl. I was hoping you'd like this."

He gives me a kiss that feels far too short, then swaps candles again.

"This one is beeswax; it's the hottest and melts around 150°F. Do you want to try it or stick with the blue paraffin?"

"I want more," I plead with him.

He leans over to nibble on my earlobe before whispering, "Be careful what you ask for, Dandy."

Still close to my face, his hand tilts the new candle straight onto my clit. I start to yell, and he quickly uses his second hand to cover my mouth.

"Shhh, remember our rule? No yelling."

I nod against his hand, and he releases me. The wax burns deeply, and as it hardens there's a thick weight on my clit. After a few seconds, Blake uses his free hand to rip off the wax. I bite my inner cheek, fighting the need to scream. After the sting fades, I find myself needy for more sensation. I squirm on the table, waiting for Blake to do something other than just watch me.

"Do you need more?"

"Yes, please."

"Then get on your knees and beg."

I push off the desk, more unsteady than I would've expected, and settle on my knees between Blake and the desk. He doesn't help me as I work his erection out of his pants. I start to drool as his veiny cock bobs in front of me, and I quickly wrap my lips around him and begin to suck. Swallowing him deep into my throat, I speak around his cock.

"Please, Blake."

He pours wax from high above me, and the gravity intensifies the sting as it lands on my ass with a forceful splash, splattering some onto my lower back. I moan and continue to suck. When I need more sensation, I beg again, receiving a harsh stream over each nipple as my reward. I continue begging until I can feel hard lines coating most of my ass and breasts. The feeling of the wax tugging on my skin satisfies me, and I work on trying to get Blake to come in my mouth.

Unexpectedly, he takes back control and shoves deep into my mouth, pushing my head back against the desk and restricting my movement. He blows out the candle, then brings it down near my face, pouring the remaining wax over my lips wrapped around his cock. I groan against him as the burning sensation covers my face, and I feel the wax cooling on my lips. He pulls out, releasing me, and I instinctively try to close my mouth. The wax only cracks slightly, causing the rest to pull on my delicate skin, and I stop.

He smiles down at me, my mouth fixed open to the shape of his dick. "So fucking beautiful. I might make you walk out like that."

There's panic in my eyes, and he chuckles. "Relax, I'm joking. Nobody gets to see you like this but me."

He pulls me up, sits me on the edge of the desk, and takes advantage of my open mouth by slipping his tongue in and tasting every corner of me. I try my best not to move beneath the wax. When he's finished, he lays me on my back again.

He uses one of the other candles to relight the beeswax one. While waiting for it to burn, he teases me with the head of his dick.

"You're so wet for me. Do you need me to fuck you?"

I nod.

"You can speak."

I utter what sounds sort of like a "yes" through the wax, and he presses into me as my reward. He fucks me unapologetically, pouring more wax over my abdomen, hips, and inner thighs. He lets a trail run down my clit and onto my labia, fucking me through the painful sensation and overwhelming my senses. He starts harshly peeling the wax off my skin, beginning with the blue trails on my arms and legs and working up to the thicker, more intimate yellowish trails from the beeswax. When I'm close to coming, I plead for him to let me. He rips the wax off my clit while pounding into me, and I can't fight it any longer, falling over the edge and throbbing around him.

He rewards me with an orgasm of his own, then gently helps me peel the wax from my face and lips as the rush fades. There are angry red lines all over my body, and I can only imagine what my face looks like.

"You look fine," he says, as if he was reading my mind about the marks. "But I do need you to get dressed quickly. We have somewhere to be."

"We do?"

"Yes, I booked us a couples' massage. We need to get going."

"Blake, I can't go like this." I use the camera in my phone and see angry red marks all over my face and bruising peeking through my makeup on my jaw.

"Yes, you can. I warned the spa about your situation in case there were any issues. They'll just think they were tears." He kisses me on the cheek. "Besides, I like how you look right now."

A blush rises to my cheeks, and I can't help but admit I love the way he looks at me when he admires his marks on my body. I allow him to help me get dressed, and he guides me to the bathroom before we head out. As we're walking out of the office, I see TJ saying goodbye to a client at the front desk before heading back to his office.

"Wait, is that David Hopkins? Like the head coach of Abilotte United, David Hopkins? What's he doing here?"

Blake just looks at me firmly. "Yes, but you did not see that. Let's go."

I can't wait to tell the girls about this and see what theories we can come up with—and if we can get any information out of TJ about it.

Saturday evening rolls around, and I'm waiting for Blake to get out of the shower so we can leave. By Thursday, I was over being cooped up in the house and had been looking for any excuse to get out. Blake has been trying to limit my activities still, knowing it would be easy for me to overdo it, but tonight is going to be full-blown fun. I already have my shoes on when Blake steps out of the bathroom in his towel and meanders over to the wardrobe.

"Wear the gray one." I try to nudge him to get dressed faster.

He turns and looks at me, not removing any shirt from his closet. "You know everyone else is going to be late. If we rush there, you'll just get less time with them before you're too tired and need to come home."

He has a point, but I don't like it. "I was just trying to help you decide."

"Sure, you were." He smirks at me. "Maybe you need a distraction to pass the time." He drops his towel and steps toward me. My hand runs over the dandelion tattoo before trailing down to his inner hip.

"Blake, I want to get going," I whine.

"Everyone will be there when we're done."

I have to touch up my hair and essentially completely redo my makeup before we're able to leave, but the ache between my legs is worth it. When we finally make it to the karaoke bar, I find TJ, Ana, and Dallas sitting around a table in booth seating lining the back wall.

The group greets us, and I learn Ari is off getting a round of shots.

"Oh, I'm sorry. I didn't know y'all were here yet. I can go get you both one." Ari starts to walk back toward the bar, but I stop her.

"Don't worry about it, we'll go grab drinks in a minute."

She slides her shot of bourbon over to Blake. "Here, you can have this. You probably need it more than I do."

"I'm good." He declines her offer.

"Fine, Logan, it's all yours then."

"No, really, it's okay. I can go grab something in a second."

She cocks her eyebrow at me and doesn't make any move to pick up the drink. After an extended stare-off, I sigh and grab the drink. She smiles, and the rest of the group clinks their glasses with mine before we throw them back. After the shot, I slide into the long booth beside Dallas, and Blake leaves to go grab us drinks.

"How's the karaoke been?" I shout over the loud music and chatter of others in the bar.

Ana replies, "Surprisingly not too bad."

"Don't worry, we can fix that." Dallas jokes.

"Should we go sign up for a song?" I ask the group.

"Count me out of anything." TJ remarks.

"Then why did you come if you're going to be lame?" Ari snarks at him.

"I'm here for moral support."

She rolls her eyes at him. "I'm going to go sign up for myself. Who wants to go with Logan?"

"I will!" Dallas answers enthusiastically. "I'll come with you so I can pick the song." She adds, and the two of them disappear into the crowd. While they're gone, I slide closer to TJ so I can hear him and Ana better.

"I miss seeing you at the club." I tell her.

"I know, but you'll be back on Monday, right?"

"That's the plan! How have things been going?"

"Okay. You can tell you're not there, but it's all been minor things."

"Why are you talking about work? This is a work-free night." TJ groans.

"Sorry, sorry." I apologize with laughter.

As the night goes on, I get drunk faster than usual, and we all perform several rounds of karaoke. Dallas and I finish a brutal attempt of "Sweet Caroline", but everyone else in the bar sings along so loudly that it mostly drowns us out.

When we make it back to the table, Ana reassures us, "That wasn't as bad as last time!"

"Do not lie to them." TJ glares at her. "My ears may have permanent damage."

Dallas and I just laugh at his comment, and Blake pulls me into his lap.

He kisses behind my ear. "Are you having a good time?"

I smile and nod my head, leaning back against him. After the next performer finishes their song, my hazy focus shifts back to Blake. I turn in his lap to face him. "Listen, I know you're still mad at him, and I am too... But I think maybe we should text Royce and see if he wants to come join us."

"I don't want him ruining your night." I can tell he doesn't want him ruining his night either, and I can feel his mood shift just at the mention of Royce, but I continue to push.

"He won't. I know he screwed up, but he's still my brother and I don't want this fight to last forever. The longer we drag it out and avoid him, the harder it will be to get back to normal."

"He doesn't deserve it to be easy."

"It's not going to be, even if we start trying to forgive him now. You know he feels guilty, and it's not like he kidnapped me."

"No, but his actions caused it to happen, and he didn't protect you."

"Neither did you." My protectiveness of Royce comes out, even with everything that happened. "But it's because nobody could've protected me. You both came to rescue me, and that's what matters."

All I get is a silent glare, but I can tell comparing him to Royce helped push him toward forgiveness, even if it stung a little.

I continue, "We did keep our relationship a secret from him, too. He's letting that go."

"Yes, us dating and him getting you almost killed and sold into the sex trade completely cancel each other out."

"I'm not saying they do. I'm saying he's trying to move on, so maybe we should, too."

He looks past me to watch the stage, marking the end of the conversation. He doesn't put up another protest, so I take that as permission to text Royce and invite him out. He takes a while to reply but agrees to come. I give him the location, and he strolls into the bar about half an hour later.

He walks up casually, but the speed of his approach lets me know he's nervous. Blake glares at him across the bar, and I scold him. "Please try to remember you've been best friends your entire lives. And maybe trust he's not a big fan of himself right now, either. I think that's something you can relate to?" Throwing a firm look at Blake over my shoulder, I jump off him to greet Royce, pulling him into a hug.

He squeezes me tightly. "Hey, Logie. How are you?"

"I'm good," I tell him honestly. "How are you?"

"I'm hanging in there." When I pull back and inspect his face, I can tell he hasn't been sleeping. Yet, he smiles at me and tries to hide the exhaustion that's audible in his voice. "Thank you for inviting me out and giving me a second chance."

"It's not like I could stay mad at you forever."

"I promise I'll do better to protect you, especially when I know there's a threat. I'm sorry I let that happen to you."

"It's not your fault, Royce. But maybe you'll think about getting out of the business now?" I ask him hopefully.

He sighs, looking at me with sad eyes. "Unfortunately, everyone's safer if I don't. But I'm going to make sure you're protected better from now on." He pauses, looking over my shoulder. "Knowing you have Blake by your side should help too."

When he looks back at me, I give him a soft smile. "Thank you for being open to the idea."

He shrugs. "I figured it'd happen eventually. Though," he chuckles, "I did kind of hope when you stopped speaking after my arrest that I dodged that bullet. Guess not." The smile reaches his eyes, and I know he's being playful with me. "You know if anything happens between you two though, you can always come to me, right?"

I shake my head at him, smiling to myself at his sincerity. "I know."

Linking arms with him, I pull him the rest of the way to the tables the group is circled around. He takes a seat beside Blake, who gives him a head nod but doesn't speak.

Royce attempts to speak to Blake behind me, but I get distracted by Ari bolting toward the stage, hovering by the side as the person currently singing wraps up their song. Looking back at the guys, Royce continues attempting to coax Blake into conversation about the night, and they talk about the last performer.

"He wasn't too bad," Royce comments.

"No, but what dude performs karaoke?"

"Us, if I go sign us up."

"You wouldn't dare."

Royce laughs at Blake's mild threat, and Blake starts to soften as the conversation becomes more comfortable. I stay quiet, hoping the two of them will work it out naturally without me interfering.

Most of the group's attention shifts to Ari performing, but Royce continues speaking. "Do you know who—" when Ari's voice reaches our ears, he stops speaking mid-sentence. His eyes dart to the stage, and he watches with intensity.

I make eye contact with Blake, who's smirking at me, and I reciprocate the gesture. If someone will knock Royce's head straight, it's Ari. Blake leans in to whisper something to Royce. I'm not sure what exactly he says, but it causes Royce to laugh and shove his forearm into Blake's shoulder. Blake chuckles, and the two chat casually, the divide between the three of us fading quickly.

I relax back into his shoulder, looking around the group to see a smiling Ana, Dallas hooting at Ari as she hits a harder note, and Ari on stage captivating the room. Blake and Royce are reconnecting, and I get to be with the man

I've loved my entire life. There's nothing else I could ask for to make my life better. It looks like everything's going to work out after all.

Then my phone vibrates with an incoming text.

Acknowledgements

I cannot believe I finished writing this book. From brainstorming and writing outlines, to the random binge writing sessions, side-quests upon side-quests to develop the world of Abilotte and create depth to the characters in it, and the hours of research into properly getting this book to fruition, I'm already excited and fearing the time I'll spend on the next one. But none of it would be possible without the support from the people around me.

Thank you, to my editor, Nicole Taylor. Thank you for being my sounding board, controlling my writer impulses for the sake of our readers, and being the "edit sober" to my "write drunk." Thank you, to my beta and ARC readers for providing me the encouragement to put this project out there and providing the final feedback and tweaks that make this better for everyone. Lastly, thank you to my husband who has had to hear more about this fictional world than anything in our real world, and who has to remind me I do in fact have a life outside these books. I love you, and I couldn't do this without your support.

Finally, thank you to everyone who supports my books through reading, sharing praise via word of mouth, online reviews, and recommendations. Writing has always been a pastime of mine that I enjoy, but nothing beats getting to share my art with you. So thank you for giving me the opportunity to share my stories with you, and thank you for investing your time in them.

Want to stay up-to-date on all things S. Belle?

Join the Serein Society for pertinent updates and information. Find us at: www.sereinliterarystudio.com.

And please, if you loved the book, drop a review on whatever platform you bought your copy through, or on GoodReads. The best praise an author can receive is a recommendation. One from you would mean the world to me.

And for those who want to know more...

Next in the Shadows of Abilotte series:

Book 2: *Red*
Anticipated Summer / Fall 2026
Your MMC? You already know and love him. Your FMC? You've met her too. Bonus: you'll get more of Blake and Logan in this next couple's book whose journey is deeply woven with theirs. Let's tie up some loose ends and fall even harder for this unexpected couple as the *Shadows of Abilotte* series continues.

You belong to us now.
We'll be seeing you.

Interested in even more from S. Belle? Follow her on Instagram at @SouthernBellePoetry

www.ingramcontent.com/pod-product-compliance
Lightning Source LLC
Chambersburg PA
CBHW010655100726
47901CB00012B/2556